Freaks on

Three Months' Rustication

R.M. Ballantyne

Alpha Editions

ISBN : 9789353296919

Design and Setting By
Alpha Editions
email - alphaedis@gmail.com

Contents

Story 1—Chapter 1

Mr Sudberry in his Counting-House

Mr John Sudberry was a successful London merchant. He was also a fat little man. Moreover, he was a sturdy little man, wore spectacles, and had a smooth bald head, over which, at the time we introduce him to the reader, fifty summers had passed, with their corresponding autumns, winters, and springs. The passage of so many seasons over him appeared to have exercised a polishing influence on the merchant, for Mr Sudberry's cranium shone like a billiard-ball. In temperament Mr Sudberry was sanguine, and full of energy. He could scarcely have been a successful merchant without these qualities. He was also extremely violent.

Now, it is necessary here to guard the reader from falling into a mistake in reference to Mr Sudberry's character. We have said that he was violent, but it must not be supposed that he was *passionate*. By no means. He was the most amiable and sweet-tempered of men. His violence was owing to physical rather than mental causes. He was hasty in his volitions, impulsive in his actions, madly reckless in his personal movements. His moral and physical being was capable of only two conditions—deep repose or wild activity.

At his desk Mr Sudberry was wont to sit motionless like a statue, with his face buried in his hands and his thoughts busy. When these thoughts culminated, he would start as if he had received an electric shock, seize a pen, and, with pursed lips and frowning brows, send it careering over the paper with harrowing rapidity, squeaking and chirping, (the pen, not the man), like a small bird with a bad cold. Mr Sudberry used quills. He was a *tremendous* writer. He could have reported the debates of the "House" in long-hand.

The merchant's portrait is not yet finished. He was a peculiar man, and men of this sort cannot be sketched off in a few lines.

Indeed, had he not been a peculiar man, it would not have been worth while to drag him thus prominently into notice.

Among other peculiarities in Mr Sudberry's character, he was afflicted with a chronic tendency to *dab* his pen into the ink-bottle and split it to the feather, or double up its point so as to render it unserviceable. This infirmity, coupled with an uncommon capacity for upsetting ink-bottles, had induced him to hire a small clerk, whose principal duties were to mend pens, wipe up ink, and, generally, to attend to the removal of *débris*.

When Mr Sudberry slept he did it profoundly. When he awoke he did it with a start and a stare, as if amazed at having caught himself in the very act of indulging in such weakness. When he washed he puffed, and gasped, and rubbed, and made such a noise, that one might have supposed a walrus was engaged in its ablutions. How the skin of his head, face, and neck stood the towelling it received is incomprehensible! When he walked he went like an express train; when he sauntered he relapsed into the slowest possible snail's-pace, but he did not graduate the changes from one to the other. When he sat down he did so with a crash. The number of chairs which Mr Sudberry broke in the course of his life would have filled a goodly-sized concert-room; and the number of tea-cups which he had swept off tables with the tails of his coat might, we believe, have set up a moderately ambitious man in the china trade.

There was always a beaming smile on the merchant's countenance, except when he was engaged in deep thought; then his mouth was pursed and his brows knitted.

The small clerk was a thin-bodied, weak-minded, timid boy, of about twelve years of age and of humble origin. He sat at Mr Sudberry's double desk in the office, opposite and in dangerous proximity to his master, whom he regarded with great admiration, alarm, and awe.

On a lovely afternoon towards the middle of May, when city men begin to thirst for a draught of fresh air, and to long for an undignified roll on the green fields among primroses, butter-cups, and daisies, Mr Sudberry sat at his desk reading the advertisements in the *Times*.

Suddenly he flung the paper away, hit the desk a sounding blow with his clinched fist, and exclaimed firmly—

"I'll do it!"

Accustomed though he was to nervous shocks, the small clerk leaped with more than ordinary tremor off his stool on this occasion, picked up the paper, laid it at his master's elbow, and sat down again, prepared to look out—nautically speaking—for more squalls.

Mr Sudberry seized a quill, dabbed it into the ink-bottle, and split it. Seizing another he dabbed again; the quill stood the shock; the small clerk ventured a sigh of relief and laid aside the inky napkin which he had pulled out of his desk expecting an upset, and prepared for the worst. A note was dashed off in two minutes,— signed, sealed, addressed, in half a minute, and Mr Sudberry leaped off his stool. His hat was thrown on his head by a species of sleight of hand, and he appeared in the outer office suddenly, like a stout Jack-in-the-box.

"I'm away, Mr Jones," (to his head clerk), "and won't be back till eleven to-morrow morning. Have you the letters ready? I am going round by the post office, and will take charge of them."

"They are here, sir," said Mr Jones, in a mild voice.

Mr Jones was a meek man, with a red nose and a humble aspect. He was a confidential clerk, and much respected by the firm of Sudberry and Company. In fact, it was generally understood that the business could not get on without him. His caution was a most salutary counteractive to Mr Sudberry's recklessness. As for "Co," he was a sleeping partner, and an absolute nonentity.

Mr Sudberry seized the letters and let them fall, picked them up in haste, thrust them confusedly into his pocket, and rushed from the room, knocking over the umbrella-stand in his exit. The sensation left in the office was that of a dead calm after a sharp squall. The small clerk breathed freely, and felt that his life was safe for that day.

Story 1—Chapter 2

Mr Sudberry at Home

"My dear," cried Mr Sudberry to his wife, abruptly entering the parlour of his villa, near Hampstead Heath, "I have done the deed!"

"Dear John, you *are* so violent; my nerves—really—*what* deed?" said Mrs Sudberry, a weak-eyed, delicate woman, of languid temperament, and not far short of her husband's age.

"I have written off to secure a residence in the Highlands of Scotland for our summer quarters this season."

Mrs Sudberry stared in mute surprise. "John! my dear! are you in earnest? Have you not been precipitate in this matter? You know, love, that I have always trusted in your prudence to make arrangements for the spending of our holiday; but really, when I think—"

"Well, my dear, 'When you think,'—pray, go on."

"Don't be hasty, dear John; you know I have never objected to any place you have hitherto fixed on. Herne Bay last year was charming, and the year before we enjoyed Margate *so* much. Even Worthing, though rather too long a journey for a family, was delightful; and, as the family was smaller then, we got over the journey on the whole better than could have been expected. But Scotland!—the Highlands!"—Mr Sudberry's look at this point induced his wife to come to a full stop. The look was not a stern look,—much less a savage look, as connubial looks sometimes are. It was an aggrieved look; not that he was aggrieved at the dubious reception given by his spouse to the arrangement he had made;— no, the sore point in his mind was that he himself entertained strong doubts as to the propriety of what he had done; and to find these doubts reflected in the mind of his faithful better half was perplexing.

"Well, Mary," said the worthy merchant, "go on. Do you state the *cons*, and I'll enumerate the *pros*, after which we will close the account, and see on which side the balance lies."

"You know, dear," said Mrs Sudberry, in a remonstrative tone, "that the journey is fearfully long. I almost tremble when I think of it. To be sure, we have the railroad to Edinburgh now; but beyond that we shall have to travel by stage, I suppose, at least I hope so; but perhaps they have no stage-coaches in Scotland?"

"Oh, yes, they have a few, I believe," replied the merchant, with a smile.

"Ah! that is fortunate; for wagons are fearfully trying. No, I really think that I could *not* stand a wagon journey after my experience of the picnic at Worthing some years ago. Think of our large family—seven of us altogether—in a wagon, John—"

"But you forget, I said that there *are* stage-coaches in Scotland."

"Well; but think of the slow and wearisome travelling among great mountains, over precipices, and through Scotch mists. Lady Knownothing assures me she has been told that the rain never ceases in Scotland, except for a short time in autumn, just to give the scanty crops time to ripen. You know, dear, that our darling Jacky's health could never stand the Scotch mists, he is so *very*, delicate."

"Why, Mary!" exclaimed Mr Sudberry, abruptly; "the doctor told me only yesterday that for a boy of five years old he was a perfect marvel of robust health—that nothing ailed him, except the result of over-eating and the want of open-air exercise; and I am sure that I can testify to the strength of his legs and the soundness of his lungs; for he kicks like a jackass, and roars like a lion."

"It is *very* wrong, *very* sinful of the doctor," said Mrs Sudberry, in a languidly indignant manner, "to give such a false report of the health of our darling boy."

At this moment the door burst open, and the "darling boy" rushed into the room—with a wild cheer of defiance at his nurse, from whom he had escaped, and who was in full pursuit—hit his head on the corner of the table, and fell flat on the floor, with a yell that might have sent a pang of jealousy to the heart of a Chippeway Indian!

Mr Sudberry started up, and almost overturned the tea-table in his haste; but before he could reach his prostrate son, nurse had him kicking in her arms, and carried him off howling.

"Darling child!" said Mrs Sudberry, with her hand on her heart. "How you do startle me, John, with your violence! That is the fifteenth tea-cup this week."

The good lady pointed to a shattered member of the set that lay on the tray beside her.

"I have just ordered a new set, my dear," said her husband, in a subdued voice. "Our poor dear boy would benefit, I think, by mountain air. But go on with the *cons*."

"Have I not said enough?" replied Mrs Sudberry, with an injured look. "Besides, they have no food in Scotland."

This was a somewhat staggering assertion. The merchant looked astonished.

"At least," pursued his wife, "they have nothing, I am told, but oatmeal. Do you imagine that Jacky could live on oatmeal? Do you suppose that your family would return to London in a condition fit to be looked at, after a summer spent on food such as we give to our horses? No doubt you will tell me they have plenty of milk,— buttermilk, I suppose, which I abhor. But do you think that I could live with pleasure on sawdust, just because I had milk to take to it?"

"But milk implies cream, my dear," interposed the merchant, "and buttermilk implies butter, and both imply cows, which are strong presumptive evidence in favour of beef. Besides—"

"Don't talk to me, Mr Sudberry. *I* know better; and Lady Knownothing, who went to Scotland last year, in the most unprejudiced state of mind, came back absolutely horrified by what she had seen. Why, she actually tells me that the natives still wear the kilt! The very day she passed through Edinburgh she met five hundred men without trousers! To be sure, they had guns on their shoulders, and someone told her they were soldiers; but the sight was so appalling that she could not get rid of the impression; she shut her eyes, and ordered the coachman to drive straight through the town, and let her know when she was quite beyond its walls. She has no doubt whatever that most, if not all, of the other inhabitants of that place were clothed—perhaps I should say unclothed—in the same way. What surprised poor Lady Knownothing most was, that she did not see nearly so many kilts in the Highlands as she saw on that occasion in Edinburgh, from which she concluded that the natives of Scotland are less barbarous in the north than they are in the south. But she *did* see a few. One man who played those hideous things called the pipes—which, she says, are so very like little pigs being killed—actually came into her presence one day, sat down before her with bare knees, and took a pinch of snuff with a salt-spoon!"

"That is a dreadful account, no doubt," said Mr Sudberry, "but you must remember that Lady Knownothing is given to exaggerating, and is therefore not to be depended on. Have you done with the *cons*?"

"Not nearly done, John, but my nervous system cannot stand the sustained contemplation of such things. I should like to recover breath, and hear what you have to say in favour of this temporary expatriation, I had almost said, of your family."

"Well, then, here goes for the *pros*," cried Mr Sudberry, while a gleam of excitement shot from his eyes, and his clinched hand came heavily down on the table.

"The sixteenth cup—*as near as possible*," observed his wife, languidly.

"Never mind the cups, my dear, but listen to me. The air of the Highlands is salubrious and bracing—"

"And piercingly cold, my dear John," interrupted Mrs Sudberry.

"In summer," pursued her husband, regardless of the interruption, "it is sometimes as clear and warm as it is in Italy—"

"And often foggy, my dear."

"The mountain scenery is grand and majestic beyond description—"

"Then why attempt to describe it, dear John?"

"The hotels in most parts of the Highlands, though rather expensive—"

"Ah! think of *that*, my dear."

"Though rather expensive, are excellent; the food is of the best quality, and the wines are passable. Beds—"

"*Have* they beds, my dear?"

"Beds are generally found to be well aired and quite clean, though of course in the poorer and more remote districts they are—"

"Hush! pray spare my feelings, my dear John."

"Remote districts, they are not so immaculate as one would wish. Then there are endless moors covered with game, and splendid lakes and rivers full of fish. Just think, Mary, what a region for our dear boys to revel in! Think of the shooting—"

"And the dreadful accidents, my dear."

"Think of the fishing—"

"And the wet feet, and the colds. Poor darling Jacky, what a prospect!"

"Think of the glorious sunrises seen from the mountain-tops before breakfast—"

"And the falling over precipices, and broken necks and limbs, dear John."

"Think of the shaggy ponies for our darling Lucy to ride on—"

"Ah! and to fall off."

"And the dew of early morning on the hills, and the mists rolling up from the lakes, and the wild uncultivated beauty of all around us, and the sketching, and walking, and driving—"

"Dreadful!"

"And bathing and boating—"

"And drowning!"

"Not to mention the—"

"Dear John, have pity on me. The *pros* are too much for me. I cannot stand the thought—"

"But, my dear, the *place is taken*. The thing is *fixed*," said Mr Sudberry, with emphasis. Mrs Sudberry was a wise woman. When she was told by her husband that a thing was *fixed*, she invariably gave in with a good grace. Her powers of dissuasion having failed,—as they always did fail,—she arose, kissed Mr Sudberry's forehead, assured him that she would try to make the most of it, since it *was* fixed, and left the room with the comfortable feeling, of having acted the part of a dutiful wife and a resigned martyr.

It was towards the close of a doubtful summer's evening, several weeks after the conversation just detailed, that a heavy stage-coach, of an old-fashioned description, toiled slowly up the ascent of one of those wild passes by which access is gained into the highlands of Perthshire.

The course of the vehicle had for some time lain along the banks of a turbulent river, whose waters, when not brawling over a rocky bed in impetuous velocity, or raging down a narrow gorge in misty spray, were curling calmly in deep pools or caldrons, the dark surfaces of which were speckled with foam, and occasionally broken by the leap of a yellow trout or a silver salmon.

To an angler the stream would have been captivating in the extreme, but his ardour would have been somewhat damped by the sight of the dense copsewood which overhung the water, and, while it added to the wild beauty of the scenery, suggested the idea of fishing under difficulties.

When the coach reached the narrowest part of the pass, the driver pulled up, and intimated that, "she would be obleeged if the leddies and gentlemen would get down and walk up the brae."

Hereupon there descended from the top of the vehicle a short, stout, elderly gentleman, in a Glengarry bonnet, green tartan shooting-coat, and shepherd's-plaid vest and pantaloons; two active youths, of the ages of seventeen and fifteen respectively, in precisely similar costume; a man-servant in pepper and salt, and a little thin timid boy in blue, a sort of confidential page without the buttons. All of them wore drab gaiters and shoes of the thickest conceivable description. From the inside of the coach there issued a delicate elderly lady, who leaned, in a helpless manner, on the arm of a young, plain, but extremely fresh and sweet-looking girl of about sixteen, whom the elder lady called Lucy, and who was so much engrossed with her mother, that some time elapsed before she could attend to the fervent remarks made by her father and brothers in regard to the scenery. There also came forth from the interior of the coach a large, red-faced angry woman, who dragged after her a little girl of about eight, who might be described as a modest sunbeam, and a little boy of about five, who resembled nothing short of an imp incarnate. When they were all out, the entire family and household of Mr Sudberry stood in the centre of that lovely Highland pass, and the coach, which was a special one hired for the occasion, drove slowly up the ascent.

What the various members of the family said in the extravagance of their excited feelings on this occasion we do not intend to reveal. It has been said that the day was doubtful: in the south the sky was red with the refulgent beams of the setting sun, which gleamed on the mountain peaks and glowed on the purple heather. Towards the north dark leaden clouds obscured the heavens, and presaged stormy weather. A few large drops began to fall as they reached the crest of the road, and opened up a view of the enclosed valley or amphitheatre which lay beyond, with a winding river, a dark overshadowed loch, and a noble background of hills. In the far distance a white house was seen embedded in the blue mountains.

"Yonder's ta hoose," said the driver, as the party overtook the coach, and resumed their places—the males on the top and the females inside.

"Oh, my dear! look! look!" cried Mr Sudberry, leaning over the side of the coach; "there is our house—the white house—our Highland home!"

At this moment a growl of distant thunder was heard. It was followed by a scream from Mrs Sudberry, and a cry of—

"You'd better send Jacky inside, my dear."

"Ah, he may as well remain where he is," replied Mr Sudberry, whose imperfect hearing led him to suppose that his spouse had said, "Jacky's inside, my dear!" whereas the real truth was that the boy was neither out nor inside.

Master Jacky, be it known, had a remarkably strong will of his own. During the journey he preferred an outside seat in all weathers. By dint of much coaxing, his mother had induced him to get in beside her for one stage; but he had made himself so insufferably disagreeable, that the good lady was thereafter much more disposed to let him have his own way. When the coach stopped, as we have described, Jacky got out, and roundly asserted that he would never get in again.

Jacky Frightened.

When the attention of the party was occupied with the gorgeous scenery at the extremity of the pass, Jacky, under a sudden impulse of wickedness, crept stealthily into the copse that lined the road, intending to give his parents a fright. In less than five minutes these parents were galloping away at the rate of ten miles an hour, each happy in the belief that the sweet boy was with the other.

Somewhat surprised at the prolonged and deathlike silence that reigned around him, Jacky returned to the road, where he actually gasped with horror on finding himself the solitary tenant of an apparently uninhabited wilderness. Sitting down on a stone, he shut his eyes, opened wide his mouth, and roared vehemently.

At the end of about five minutes he ventured to re-open his eyes. His face instantly assumed an expression of abject terror, and the roar was intensified into a piercing shriek when he beheld a fierce little black cow staring at him within a yard of his face.

A drove of shaggy Highland cattle had come suddenly round a turn in the pass while Jacky's eyes had been shut. They now filed slowly and steadily past the transfixed boy, as if they were a regiment and he a reviewing general. Each animal as it came up, stopped, stared for a few seconds, and passed slowly on with its head down, as if saddened by the sight of such a melancholy spectacle.

There were upwards of a hundred animals in the drove; the prolonged and maddening agony which Jacky endured may therefore be conceived but cannot be described.

Last of all came the drover, a kilted, plaided, and bonneted Highlander, quite as shaggy as the roughest of his cattle, and rather fiercer in aspect. He was not so in reality however, for, on coming to the place where the poor boy sat, he stopped and stared as his predecessors had done.

"Fat is she doin' there?" said he.

Jacky paused, and gazed for one moment in mute surprise, then resumed his roar with shut eyes and with tenfold vigour.

As it was evident that any farther attempt at conversation must prove fruitless, the drover took Jacky in his arms, carried him to the extremity of the pass, set him down, and, pointing to the white house in the blue distance, said—

"Yonder's ta hoose; let her see how she can rin."

Jacky fixed his eyes on the house with the stare of one who regarded it as his last and only refuge, and ran as he had never done before, roaring while he ran.

"She's a clever callant," observed the drover with a grim smile, as he turned to follow his cattle.

Meanwhile the Sudberry Family reached the White House in the midst of increasing rain and mists and muttering thunder. Of course Jacky's absence was at once discovered. Of course the females screamed and the males shouted, while they turned the mail-coach entirely inside out in a vain search for the lost one. The din was increased by nine shepherd dogs, which rushed down the mountain-side, barking furiously with delight, (probably), and with excitement, (certainly), at the unwonted sight of so many strangers in that remote glen. Presently the coach was turned round, and the distracted father galloped back towards the pass. Of course he almost ran over his youngest son in less than five minutes! Five minutes more placed the recovered child in its mother's arms. Then followed a scene of kissing, crying, laughing, barking, and excitement, which is utterly indescribable, accompanied by thunder, lightning, and rain, in the midst of which tempestuous mental and elemental commotion, the Sudberry Family took possession of their Highland home.

Story 1—Chapter 3

First Impressions

Next morning the Sudberrys were awakened to a sense of the peculiar circumstances into which they had plunged, by the lowing of cattle, the crowing of cocks, and the furious barking of collie dogs, as the household of Donald McAllister commenced the labours of a new day.

Of course every member of the Sudberry Family, with the exception of "mamma," rushed to his or her respective window.

"Oh! how beautiful!" gushed from the heart and lips of Lucy, as she gazed in wonder through the casement, and a shriek burst from Jacky, as he stared in wild delight upon the gorgeous scene that met his view.

We have said that the White House was embedded among the blue hills. It was an old and extremely simple building, having an oblong front, two sides, and a back; two stories, six windows, and one door; which last, imbued, apparently, with a dislike to being shut, was always open. The house appeared to have an insatiable thirst for mountain air, and it was well supplied with this fresh and exhilarating beverage; for it stood in an elevated position on the slope of a mountain, and overlooked a wide tract of flood and fell, on which latter there was little wood, but a luxuriant carpet of grass and heather.

The weather had evidently resolved to make amends for its surly reception of the strangers the previous evening, by greeting them with one of its sweetest Highland smiles in the morning.

When Mr Sudberry, in the exuberance of his delight, ran without hat or coat to a neighbouring knoll, accompanied by all his children, the scene that met his eye was one of surpassing grandeur and beauty. The mists of early morning were rolling up from the loch in white, fleecy clouds, which floated over and partly concealed the sides of the mountains. The upper wreaths of these clouds, and the crags and peaks that pierced through them were set on fire by the rising sun. Great fissures and gorges in the hills, which at other times lay concealed in the blue haze of distance, were revealed by the mists and the slanting rays of the sun, and the incumbent cliffs, bluff promontories, and capes, were in some places sharply defined, in others luminously softened, so that the mountains displayed at once that appearance of solid reality, mingled with melting mystery, which is seen at no period of the day but early morning. The whole scene—water, earth, and sky—was so involved, that no lines of demarcation could be traced anywhere; only bold startling points, melting into blue and white masses that mingled with each other in golden and pearly greys of every conceivable variety. Having said thus much, we need scarcely add that the scene cannot be adequately described.

A light fragrant air met the stout Englishman as he crested the hill, and filled his unaccustomed nostrils with sensations that could not have been excelled had he been greeted by one of "Afric's spicy gales." The same air, with telegraphic speed, conveyed to the collie dogs of the place the information that the Sudberrys were abroad; whereupon the whole pack—nine in number—bounded open-mouthed up the hill, with noise and ferocity enough to have alarmed the bravest of the brave. No wonder then that poor Jacky rushed into his father's knees, being too small to run into his arms. But these seemingly ferocious dogs were in reality the gentlest and meekest of animals.

"Down, Topper, down! down, Lively, lass; come into heel, Swaney," cried Donald McAllister, as he approached his tenants. "Good-mornin', miss; mornin', gentlemen. The Ben has on its nightcap, but I'm thinkin' it'll soon take it off."

Donald McAllister's English was excellent, but he spoke in a slow, deliberate manner, and with a slightly nasal drawl, which sounded very peculiar in the ears of the Sudberrys,—just as peculiar, in fact, as their speech sounded in the ears of McAllister.

"Ah! you call the white cloud on the mountain-top a nightcap?—good, very good," cried Mr Sudberry, rubbing his hands. "What a charming place this is, a paradisaical place, so to speak. The dogs won't bite, will they?" said he, patting the alarmed Jacky on the head.

"No fear o' the dogs, sir," returned McAllister; "they're like lambs. It's just their way. Ye'll be for a row on the loch the day, no doot." The Highlander addressed this remark to George and Fred.

"What!" exclaimed the former, "is there a boat that we can have the use of?"

"'Deed is there, a good safe boat too, that can hold the whole of ye. I'll show you where the oars lie after breakfast."

"Capital," cried Mr Sudberry, rubbing his hands.

"Charming," exclaimed Lucy, with sparkling eyes.

Master Jacky expressed his glee with a characteristic cheer or yell, that at once set fire to the easily inflamed spirits of the dogs, causing them to resume their excited gambols and furious barking. This effectually stopped the conversation for five minutes.

"I delight in boating," observed Fred, when McAllister had quelled the disturbance.

"So do I," said his father; "but fishing is the thing for me. There's nothing like fishing. You have fine trout in the lake, I believe?"

"Ay, an' salmon too," answered McAllister.

"So I've heard, so I've heard," said Mr Sudberry, with a glow of excitement and pleasure on his round visage. "We must get our rods and tackle unpacked at once, George. You are a great fisher, no doubt, Mr McAllister?"

"Well, not just that, but I do manage to fill a basket now and then, an' whiles to land a g'ilse."

"A gilse!" cried George in surprise, "what is that?"

"It is a small salmon—"

"Oh! you mean a grilse," interposed Mr Sudberry.

"Yes, I mean that, an' I said that," returned McAllister, slowly and with emphasis. "Scienteefic men are not agreed whether the g'ilse is a small salmon or not; I'm of opeenion that it is. But whether or not, it's a famous fish on the table, and lively enough on the line to delight the heart of every true disciple of Isaac Walton."

"What, you have read that charming book?" exclaimed Mr Sudberry, looking at the rugged Highlander in some surprise.

"Yes," replied the other, in the grave quiet manner that was peculiar to him; "I took to it one winter as a sort o' recreation, after readin' through 'Paley's Evidences.'"

"What!" cried Mr Sudberry, "whose Evidences did you say?"

"Paley's; ye've heard o' him, dootless."

"Why, yes," replied Mr Sudberry, "I have heard of him, but I—I must confess that I have not read him."

At this point, Jacky's eye fell on a shaggy little cow which had strayed near to the party, and stood regarding him with a stern inquisitive glance. Remembering the fright he had received so recently from a similar creature, he uttered a tremendous roar, and again sought refuge in his father's knees. The discussion on Paley was thus cut short; for the dogs—whose chief delight was to bark, though *not* to bite, as has been libellously asserted of all dogs by Dr Watts—sprang to their feet, divided their forces, and, while two of the oldest kept frisking round and leaping upon the party in a promiscuous manner, as if to assure them of protection in the event of danger, the remainder ran open-mouthed and howling at the cow. That curly-headed, long-horned creature received them at first with a defiant look and an elevated tail, but ultimately took to her heels, to the immense delight of Jacky, whose soul was imbued with a deep and altogether unutterable horror of cattle, especially black cows.

The service which the dogs rendered to him on this occasion induced the boy to make advances of a friendly nature, which were met more than halfway, and the result was the establishment of a good understanding between the Sudberrys and the collie dogs, which ultimately ripened into a lasting friendship, insomuch that when the family quitted the place, Lucy carried away with her a lock of Lively's hair, cut from the pendent tip of her right ear.

Presently Mr Sudberry pulled out his watch, and, exclaiming that it was breakfast-time, trotted down the hill, followed by his family and escorted by the dogs.

We will pause here to describe Mr Sudberry's family briefly.

George was the merchant's eldest son. He was bold, stout, active, middle-sized, and seventeen years of age; full of energy and life, a crack rower, a first-rate cricketer, and generally a clever fellow. George was always jolly.

Fred was about the same height as his brother, two years younger, slender in form, and gentle in disposition, but active, too, when occasion required it. His forte was drawing and painting. Fred was generally quiet and grave. Both brothers were musical.

Lucy had reached the interesting age of sixteen. She was plain, decidedly, but sweet-tempered in the extreme. Her mouth was good, and her eyes were good, and her colour was good, but her nose was a snub,—an undeniable and incurable snub. Her mother had tried to amend it from the earliest hours of Lucy's existence by pulling the point gently downwards and pinching up the bridge,—or, rather, the hollow where the bridge ought to have been,—but all in vain; the infant turned up its eyes when the operation was going on, and still turned up its nose when it was over. Yes, although there were many of the elements of beauty about Lucy, she was plain—but sweet; always bear that in mind. She was funny too. Not that she made fun of her own free will; but she appreciated fun in others so intensely that she looked funny herself; and she giggled. This was her only fault, she giggled. When the spirit of fun was roused, nothing could stop her. But don't suppose that she was always giggling; by no means. She was always good and amiable, often grave, and sometimes deeply serious.

Matilda, commonly called Tilly, was a meek, delicate, pretty little girl of eight years old. She was charmingly innocent and ignorant. In the last respect she resembled her mother, who was the only other stupid member of Mr Sudberry's family. Being deeply impressed with the fact of her ignorance and stupidity, Mrs Sudberry went on the tack of boldly admitting the same, and holding, or affecting to hold, ability and general acquirements in contempt.

Mrs Brown was a female dragon, nurse to Master Jacky and Miss Tilly; she tormented the former, whom she disliked, and spoiled the latter, whom she loved.

Hobbs was the man-servant of the family. He was characterised chiefly by a tendency to drop his h's in conversation, out of words to which they naturally belonged, and to pick them up and insert them in the most contradictory manner in words with which they had no connection whatever. He was also marked by the strong regard and esteem which he had for his master and family; the stronger regard and esteem which he had for himself; and the easy, good-humoured way in which he regarded the remainder of the world at large as an inferior order of beings.

As for Peter, he has already been described as the timid clerk of humble origin, whose chief duties, while in London, were to wipe up ink and clear away *débris*. He had been taken with the family to act the part of a page in buttons without the buttons—and to make himself generally useful. Hitherto the page's bosom had, since leaving London, been a chamber of indescribable terrors. Truly, if, as is said, the anticipation of death be worse than the reality, poor Peter must have suffered a prolonged and continuous death during the last few days. Never having been on a railway before, the first shriek of the whistle pierced him like a knife, the shock of starting rent him, (figuratively), like a thunderbolt. Thereafter, every passing train was an excruciating arrow in his quivering heart, every tunnel was a plunge into the horrible anticipation that "here it was coming at last!" But Peter's trials were now, for a time, he fondly hoped, at an end. Poor boy! he little knew what was in store for him.

Story 1—Chapter 4

First Comers served first, etcetera

When Mr Sudberry reached the breakfast parlour, and put his head in at the door to see whether his faithful wife were there, he was struck absolutely dumb by the amazing *tableau vivant* that met his vision.

There was nothing in the aspect of the room itself to surprise him. It was homely and neat. The table was spread with a clean white cloth, on which the breakfast equipage was displayed with a degree of care and precision that betrayed the master-hand of Hobbs; but on the edge of the table sat a large black cat, calmly breakfasting off a pat of delicious fresh butter. Beside the table, with its fore-legs thereon and its hind-legs on the floor, stood a large nanny-goat, which was either looking in vain for something suited to its own particular taste, or admiring with disinterested complacency the energy with which two hens and a bantam cock pecked out the crumb of a wheaten loaf. If the latter were the goat's occupation, it must have been charmed beyond expression; for the half of the loaf had been devoured by the audacious trio, and, just at the moment of Mr Sudberry's appearance, the bantam's body was buried over the shoulders, and nothing of it was visible to the horrified master of the house save its tail, appearing over the edge of the loaf.

"He was struck absolutely dumb by the amazing 'tableau vivant' that met his vision."

"She—ee—ew!" roared Mr Sudberry, rushing into the room and whirling his arms like the sails of a windmill. The cat vanished through the window like a black vision galvanised and made awfully real. The poultry, thrown into convulsions of terror, flew screaming round the room in blind haste, searching for a door or window of escape; while the goat, true to its nature, ran at the enemy on its hind-legs, and, with its head down, attempted to punch him on the stomach. By an active leap to one side, the enemy escaped this charge; but the goat, nothing daunted, turned to renew the attack; next moment George, Fred, and Hobbs, rushing into the room, diverted its attention. Intimidated by overwhelming numbers, the animal darted through the doorway, along the passage and out at the front door, where it met Peter unexpectedly, and wreaked its disappointed vengeance on him by planting on his chest the punch which had been intended for his master. By this means that timid and hapless youth was laid flat on the green grass.

"Is Jacky safe?" cried Mrs Sudberry, running into the room with terror on her countenance, and falling down on the sofa in a semi-swoon on being informed that he was. She was followed by Lucy and Tilly, with scent-bottles, and by nurse, who exhibited a tendency to go off into hysterics; but who, in consequence of a look from her master, postponed that luxury to a more convenient season.

Thus the "expatriated" family assembled to morning prayers, and to partake of their first Highland breakfast.

Of course that day, being their first, was spent in an excited and rambling endeavour to master the localities and ascertain the most interesting points about their new home.

Mrs Sudberry and her daughters examined the interior accommodation of the White House minutely, and, with the assistance of Mrs Brown, Hobbs, and the page, disposed their goods and chattels to the best advantage; while her husband and sons went out to introduce themselves to the farmer and his family. They lived in a small cottage, or off-shoot, at the back of the principal dwelling, in close proximity to which were the byre, stable, and barns.

It would occupy too much space to relate in detail all the things and sights that called forth the delight and surprise of the excitable Mr Sudberry. How he found to his amazement that the byre was under the same roof with the farmer's kitchen, and only separated therefrom by a wooden partition with a door in it. How he was assailed by the nine collie dogs the moment he entered the kitchen, with threats of being torn to pieces, yet was suffered to pass unscathed. How he and his sons were introduced by Mr McAllister to his mother, a grave, mild old woman, who puzzled them beyond measure; because, although clad in homely and unfashionable garments, and dwelling in a hut little better than the habitation of the cattle, except in point of cleanliness, she conversed and conducted herself towards them with a degree of unaffected ease and urbanity that might have graced any lady in the land. How this old lady astonished them with the amount of general knowledge that leaked out in the course of a few minutes' talk. How she introduced the dogs by name, one by one, to Jacky, which delighted him immensely; and how, soon after that, Jacky attempted to explore out-of-the-way corners of the farm-yard, and stepped suddenly up to the knees in a mud-hole, out of which he emerged with a pair of tight-fitting Wellington boots, which filled him with ecstasy and his father with disgust.

All this and a great deal more might be dilated on largely; but we are compelled to dismiss it summarily, without further remark.

In the course of that day Mr Sudberry and his boys learned a great deal about their new home from McAllister, whom they found intelligent, shrewd, and well-informed on any topic they chose to broach; even although he was, as Mr Sudberry said in surprise, "quite a common man, who wore corduroy and wrought in his fields like a mere labourer." After dinner they all walked out together, and had a row on the lake under his guidance; and in the evening they unexpectedly met Mr Hector Macdonald, who was proprietor of the estate on which the White House stood, and who dwelt in another white house of much larger size at the head of the loch, distant about two miles. Mrs Sudberry had expected to find this Highland gentleman a very poor and proud sort of man, with a rough aspect, a superabundance of red hair, and, possibly, a kilt. Judge, then, her surprise when she found him to be a young gentleman of refined mind, prepossessing manners, elegant though sturdy appearance, and clad in grey tweed shooting-coat, vest, and trousers, the cut of which could not have been excelled by her own George's tailor, and George was particular in respect to cut.

Mr Macdonald, who carried a fishing-rod, introduced himself; and accompanied his new friends part of the way home; and then, saying that he was about to take a cast in the river before sunset, offered to show the gentlemen the best pools. "The gentlemen" leaped at the offer more eagerly than ever trout leaped at an artificial fly; for they were profoundly ignorant of the gentle art, except as it is practised on the Thames, seated on a chair in a punt, and with bait and float.

Hector Macdonald not only showed his friends where to fish, but *how* to fish; and the whole thing appeared so easy as practised and explained by him, that father and sons turned their steps homeward about dusk, convinced that they could "do it" easily, and anticipating triumph on the morrow.

On the way home, after parting from Hector, they passed a solitary hut of the rudest description, which might have escaped observation had not a bright stream of light issued from the low doorway and crossed their path.

"I would like to peep into this cottage, father," said Fred, who cherished strong sympathies with poor people.

"Come then," cried Mr Sudberry, "let us explore."

Jacky, who was with them, felt timid, and objected; but being told that he might hang about outside, he gave in.

They had to bend low on entering the hovel, which was mean and uncomfortable in appearance. The walls were built of unhewn stones, gathered from the bed of the river hard by; and the interstices were filled up with mud and straw. Nothing graced these walls in the shape of ornament; but a few mugs and tin pots and several culinary implements hung from rusty nails and wooden pegs. The floor was of hard mud. There was no ceiling, and the rafters were stained black by the smoke of the peat fire which burned in the middle of the floor, and the only chimney for which was a small hole in the roof. A stool, a broken chair, and a crooked table, constituted the entire furniture of the miserable place; unless we may include a heap of straw and rags in a corner, which served for a bed.

Seated on the stool, and bending over the fire,—was an old woman, so wild and shrivelled in her appearance that a much less superstitious urchin than Jacky might have believed her to be a witch. Her clothing may be described as a bundle of rags, with the exception of a shepherd's-plaid on her shoulders, the spotless purity of which contrasted strangely with the dirtiness of every thing else around. The old creature was moaning and moping over the fire, and drawing the plaid close round her as if she were cold, although the weather was extremely warm. At first she took no notice whatever of the entrance of her visitors, but kept muttering to herself in the Gaelic tongue.

"A fine evening, my good woman," said Fred, laying his hand gently on her shoulder.

"How do ye know I'm good?" she cried, turning her gleaming eyes sharply on her questioner.

"Don't be angry, granny," put in Mr Sudberry, in a conciliatory tone.

The effect of this remark on the old woman was the reverse of what had been expected.

"Granny! granny!" she shrieked fiercely, holding up her skinny right arm and shaking her fist at Mr Sudberry, "who dares to ca' me granny?"

"My dear woman, I meant no offence," said the latter, much distressed at having unwittingly roused the anger of this strange creature, who continued to glare furiously at the trio.

Jacky kept well in the background, and contented himself with peeping round the door-post.

"No offence! no offence! an' you dare to ca' me granny! Go! go! *go!*"

As she uttered these three words with increasing vehemence, the last syllable was delivered in a piercing scream. Rising suddenly from her stool, she pointed to the door with an air of command that would have well become the queen of the witches.

Not wishing to agitate the poor woman, whom he now regarded as a lunatic, Mr Sudberry turned to go, but a wonderful change in the expression of her face arrested him. Her eye had fallen on the round visage of Jacky, and a beaming smile now lighted up and beautified the countenance which had so recently been distorted with passion. Uttering some unintelligible phrase in Gaelic, she held out her skinny arms towards the child, as if entreating him to come to her. Strange to say, Jacky did not run away or scream with fright as she approached him and took him in her arms. Whether it was that he was too much petrified with horror to offer any resistance, or that he understood the smile of affection and reciprocated it, we cannot tell; but certain it is that Jacky suffered her to place him on her knee, stroke his hair, and press him to her old breast, as unresistingly and silently as if she had been his own mother, instead of a mad old woman.

Fred availed himself of this improved state of things to attempt again to open an amicable conversation; but the old woman appeared to have turned stone deaf; for she would neither look at nor reply to him. Her whole attention was devoted to Jacky, into whose wondering ears she poured a stream of Gaelic, without either waiting for, or apparently expecting, a reply.

Suddenly, without a word of warning, she pushed Jacky away from her, and began to wring her hands and moan as she bent over the fire. Mr Sudberry seized the opportunity to decamp. He led Jacky quietly out of the hut, and made for the White House at as rapid a pace as the darkness of the night would allow. As they walked home, father and sons felt as if they had recently held familiar converse with a ghost or an evil spirit.

But that feeling passed away when they were all seated at tea in the snug parlour, relating and listening to the adventure; and Jacky swelled to double his size, figuratively, on finding himself invested with sudden and singular importance as the darling of an "old witch." Soon, however, matters of greater interest claimed the attention of Mr Sudberry and his sons; for their bosoms were inflamed with a desire to emulate the dexterous Hector Macdonald.

Rods and tackle were overhauled, and every preparation made for a serious expedition on the morrow. That night Mr Sudberry dreamed of fishing.

Story 1—Chapter 5

Some Account of a Great Fishing Expedition

There was an old barometer of the banjo type in the parlour of the White House, which, whatever might have been its character for veracity in former days, had now become such an inveterate story-teller, that it was pretty safe to accept as true exactly the reverse of what it indicated. One evening Mr Sudberry kept tapping that antique and musical-looking instrument, with a view to get it to speak out its mind freely. The worthy man's efforts were not in vain, for the instrument, whether out of spite or not, we cannot say, indicated plainly "much rain."

Now, it must be known that Mr Sudberry knew as much about trout and salmon-fishing as that celebrated though solitary individual, "the man in the moon." Believing that bright, dry, sunny weather was favourable to this sport, his heart failed him when the barometer became so prophetically depressed, and he moved about the parlour with quick, uneasy steps, to the distress of his good wife, whose work-box he twice swept off the table with his coat-tails, and to the dismay of George, whose tackle, being spread out for examination, was, to a large extent, caught up and hopelessly affixed to the same unruly tails.

Supper and repose finally quieted Mr Sudberry's anxious temperament; and when he awoke on the following morning, the sun was shining in unclouded splendour through his window. Awaking with a start, he bounced out of bed, and, opening his window, shouted with delight that it was a glorious fishing-day.

The shout was addressed to the world at large, but it was responded to only by Hobbs.

"Yes, sir, it *is* a hexquisite day," said that worthy; "what a day for the Thames, sir! It does my 'art good, sir, to think of that there river."

Hobbs, who was standing below his master's window, with his coat off, and his hands in his waistcoat-pockets, meant this as a happy and delicate allusion to things and times of the past.

"Ah! Hobbs," said Mr Sudberry, "you don't know what fishing in the Highlands is, yet; but you shall see. Are the rods ready?"

"Yes, sir."

"And the baskets and books?"

"Yes, sir."

"And, ah! I forgot—the flasks and sandwiches—are they ready, and the worms?"

"Yes, sir; Miss Lucy's a makin' of the san'wiches in the kitchen at this moment, and Maclister's a diggin' of the worms."

Mr Sudberry shut his window, and George, hearing the noise, leaped out of bed with the violence that is peculiar to vigorous youth. Fred yawned.

"What a magnificent day!" said George, rubbing his hands, and slapping himself preparatory to ablutions; "I will shoot."

"Will you—a–ow?" yawned Fred: "I shall sketch. I mean to begin with the old woman's hut."

"What! do you mean to have your nose plucked off and your eyes torn out at the beginning of our holiday?"

"Not if I can help it, George; but I mean to run the risk—I mean to cultivate that old woman."

"Hallo! hi!" shouted their father from below, while he tapped at the window with the end of a fishing-rod. "Look alive there, boys, else we'll have breakfast without you."

"Ay, ay, father!" Fred was up in a moment.

About two hours later, father and sons sallied out for a day's sport, George with a fowling-piece, Fred with a sketch-book, and Mr Sudberry with a fishing-rod, the varnish and brass-work on which, being perfectly new, glistened in the sun.

"We part here, father," said George, as they reached a rude bridge that spanned the river about half a mile distant from the

White House. "I mean to clamber up the sides of the Ben, and explore the gorges. They say that ptarmigan and mountain hares are to be found there."

The youth's eye sparkled with enthusiasm; for, having been born and bred in the heart of London, the idea of roaming alone among wild rocky glens up among the hills, far from the abodes of men, made him fancy himself little short of a second Crusoe. He was also elated at the thought of firing at *real* wild birds and animals—his experiences with the gun having hitherto been confined to the unromantic practice of a shooting-gallery in Regent Street.

"Success to you, George," cried Mr Sudberry, waving his hand to his son, as the latter was about to enter a ravine.

"The same to you, father," cried George, as he waved his cap in return, and disappeared.

Five minutes' walk brought them to the hut of the poor old woman, whose name they had learned was Moggy.

"This, then, is my goal," said Fred, smiling. "I hope to scratch in the outline of the interior before you catch your first trout."

"Take care the old woman doesn't scratch out your eyes, Fred," said the father, laughing. "Dinner at five—*sharp*, remember."

Fred entered the hovel, and Mr Sudberry, walking briskly along the road for a quarter of a mile, diverged into a foot-path which conducted him to the banks of the river, and to the margin of a magnificent pool where he hoped to catch his first trout.

And now, at last, had arrived that hour to which Mr Sudberry had long looked forward with the most ardent anticipation. To stand alone on a lovely summer's day, rod in hand, on the banks of a Highland stream, had been the ambition of the worthy merchant ever since he was a boy. Fate had decreed that this ambition should not be gratified until his head was bald; but he did not rejoice the less on this account. His limbs were stout and still active, and his enthusiasm was as strong as it was in boyhood. No one knew the powerful spirit of angling which dwelt in Mr Sudberry's breast. His wife did not, his sons did not. He was not fully aware of it himself, until opportunity revealed it in the most surprising manner. He had, indeed, known a little of the angler's feelings in the days of his youth, but he had a soul above punts, and chairs, and floats, and such trifles; although, like all great men, he did not despise little things. Many a day had he sat on old Father Thames, staring, with eager expectation, at a gaudy float, as if all his earthly hopes were dependent on its motions; and many a struggling fish had he whipped out of the muddy waters with a shout of joy. But he thought of those days, now, with the feelings of an old soldier who, returning from the wars to his parents' abode, beholds the drum and pop-gun of his childhood. He recalled the pleasures of the punt with patronising kindliness, and gazed majestically on crag, and glen, and bright, glancing stream, while he pressed his foot upon the purple heath, and put up his fishing-rod!

Mr Sudberry was in his element now. The deep flush on his gladsome countenance indicated the turmoil of combined romance and delight which raged within his heaving chest, and which he with difficulty prevented from breaking forth into an idiotic cheer. He was alone, as we have said. He was purposely so. He felt that, as yet, no member of his family could possibly sympathise with his feelings. It was better that they should not witness emotions which they could not thoroughly understand. Moreover, he wished to surprise them with the result of his prowess—in regard to which his belief was unlimited. He felt, besides, that it was better there should be no witness to the trifling failures which might be expected to occur in the first essay of one wholly unacquainted with the art of angling, as practised in these remote glens.

The pool beside which Mr Sudberry stood was one which Hector Macdonald had pointed out as being one of the best in the river. It lay at the tail of a rapid, had an eddy in it, and a rippling, oily surface. The banks were in places free from underwood, and only a few small trees grew near them. The shadow of the mountain, which reared its rugged crest close to it, usually darkened the surface, but, at the time we write of, a glowing sun poured its rays into the deepest recesses of the pool—a fact which filled Mr Sudberry, in his ignorance, with delight; but which, had he known better, would have overwhelmed him with dismay. In the present instance it happened that "ignorance was bliss," for as every fish in the pool was watching the angler with grave upturned eyes while he put up his rod, and would as soon have attempted to swallow Mr Sudberry's hat as leap at his artificial flies, it was well that he was not aware of the fact, otherwise his joy of heart would have been turned into sorrow sooner than there was any occasion for.

Musing on piscatorial scenes past, present, and to come, Mr Sudberry passed the line through the rings of his rod with trembling and excited fingers.

While thus engaged, he observed a break on the surface of the pool, and a fish caused a number of rings to form on the water; those floated toward him as if to invite him on. Mr Sudberry was red-hot now with hope and expectation. It was an *enormous* trout that had risen. Most trouts that are seen, but not caught, are enormous!

There is no pleasure without its alloy. It could not be expected that the course of true sport, any more than that of true love, should run smooth. Mr Sudberry's ruddy face suddenly turned pale when he discovered that he had forgotten his fishing book! Each pocket in his coat was slapped and plunged into with vehement haste, while drops of cold perspiration stood on his forehead. It was not to be found. Suddenly he recollected the basket at his back: wrenching it open, he found the book there, and joy again suffused his visage.

Selecting his best line and hooks—as pointed out to him by Hector—Mr Sudberry let out a few yards of line, and prepared for action. Remembering the advice and example of his friend, he made his first cast.

Ha! not so bad. The line fell rather closer to the bank on which he stood than was consistent with the vigour of the cast; but never mind, the next would be better! The next *was* better. The line went out to its full extent, and came down on the water with such a splash that no trout in its senses would have looked at the place for an hour afterwards. But Mr Sudberry was ignorant of this, so he went on hopefully.

As yet the line was short, so he let out half a dozen yards boldly, and allowed the stream to draw it straight. Then, making a violent effort, he succeeded in causing it to descend in a series of circles close to his feet! This, besides being unexpected, was embarrassing. Determined to succeed, he made another cast, and caught the top branch of a small tree, the existence of which he had forgotten. There the hooks remained fixed.

A deep sigh broke from the excited man, as he gazed ruefully up at the tree. Under a sudden and violent impulse, he tried to pull the tackle forcibly away. This would not do. He tried again till the rod bent almost double, and he was filled with amazement to find that the casting-line, though no thicker than a thread, could stand such a pull. Still the hooks held on. Laying down his rod, he wiped his forehead and sighed again.

But Mr Sudberry was not a man to be easily thwarted. Recalling the days of his boyhood, he cast off his coat and nimbly shinned up the trunk of the tree. In a few minutes he reached the top branch and seized it. At that moment the bough on which he stood gave way, and he fell to the ground with a terrible crash, bringing the top branch with him! Gathering himself up, he carefully manipulated his neck, to ascertain whether or not it was broken. He found that it was not; but the line was, so he sat down quietly on the bank and replaced it with a new one.

Before Mr Sudberry left that spot on the bank beside the dark pool, he had caught the tree four times and his hat twice, but he had caught no trout. "They're not taking to-day, that's it," he muttered sadly to himself; "but come, cheer up, old fellow, and try a new fly."

Thus encouraged by himself, Mr Sudberry selected a large blue fly with a black head, red wings, and a long yellow tail. It was a gorgeous, and he thought a tempting creature; but the trout were evidently not of the same opinion. For several hours the unfortunate piscator flogged the water in vain. He became very hot during this prolonged exertion, stumbled into several holes, and wetted both legs up to the knees, had his cap brushed off more than once by overhanging branches, and entangled his line grievously while in the act of picking it up, bruised his shins several times, and in short got so much knocked about, battered, and worried, that he began to feel in a state of mental and physical dishevelment.

Still his countenance did not betray much of his feelings. He found fishing more difficult in all respects than he had expected;

but what then? Was he going to give way to disgust at the first disappointment? Certainly not. Was he going to fail in perseverance now, after having established a reputation for that quality during a long commercial life in the capital of England? Decidedly not. Was that energy, that vigour, that fervour of character for which he was noted, to fail him here—here, in an uncivilised country, where it was so much required—after having been the means of raising him from a humble station to one of affluence; after having enabled him to crush through all difficulties, small or great, as well as having caused him to sweep hecatombs of crockery to destruction with his coat tails? Indubitably not!

Glowing with such thoughts, the dauntless man tightened his cap on his brow, pressed his lips together with a firm smile, frowned good-humouredly at fate and the water, and continued his unflagging, though not unflogging, way.

So, the hot sun beat down upon him until evening drew on apace, and then the midges came out. The torments which Mr Sudberry endured after this were positively awful, and the struggles that he made, in the bravery of his cheerful heart, to bear up against them, were worthy of a hero of romance. His sufferings were all the more terrible and exasperating, that at first they came in the shape of an effect without a cause. The skin of his face and hands began to inflame and to itch beyond endurance—to his great surprise; for the midges were so exceedingly small and light, that, being deeply intent on his line, he did not observe them. He had heard of midges, no doubt; but never having seen them, and being altogether engrossed in his occupation, he never thought of them for a moment. He only became aware of ever-increasing uneasiness, and exhibited a tendency to rub the backs of his hands violently on his trousers, and to polish his countenance with his cuffs.

It must be the effect of exposure to the sun, he thought—yes, that was it; of course, that would go off soon, and he would become case-hardened, a regular mountaineer! Ha! was that a trout? Yes, that must have been one at last; to be sure, there were several stones and eddies near the spot where it rose, but he knew the difference between the curl of an eddy now and the splash of a trout; he would throw over the exact spot, which was just a foot or two above a moss-covered stone that peeped out of the water; he did so, and caught it—the stone, not the trout—and the hooks remained fixed in the slimy green moss.

Mr Sudberry scratched his head and felt inclined to stamp. He even experienced a wild desire to cast his rod violently into the river, and walk home with his hands in his pockets; but he restrained himself. Pulling on the line somewhat recklessly, the hook came away, to his immense delight, trailing a long thread of the green moss along with it.

Mr Sudberry now took to holding a muttered conversation with himself—a practice which was by no means new to him, and in the course of which he was wont to address himself in curiously disrespectful terms. "Come, come, John, my boy, don't be cast down! Never say die! Hope, ay, hope told a flatter— Hallo! was that a rise? No, it must have been another of these—what can be the matter with your skin to-day, John? I don't believe it's the sun, after all. The sun never drove anyone frantic. Never mind; cheer up, old cock! That seems a very likely hole—a beautiful—beau– ti—steady! That was a good cast—the best you've made to-day, my buck; try it again—ha! s–s–us! caught again, as I'm a Dutchman. This is too bad. Really, you know—well, you've come off easier than might have been expected. Now then, softly. What *can* be the matter with your face?—surely—it cannot be," (Mr Sudberry's heart palpitated as he thought), "the *measles*! Oh! impossible, pooh! pooh! you had the measles when you were a baby, of course—d'ye know, John, you're not quite sure of that. Fevers, too, occasionally come on with extreme—dear me, how hot it is, and what a time you have been fishing, you stupid fellow, without a rise! It must be getting late."

Mr Sudberry stopped with a startled look as he said this. He glanced at the sun, pulled out his watch, gazed at it with unutterable surprise, put it to his ear, and groaned.

"Too late! half-past five; dinner at five—punctually! Oh! Mary, Mary, won't I catch it to-night!"

A cloud passed over the sun as he spoke. Being very susceptible to outward influences, the gloom of the shadow descended on his spirits as well as his person, and for the first time that day a look of deep dejection overspread his countenance.

Suddenly there was a violent twitch at the end of the rod, the reel spun round with a sharp whirr–r, and every nerve in Mr Sudberry's system received an electric shock as he bent forward, straddled his legs, and made a desperate effort to fling the trout over his head.

The slender rod would not, however, permit of such treatment. It bent double, and the excited piscator was fain to wind up—an operation which he performed so hastily that the line became entangled with the winch of the reel, which brought it to a deadlock. With a gasp of anxiety he flung down the rod, and seizing the line with his hands, hauled out a beautiful yellow trout of about a quarter of a pound in weight, and five or six inches long.

To describe the joy of Mr Sudberry at this piece of good fortune were next to impossible. Sitting down on his fishing-basket, with the trout full in view, he drew forth a small flask of sherry, a slice of bread, and a lump of cheese, and proceeded then and there to regale himself. He cared nothing now for the loss of his dinner; no thought gave he to the anticipated scold from neglected Mrs Sudberry. He gave full scope to his joy at the catching of this, his first trout. He looked up at the cloud that obscured the sun, and forgave it, little thinking, innocent man, that the said cloud had done him a good turn that day. He smiled benignantly on water, earth, and sky. He rubbed his face, and when he did so he thought of the measles and laughed—laughed heartily, for by that time he had discovered the true cause of his misery; and although we cannot venture to say that he forgave the midges, sure we are that he was greatly mollified towards them.

Does any ignorant or cynical reader deem such an extravagance of delight inconsistent with so trifling an occasion? Let him ponder before he ventures to exclaim, "Ridiculous!" Let him look round upon this busy, whirling, incomprehensible world, and note how its laughing and weeping multitudes are oft-times tickled to uproarious merriment, or whelmed in gloomy woe, by the veriest trifles, and then let him try to look with sympathy on Mr Sudberry and his first trout.

Having carefully deposited the fish in his basket, he once more resumed his rod and his expectations.

But if the petty annoyances that beset our friend in the fore part of that day may be styled harassing, those with which he was overwhelmed towards evening may be called exasperating. First of all he broke the top of his rod, a misfortune which broke his heart entirely. But recollecting suddenly that he had three spare top-pieces in the butt, his heart was cemented and bound up, so to speak, in a rough and ready manner. Next, he stepped into a hole, which turned out to be three feet deep, so that he was instantly soaked up to the waist. Being extremely hot, besides having grown quite reckless, Mr Sudberry did not mind this; it was pleasantly cooling. He was cheered, too, at the moment, by the re-appearance of the sun, which shone out as bright as ever, warming his heart, (poor, ignorant man!) and, all unknown to him, damaging his chance of catching any more fish at that time.

Soon after this he came to a part of the river where it flowed through extremely rugged rocks, and plunged over one or two precipices, sending up clouds of grey mist and a dull roar which overawed him, and depressed his spirits. This latter effect was still further increased by the bruising of his shins and elbows, which resulted from the rough nature of the ground. He became quite expert now in hanking on bushes and disentangling the line, and experienced a growing belief in the truth of the old saying that "practice makes perfect." He cast better, he hanked oftener, and he disentangled more easily than he had done at an earlier period of the day. The midges, too, increased as evening advanced.

Presently he came upon a picturesque portion of the stream where the waters warbled and curled in little easy-going rapids, miniature falls, and deep oily pools. Being an angler by nature, though not by practice, (as yet), he felt that there must be *something* there. A row of natural stepping-stones ran out towards a splendid pool, in which he felt assured there must be a large trout—perhaps a grilse. His modesty forbade him to hint "a salmon," even to himself.

It is a very difficult thing, as everyone knows, to step from one stone to another in a river, especially when the water flowing between runs swift and deep. Mr Sudberry found it so. In his effort to approach the pool in question, which lay under the opposite bank, he exhibited not a few of the postures of the rope-dancer and the acrobat; but he succeeded, for Mr Sudberry was a man of indomitable pluck.

Standing on a small stone, carefully balanced, and with his feet close together, he made a beautiful cast. It was gracefully done; it was vigorously, manfully done—considering the difficulty of the position, and the voracity of the midges—and would have been undoubtedly successful but for the branch of a tree which grew on the opposite bank and overhung the stream. This branch Mr Sudberry, in his eagerness, did not observe. In casting, he thrust the end of his rod violently into it; the line twirled in dire confusion round the leaves and small boughs, and the drag hook, as if to taunt him, hung down within a foot of his nose.

Mr Sudberry, in despair, made a desperate grasp at this and caught it. More than that—it caught him, and sunk into his forefinger over the barb, so that he could not get it out. The rock on which he stood was too narrow to admit of much movement, much less to permit of his resting the butt of his rod on it, even if that had been practicable—which it was not, owing to the line being fast to the bough, and the reel in a state of dead-lock from some indescribable manoeuvre to which it had previously been subjected.

There he stood, the very personification of despair; but while standing there he revolved in his mind the best method of releasing his line without breaking it or further damaging his rod. Alas! fortune, in this instance, did not favour the brave. While he was looking up in rueful contemplation of the havoc above, and then down at his pierced and captured finger, his foot slipped and he fell with a heavy plunge into deep water. That settled the question. The whole of his tackle remained attached to the fatal bough excepting the hook in his finger, with which, and the remains of his fishing-rod, he floundered to the shore.

Mr Sudberry's first act on gaining the land was to look into his basket, where, to his great relief, the trout was still reposing. His next was to pick up his hat, which was sailing in an eddy fifty yards down the stream. Then he squeezed the water out of his garments, took down his rod, with a heavy sigh strangely mingled with a triumphant smile, and turned his steps home just as the sun began to dip behind the peaks of the distant hills.

"The rock on which he stood was too narrow to admit of much movement."

To his surprise and relief; Mrs Sudberry did *not* scold when, about an hour later, he entered the hall or porch of the White House with the deprecatory air of a dog that knows he has been misbehaving, and with the general aspect of a drowned rat. His wife had been terribly anxious about his non-arrival, and the joy she felt on seeing him safe and well, induced her to forget the scold.

"Oh! John dear, quick, get off your clothes," was her first exclamation.

As for Jacky, he uttered a cheer of delight and amazement at beholding his father in such a woeful plight; and he spent the remainder of the evening in a state of impish triumph; for, had not his own father come home in the same wet and draggled condition as that in which he himself had presented himself to Mrs Brown earlier in the day, and for which he had received a sound whipping? "Hooray!" and with that the amiable child went off to inform his worthy nurse that "papa was as bad a boy as himself—badder, in fact; for he, (Jacky), had only been in the water up to the waist, while papa had gone into it head and heels!"

Story 1—Chapter 6

The Picnic

A Vision of beauty now breaks upon the scene! This vision is tall, graceful, and commanding in figure. It has long black ringlets, piercing black eyes, a fair delicate skin, and a bewitching smile that displays a row of—of "pearls!" The vision is about sixteen years of age, and answers to the romantic name of Flora Macdonald. It is sister to that stalwart Hector who first showed Mr Sudberry how to fish; and stately, sedate, and beautiful does it appear, as, leaning on its brother's arm, it ascends the hill towards the White House, where extensive preparations are being made for a picnic.

"Good-morning, Mr Sudberry," cries Hector, doffing his bonnet and bowing low to Lucy. "Allow me to introduce my sister, Flora; but," (glancing at the preparations), "I fear that my visit is inopportune."

Mr Sudberry rushes forward and shakes Hector and sister heartily by the hand.

"My dear sir, my dear madam, inopportune! impossible! I am charmed. We are just going on a picnic, that is all, and you will go with us. Lucy, my dear, allow me to introduce you to Miss Macdonald—"

"*Flora*, my good sir; pray do not let us stand upon ceremony," interposes Hector.

Lucy bows with a slight air of bashful reserve; Flora advances and boldly offers her hand. The blue eyes and the black meet; the former twinkle, the latter beam, and the knot is tied; they are fast friends for life!

"Glorious day," cries Mr Sudberry, rubbing his hands.

"Magnificent," assents Hector. "You are fortunate in the weather, for, to say truth, we have little enough of sunshine here.

Sometimes it rains for three or four weeks, almost without cessation."

"Does it indeed?"

Mr Sudberry's visage elongates a little for one moment. Just then George and Fred come out of the White House laden with hampers and fishing-baskets full of provisions. They start, gaze in surprise at the vision, and drop the provisions.

"These are my boys, Miss Macdonald—Hector's sister, lads," cries Mr Sudberry. "You'll join us I trust?" (to Hector.)

Hector assents "with pleasure." He is a most amiable and accommodating man. Meanwhile George and Fred shake hands with Flora, and express their "delight, their pleasure, etcetera, at this unexpected meeting which, etcetera, etcetera." Their eyes meet, too, as Lucy's and Flora's had met a minute before. Whether the concussion of that meeting is too severe, we cannot say, but the result is, that the three pair of eyes drop to the ground, and their owners blush. George even goes the length of stammering something incoherent about "Highland scenery," when a diversion is created in his favour by Jacky, who comes suddenly round the corner of the house with a North-American-Indian howl, and with the nine dogs tearing after him clamorously.

Jacky tumbles over a basket, of course, (a state of disaster is his normal condition), bruises his shins, and yells fearfully, to the dismay of his mother, who runs shrieking to the window in her dressing-gown, meets the gaze of Hector and Flora Macdonald, and retires precipitately in discomfiture.

No such sensibility affects the stern bosom of Mrs Brown, who darts out at the front door, catches the unhappy boy by one arm, and drags him into the house by it as if *it* were a rope, the child a homeward-bound vessel, and *she* a tug-steamer of nine hundred horse-power. The sounds that proceed from the nursery thereafter are strikingly suggestive: they might be taken for loud clapping of hands, but the shrieks which follow forbid the idea of plaudits.

Poor Tilly, who is confused by the uproar, follows the nurse timidly, bent upon intercession, for she loves Jacky dearly.

The nine dogs—easy-going, jovial creatures—at once jump to the conclusion that the ham and cold chicken have been prepared and laid out there on the green hill-side for their special entertainment. They make a prompt dash at the hampers. Gentlemen and ladies alike rush to the rescue, and the dogs are obliged to retire. They do so with a surprised and injured look in their innocent eyes.

"Have you one or two raw onions and a few cold boiled potatoes?" inquires Hector.

"I'll run and see," cries George, who soon returns with the desired edibles in a tin can.

"That will do. Now I shall let you taste a potato salad; meanwhile I will assist in carrying the baskets down to the boat."

Hector's and Lucy's eyes meet as this is said. There must be some unaccountable influence in the atmosphere this morning, for the meeting of eyes, all round, seems to produce unusual results!

"Will Mr McAllister accompany us?" says Mr Sudberry.

Mr McAllister permits a quiet smile to disturb the gravity of his countenance, and agrees to do so, at the same time making vague reference to the groves of Arcadia, and the delight of dining *alfresco*, specially in wet weather,—observations which surprise Mr Sudberry, and cause Hector and the two brothers to laugh.

Mrs Sudberry is ready at last! The gentlemen and Hobbs load themselves, and, followed by Jacky and the ladies, proceed to the margin of the loch, which sheet of water Mr Sudberry styles a "lock," while his better half deliberately and obstinately calls it a "lake." The party is a large one for so small a boat, but it holds them all easily. Besides, the day is calm and the water lies like a sheet of pure glass; it seems almost a pity to break such a faithful mirror with the plashing oars as they row away.

Thus, pleasantly, the picnic began!

George and Fred rowed, Hector steered, and the ladies sang,— Mr Sudberry assisting with a bass. His voice, being a strong baritone, was overwhelmingly loud in the middle notes, and sank into a muffled ineffective rumble in the deep tones. Having a bad ear for tune, he disconcerted the ladies—also the rowers. But what did that matter? He was overflowing with delight, and apologised for his awkwardness by laughing loudly and begging the ladies to begin again. This they always did, with immense good humour. Mrs Sudberry had two engrossing subjects of contemplation. The one was the boat, which, she was firmly persuaded, was on the point of upsetting when any one moved ever so little; the other was Jacky, who, owing to some strange impulse natural to his impish character, strove to stretch as much of his person beyond the side of the boat as was possible without absolutely throwing himself overboard.

The loch was upwards of three miles in length; before the party had gone half the distance Mr Sudberry senior had sung himself quite hoarse, and Master Sudberry junior had leaped three-quarters of his length out of the boat six times, and in various other ways had terrified his poor mother almost into fits, and imperilled the lives of the party more than once.

"By the way," said Fred, when his father concluded a fine old boat-song with a magnificent flourish worthy of an operatic *artiste*, "can any one tell me any thing about the strange old woman that lives down in the hut near the bridge?"

"Ha! ha!" laughed George, "I can tell you that she's an old witch, and a very fierce one too."

A slight frown gathered on Flora's white forehead, and a flash shot from her dark eyes, as George said this, but George saw it not. Lucy did, however, and became observant, while George continued—

"But methinks, Fred, that the long visit you paid her lately must have been sadly misapplied if you have not pumped her history out of her."

"I went to paint, not to pump. Perhaps Mr Macdonald can tell me about her."

"Not I," said Hector, lighting a cigar. "I only know that she lost her grandson about six years ago, and that she's been mad ever since, poor thing."

"For shame, Hector," said Flora; "you know that poor old Moggy is no more mad than yourself."

"Possibly not, sweet sister, but as you often tell me that I *am* mad, and as I never deny the charge, it seems to me that you have said nothing to vindicate the old woman's character for sanity."

"Poor thing," said Flora, turning from her brother, and speaking with warmth to Fred; "if you knew how much that unhappy old creature has suffered, you would not be surprised to find her somewhat cross at times. She is one of my people, and I'm very glad to find that you take an interest in her."

"'My people!' Flora then takes an interest in the poor," thought the observant Lucy. Another link was added to the chain of friendship.

"Do tell us about her, please," cried George. "There is nothing that I love so much as a story—especially a horrible one, with two or three dreadful murders to chill one's blood, and a deal of retributive justice to warm it up again. I'm dying to know about old Moggy."

"Are you?" said Flora saucily. "I'm glad to hear that, because I mean to keep you in a dying state. I will tell the story as a dead secret to Lucy, when I take her to see my poor people, and you sha'n't hear it for weeks to come."

George cast up his eyes in affected despair, and said with a groan, that he "would endeavour to exist notwithstanding."

"Oh! *I* know all about old Moggy," cried Jacky with energy.

Everyone looked at the boy in surprise. In the midst of the foregoing dialogue he had suddenly ceased to tempt his fate, and sat down quietly with a hand on each knee and his eyes fixed intently on Flora Macdonald—to the surprise and secret joy of his mother, who, being thus relieved from anxiety on his account, had leisure to transfer the agony of her attention to the boat.

"What do *you* know about her, child?" asked Flora.

"She's jolly," replied the boy with prompt vivacity.

"Most genuine testimony in her favour," laughed Hector, "though the word is scarcely appropriate to one whose temper is sour."

"Why do you think her jolly, my boy?" said Flora.

"'Cause I do. She's a old brick!"

"Jacky, darling," said Mrs Sudberry, "do try to give up those ugly slang words—they're *so* naughty—that is to say—at least—they are very ugly if they're not positively naughty."

"She's a jolly old brick," retorted Jacky, with a look at his mother that was the concentrated essence of defiance.

"Dear child!"

Lucy snickered and coughed somewhat violently into her handkerchief; while Flora, repressing a smile, said—

"But why does Jacky like old Moggy so much?"

"Hallo! don't run us ashore," shouted Mr Sudberry, starting up with a sudden impetuosity which shook the boat and sent a pang to the heart of his wife, the sharpness of which no words can convey. A piercing shriek, however, betrayed the state of her feelings as the boat was swept violently round by George to avoid a point of rock. As they were now drawing near to the spot where it was proposed that they should picnic, Jacky suddenly became alive to the fact that in his interest about old Moggy he had been betrayed into a forgetfulness of his opportunities. No time was to be lost. Turning round with a cheer, he made a desperate plunge at the water and went much farther over than he had intended, insomuch that he would certainly have taken a "header" into its depths, had not McAllister grasped him by the baggy region of his trousers and gravely lifted him into his mother's lap. Next moment the boat's keel grated sharply on the gravel, to the horror of Mrs Sudberry, who, having buried her face in the bosom of her saved son, saw not what had occurred, and regarded the shock as her death-warrant.

Thus agreeably the picnic continued!

Story 1—Chapter 7

The Picnic Concluded

What a glorious day it was, and what spirits it put everybody in! The sun shone with an intensity almost torrid; the spot on which they had landed was green and bright, like a slice out of the realms of Fairy-land. No zephyr dared to disturb the leaves or the glassy water; great clouds hung in the bright blue sky—rotund, fat, and heavy, like mountains of wool or butter. Everything in nature seemed to have gone to sleep at noon, as if Spanish principles had suddenly imbued the universe.

And what a business they had, to be sure, with the spreading of the viands and the kindling of the fire! The latter was the first duty. Hector said he would undertake it, but after attempting to light it with damp sticks he gave it up and assisted the ladies to lay the cloth on the grass. Then George and Fred got the fire to kindle, and Mr Sudberry, in attempting to mend it, burnt his fingers and put it out; whereupon McAllister came to his rescue and got it to blaze in right earnest. Jacky thereafter tried to jump over it, fell into it, and was saved from premature destruction by being plucked out and quenched before having received any further damage than the singeing of his hair and eyelashes. He was thus rendered a little more hideous and impish-like than Nature had intended him to be.

Jacky happened to be particularly bad that day. Not only was he more bent on mischief than usual, but Fortune seemed to enhance the value, (so to speak), of his evil doings, by connecting them with disasters of an unexpected nature. He tried to leap over a small stream, (in Scotland styled a burn), and fell into it. This necessitated drying at the fire—a slow process and disagreeable in all circumstances, but especially so when connected with impatience and headstrong obstinacy. Then he put his foot on a plate of sandwiches, and was within an ace of sitting down on a jam tart, much to his own consternation, poor boy, for had he destroyed *that*, the chief source of his own prospective felicity would have been dried up.

It is not to be supposed that everyone regarded Jacky's eccentricities with the forgiving and loving spirit of his mother. Mr Sudberry, good man, did not mind much; he was out for a day's enjoyment, and having armed himself *cap-à-pie* with benevolence, was invulnerable. Not so the other members of the party, all of whom had to exercise a good deal of forbearance towards the boy. McAllister took him on his knee and gravely began to entertain him with a story, for which kindness Jacky kicked his shins and struggled to get away; so the worthy man smiled sadly, and let him go, remarking that Ovid himself would be puzzled to metamorphose him into a good boy—this in an undertone, of course.

Hector Macdonald was somewhat sanguine and irascible in temper. He felt a tingling in his fingers, and an irresistible desire to apply them to the ears of the little boy.

"Come here, Jacky!" said he.

Flora, who understood his feelings, smiled covertly while she busied herself with cups, plates, and pannikins. Lucy, who did not understand his feelings, thought, "he must be a good-natured fellow to speak so kindly to a child who had annoyed him very much." Lucy did not admit that she herself had been much annoyed by her little brother's pertinacity in interrupting conversation between her and Hector, although she might have done so with perfect truth.

Jacky advanced with hesitation. Hector bent down playfully and seized him by both arms, turning his back upon the party, and thus bringing his own bulky figure between them and young Hopeful.

"Jack, I want you to be good."

"I won't!" promptly said, and with much firmness.

"Oh, yes, you will!" A stern masculine countenance within an inch of his nose, and a vigorous little shake, somewhat disconcerted Jacky, who exhibited a tendency to roar; but Hector closed his strong hands on the little arms so suddenly and so powerfully, that, being unexpectedly agonised, Jacky was for a moment paralysed. The awful glare of a pair of bright blue eyes, and the glistening of a double row of white teeth, did not tend to re-assure him.

"Oh, yes, you will, my little man!" repeated Hector, tumbling him over on his back with a smile of ineffable sweetness, but with a little touch of violence that seemed inconsistent therewith.

Jacky rose, gasped, and ran away, glancing over his shoulder with a look of alarm. This little piece of by-play was not observed by any one but Flora, who exchanged a bright glance and a smile with her brother.

The imp was quelled—he had met his match! During the remainder of the picnic he disturbed no one, but kept at the farthest possible distance from Hector that was consistent with being one of the party. But it is not to be supposed that his nature was changed. No—Jacky's wickedness only sought a new channel in which to flow. He consoled himself with thoughts of the dire mischief he would perpetrate when the dinner was over. Meanwhile, he sat down and gloated over the jam tart, devouring it in imagination.

"Is that water boiling yet?" cried Mr Sudberry.

"Just about it. Hand me the eggs, Fred."

"Here they are," cried Flora, going towards the fire with a basket.

She looked very sweet at that moment, for the active operations in which she had been engaged had flushed her cheeks and brightened her eyes.

George and Fred gazed at her in undisguised admiration. Becoming suddenly aware of the impoliteness of the act, the former ran to relieve her of the basket of eggs; the latter blushed, and all but upset the kettle in an effort to improve the condition of the fire.

"Fred, you goose, leave alone, will you?" roared George, darting forward to prevent the catastrophe.

"This is really charming, is it not, Mr Macgregor?" said Mrs Sudberry, with a languid smile.

"Macdonald, madam, if I may be allowed to correct you," said Hector, with a smile and a little bow.

"Ah, to be sure!" (with an attempt at a laugh.) "I have such a stupid habit of misnaming people."

If Mrs Sudberry had told the exact truth she would have said, "I have such difficulty in remembering people's names that I have made up my mind to call people by any name that comes first into my head rather than confess my forgetfulness." But she did not say this; she only went on to observe that she had no idea it would have been so charming.

"To what do you refer?" said Hector,—"the scenery, the weather, or the prospect of dinner?"

"Oh! you shocking man, how *can* you talk of food in the same breath with—"

"The salt!" exclaimed Lucy with a little shriek. Was there ever a picnic at which the salt was not forgotten, or supposed to have been forgotten? Never!

Mr Sudberry's cheerful countenance fell. He had never eaten an egg without salt in his life, and did not believe in the possibility of doing so. Everyone ransacked everything in anxious haste.

"Here it is!" (hope revived.)

"No, it's only the pepper." (Mitigated despair and ransacking continued.)

"Maybe it'll be in this parcel," suggested McAllister, holding up one which had not yet been untied.

"Oh! bring it to me, Mr Macannister!" cried Mrs Sudberry with unwonted energy, for her happiness was dependent on salt that day, coupled, of course, with weather and scenery. "Faugh! no, it's your horrid onions, Mr MacAndrews."

"Why, you have forgotten the potato salad, Mr Macdonald," exclaimed Lucy.

"No, I have not: it can be made in five minutes, but not without salt. Where *can* the salt be? I am certain it could not have been forgotten."

The only individual of the party who remained calmly indifferent was Master Jacky. That charming creature, having made up his mind to feed on jam tart, did not feel that there was any need for salt. An attentive observer might have noticed, however, that Jacky's look of supreme indifference suddenly gave place to one of inexpressible glee. He became actually red in the face with hugging himself and endeavouring to suppress all visible signs of emotion. His eye had unexpectedly fallen on the paper of salt which lay on the centre of the table-cloth, so completely exposed to view that nobody saw it!

"Why, here it is, actually before our eyes!" shouted George, seizing the paper and holding it up.

A small cheer greeted its discovery. A groan instantly followed, as George spilt the whole of it. As it fell on the cloth, however, it was soon gathered up, and then Mr Sudberry ordered everyone to sit down on the grass in a circle round the cloth.

"What a good boy Jacky has suddenly become!" remarked Lucy in some surprise.

"Darling!" ejaculated his mother.

"A *very* good little fellow," said Flora, with a peculiar smile.

Jacky said nothing. Hector's eye was upon him, as was his upon Hector. Deep unutterable thoughts filled his swelling heart, but he spoke not. He merely gazed at the jam tart, a large portion of which was in a few minutes supplied to him. The immediate result was crimson hands, arms, and cheeks.

While Hector was engaged in concocting the potato salad the kettle upset, extinguished the fire, and sent up a loud triumphant hiss of steam mingled with ashes. Fortunately the potatoes were cooked, so the dinner was at last begun in comfort—that is to say, everyone was very hot, very much exhausted and excited, and very thirsty. Jacky gorged himself with tart in five minutes, and then took an opportunity of quietly retiring into the bushes, sheltered by which he made a détour unseen towards the place where the boat had been left.

Alas for the picnic party that day, that they allowed Hector to prevail on them to begin with his potato salad! It was partly composed of raw onions. After having eaten a few mouthfuls of it, their sense of taste was utterly destroyed! The chickens tasted of onions, so did the cheese and the bread. Even the whiskey was flavoured with onions. The beefsteak-pie might as well have been an onion-pie; indeed, no member of the party could, with shut eyes, have positively said that it was not. The potatoes harmonised with the prevailing flavour; not so the ginger-bread, however, nor the butter. Everything was oniony; they finished their repast with a sweet onion-tart! To make things worse, the sky soon became overcast, a stiff breeze began to blow, and Mr McAllister "opined" that there was going to be a squall.

A piercing shriek put an abrupt termination to the meal!

Intent on mischief; the imp had succeeded in pushing off the boat and clambering into it. For some time he rowed about in a circle with one oar, much delighted with his performances. But when the breeze began to increase and blow the boat away he became alarmed; and when the oar missed the water and sent him sprawling on his back, he gave utterance to the shriek above referred to. Luckily the wind carried him past the place where they were picnicking. There was but one mode of getting at the boat. It was at once adopted. Hector threw off his coat and vest, and swam out to it!

Ten minutes later, they were rowing at full speed for the foot of the loch. The sky was dark and a squall was tearing up the waters of the lake. Then the rain came down in torrents. Then it was discovered that the cloaks had been left at Hazlewood Creek, as the place where they had dined was named. To turn back was impossible. The gentlemen's coats were therefore put on the ladies' shoulders. All were soaked to the skin in a quarter of an hour. Jacky was quiet—being slightly overawed, but not humbled! His mother was too frightened to speak or scream. Mr Sudberry rubbed his hands and said, "Come, I like to have a touch of all sorts of weather, and *won't* we have a jolly tea and a rousing fire when we get home?" Mrs Sudberry sighed at the word "home." McAllister volunteered a song, and struck up the "Callum's Lament," a dismally cheerful Gaelic ditty. In the midst of this they reached the landing-place, from which they walked through drenched heather and blinding rain to the White House.

Thus, drearily, the picnic ended!

Story 1—Chapter 8

Concerning Fowls and Pools

One morning the Sudberry Family sat on the green hill-side, in front of the White House, engaged in their usual morning amusement—feeding the cocks and hens.

It is astonishing what an amount of interest may be got up in this way! If one goes at it with a sort of philanthropico-philosophical spirit, a full hour of genuine satisfaction may be thus obtained—not to speak of the joy imparted to the poultry, and the profound glimpses obtained into fowl character.

There were about twenty hens, more or less, and two cocks. With wonderful sagacity did these creatures come to perceive that when the Sudberrys brought out chairs and stools after breakfast, and sat down thereon, they, the fowls, were in for a feed! And it was surprising the punctuality with which they assembled each fine morning for this purpose.

Most of the family simply enjoyed the thing; but Mr Sudberry, in addition to enjoying it, studied it. He soon came to perceive that the cocks were cowardly wretches, and this gave him occasion to point out to his wife the confiding character and general superiority of female nature, even in hens. The two large cocks could not be prevailed on to feed out of the hand by any means. Under the strong influence of temptation they would strut with bold aspect, but timid, hesitating step, towards the proffered crumb, but the slightest motion would scare them away; and when they did venture to peck, they did so with violent haste, and instantly fled in abject terror.

It was this tendency in these ignoble birds that exasperated poor Jacky, whose chief delight was to tempt the unfortunate hens to place unlimited confidence in him, and then clutch them by the beaks or heads, and hold them wriggling in his cruel grasp; and it was this tendency that induced him, in the heat of disappointment, and without any reference whatever to sex, to call the cocks "big hens!"

The hens, on the other hand, exhibited gentle and trusting natures. Of course there was vanity of character among them, as there is among ladies; but, for the most part, they were wont to rush towards their human friends in a body, and peck the crumbs—at first timidly, then boldly—from their palms. There was one hen—a black and ragged one, with only half a tail, and a downtrodden aspect—which actually went the length of jumping up on little Tilly's knee, and feeding out of her lap. It even allowed her to stroke its back, but it evidently permitted rather than enjoyed the process.

On the morning in question, the black hen was bolder than usual; perhaps it had not breakfasted that day, for it was foremost in the rush when the family appeared with chairs and stools, and leaped on Tilly's knee, without invitation, as soon as she was seated; whereupon Tilly called it "a dear darling pretty 'ittle pet," and patted its back.

"Why, the creature seems quite fond of you, my child," said Mrs Sudberry.

"So it is, mamma. It loves me, I know, by the way it looks at me with its beautiful black eye. What a pity the other is not so nice! I think the poor darling must be blind of that eye."

There was no doubt about that. Blackie's right eye was blinder than any bat's; it was an opaque white ball—a circumstance which caused it no little annoyance, for the other eye had to do duty for both, and this involved constant screwing of the head about, and unwearied watchfulness. It was as if a solitary sentinel were placed to guard the front and back doors of a house at one and the same time. Despite Blackie's utmost care, Jacky got on her blind side more than once, and caught her by the remnant of her poor tail. This used to spoil Tilly's morning amusement, and send her sorrowful into the house. But what did that matter to Jacky? He sometimes broke out worse than usual, and set the whole brood into an agitated flutter, which rather damaged the happiness of the family. But what did that matter to Jacky?

Oh! he was a "darling child," *according to his mother.*

For some time the feeding went on quietly enough. The fowls were confiding. Mr Sudberry was becoming immensely philosophical; Mrs Sudberry was looking on in amiable gratification; George had prevailed on a small white hen to allow him to scratch her head; Fred was taking a rapid portrait of the smallest cock; Lucy had drawn the largest concourse towards herself by scattering her crumbs on the ground; Jacky had only caught two chickens by their beaks and one hen by its tail, and was partially strangling another; and the nine McAllister dogs were ranged in a semicircle round the group, looking on benignantly, and evidently inclined to put in for a share, but restrained by the memory of past rebuffs—when little Blackie, standing on Tilly's knee, and having eaten a large share of what was going, raised itself to its full height, flapped its wings, and gave utterance to a cackle of triumph! A burst of laughter followed—and Tilly gave a shriek of delighted surprise that at once dissolved the spell, and induced the horrified fowl to seek refuge in precipitate flight.

"By the way," said Mrs Sudberry, "that reminds me that this would be a most charming day for your excursion over the mountains to that Lake What-you-may-call-it."

What connection there was between the little incident just described and the excursion to Lake "What-you-may-call-it" we cannot pretend to state; but there must have been some sort of connection in Mrs Sudberry's brain, and we record her observation because it was the origin of this day's proceedings. Mr Sudberry had, for some time past, talked of a long walking excursion with the whole family to a certain small loch or tarn among the hills. Mrs Sudberry had made up her mind,—first, that she would not go; and second, that she would get everyone else to go, in order to let Mrs Brown and Hobbs have a thorough cleaning-up of the house. This day seemed to suit for the excursion—hence her propounding of the plan. Poor delicate Tilly seldom went on long expeditions,—she was often doomed to remain at home.

Mr Sudberry shouted, "Capital! huzza!" clapped his hands, and rushed into the house to prepare, scattering the fowls like chaff in a whirlwind. Fired by his example, the rest of the family followed.

"But we must have our bathe first, papa," cried Lucy.

- 53 -

"Certainly, my love, there will be time for that." So away flew Lucy to the nursery, whence she re-issued with Jacky, Tilly, Mrs Brown, and towels.

The bathing-pool was what George called a "great institution." In using this slang expression George was literally correct, for the bathing-pool was not a natural feature of the scenery: it was artificial, and had been instituted a week after the arrival of the family. The loch was a little too far from the house to be a convenient place of resort for ablutionary purposes. Close beside the house ran a small burn. Its birthplace was one of those dark glens or "corries" situated high up among those mountains that formed a grand towering background in all Fred's sketches of the White House. Its bed was rugged and broken—a deep cutting, which the water had made on the hill-side. Here was quite a forest of dwarf-trees and shrubs; but so small were they, and so deep the torrent's bed, that you could barely see the tree-tops as you approached the spot over the bare hills. In dry weather this burn tinkled over a chaos of rocks, forming myriads of miniature cascades and hosts of limpid little pools. During heavy rains it ran roaring riotously over its rough bed with a force that swept to destruction whatever chanced to come in its way.

In this burn, screened from observation by an umbrageous coppice, was the bathing-pool. No pool in the stream was deep enough, in ordinary weather, to take Jacky above the knees; but one pool had been found, about two hundred yards from the house, which was large enough, if it had only been deeper. To deepen it, therefore, they went—every member of the family.

Let us recall the picture:—

Father, in shirt sleeves rolled up to the shoulders, and trousers rolled up to the knees, in the middle of the pool, trying to upheave from the bottom a rock larger than himself—if he only knew it! But he doesn't, because it is deeply embedded, therefore he toils on in hope. George building, with turf and stone, a strong embankment with a narrow outlet, to allow the surplus water to escape. Fred, Lucy, Tilly, and Peter cutting turf and carrying stones. Mother superintending the whole, and making remarks. Jacky making himself universally disagreeable, and distracting his mother in a miscellaneous sort of way.

"It's as good as Robinson Crusoe any day!" cries father, panting and wiping his bald forehead. "What a stone! I can't budge it." He stoops again, to conquer, if possible; but the great difficulty with father is, that the water comes so near to his tucked-up trousers that he cannot put forth his full strength without wetting them; and mother insists that this must not be done. "Come, George and Fred, bring the pick-axe and the iron lever, we *must* have this fellow out, he's right in the middle of the pool. Now, then, heave!"

The lads obey, and father straddles so fiercely that one leg slips down.

"Hah! *there*, you've done it now!" from mother.

"Well, my dear, it can't be helped," meekly, from father, who is secretly glad, and prepares to root out the stone like a Hercules. Jacky gets excited, and hopes the other leg will slip down and get wet, too!

"Here, hand me the lever, George; you don't put enough force to it." George obeys and grins. "Now then, once more, with will—ho! hi! hup!" Father strains at the lever, which, not having been properly fixed, slips, and he finds himself suddenly in a sitting posture, with the water round his waist. As the cool element embraces his loins, he "h–ah–ah!" gasps, as every bather knows how; but the shock to his system is nothing compared with the aggravation to his feelings when he hears the joyful yell of triumph that issues from the brazen lungs of his youngest hope.

"Never mind, I'll work all the better now—come, let us be jolly, and clear out the rest of the pool." Good man! nothing can put him out. Gradually the bottom is cleared of stones, (excepting the big one), and levelled, and the embankment is built to a sufficient height.

"Now for the finishing touch!" cries George; "bring the turf; Fred—I'm ready!" The water of the burn is rushing violently through the narrow outlet in the "dike." A heavy stone is dropped into the gap, and turf is piled on.

"More turf! more stones! quick, look alive!—it'll burst everything—there, that's it!"

All hands toil and work at the opening, to smother it up. The angry element leaks through, bursts, gushes—is choked back with a ready turf; and squirts up in their faces. Mother is stunned to see the power of so small a stream when the attempt is made to check it thoroughly; she is not mechanically-minded by nature, and has learned nothing in that way by education. It is stopped at last, however.

For a quarter of an hour the waters from above are cut off from those below, as completely as were those of the Jordan in days of old. They all stand panting and silent, watching the rising of the water, while George keeps a sharp eye on the dike to detect and repair any weakness. At last it is full, and the surplus runs over in a pretty cascade, while the accommodating stream piles mud and stones against the dike, and thus unwittingly strengthens the barrier. The pool is formed, full three feet deep by twenty broad. Jacky wants to bathe at once.

"But the pool is like pea-soup, my pet—wait until it clears."

"I won't—let me bathe!"

"O Jacky, my darling!"

He does; for in his struggles he slips on the bank, goes in head foremost, and is fished out in a disgusting condition!

So the bathing-pool was made. It was undoubtedly a "great institution;" they did not know at the time, that, like many such institutions, it was liable to destruction; but they lived to see it.

Meanwhile, to return from this long digression, Lucy, Tilly, and Jacky bathed, while Mrs Brown watched and scolded. This duty performed, they returned to the house, where they found the remainder of the party ready for a journey on foot to Lake "What-you-may-call-it," which lake Lucy named the Lake of the Clouds, its Gaelic cognomen being quite unpronounceable.

Story 1—Chapter 9

A Grand Excursion over the Mountains

Little did good Mr Sudberry think what an excursion lay before him that day, when, in the pride of untried strength and unconquerable spirits, he strode up the mountain-side, with his dutiful family following like a "tail" behind him. There was a kind of narrow sheep-path, up which they marched in single file. Father first, Lucy next, with her gown prettily tucked-up; George and Fred following, with large fishing-baskets stuffed with edibles; Jacky next, light and active, but as yet quiescent; timorous Peter bringing up the rear. He, also, was laden, but not heavily. Mr Sudberry carried rod and basket, for he had been told that there were large trout in the Lake of the Clouds.

Ever and anon the party halted and turned round to wave hats and kerchiefs to Mrs Sudberry, Tilly, and Mrs Brown, who returned the salute with interest, until the White House appeared a mere speck in the valley below, and Mrs Brown became so small, that Jacky, for the first time in his life, regarded her as a contemptible *little* thing! At last a shoulder of the hill shut out the view of the valley, and they began to *feel* that they were in a deep solitude, surrounded by wild mountain peaks.

It is a fact, that there is something peculiarly invigorating in mountain air. What that something is we are not prepared to say. Oxygen and ozone have undoubtedly something to do with it, but in what proportions we know not. Scientific men could give us a learned disquisition on the subject, no doubt; we therefore refer our readers to scientific men, and confine our observations to the simple statement of the fact, that there is something extremely invigorating in mountain air. Every mountaineer knows it; Mr Sudberry and family proved it that day beyond dispute, excepting, by the way, poor Peter, whose unfortunate body was not adapted for rude contact with the rough elements of this world.

The whole party panted and became very warm as they toiled upwards; but, instead of growing fatigued, they seemed to gather fresh strength and additional spirit at every step—always excepting Peter, of course. Soon a wild spirit came over them. On gaining a level patch of springy turf, father gave a cheer, and rushed madly, he knew not, and cared not, whither. Sons and daughters echoed the cheer, and followed his example. The sun burst forth at the moment, crisping the peaks, gorges, and clouds—which were all mingled together—with golden fires. Each had started off without definite intention, and they were scattered far and wide in five minutes, but each formed the natural resolve to run to the nearest summit, in order to devour more easily the view. Thus they all converged again and met on a neighbouring knoll that overtopped a terrific precipice which over hung a small lake.

"The—Lake—of the—Clouds!" exclaimed Lucy, as she came up, breathless and beaming.

"Impossible!" cried her father; "McAllister says it is on the other side of the ridge, and we're not near the top yet. Where are Peter and Jacky?"

"I cannot see them!" said George and Fred, in a breath.

"No more can I," cried Lucy.

No more could anybody, except a hunter or an eagle, for they were seated quietly among grey rocks and brown ferns, which blended with their costume so as to render them all but invisible.

The party on the knoll were, however, the reverse of invisible to Jacky and his exhausted companion. They stood out, black as ink, against the bright blue sky, and were so sharply defined that Jacky declared he could see the "turn-up of Lucy's nose."

The reader must not suppose that Master Jacky was exhausted, like his slender companion. A glance at his firm lip, flushed cheek, sturdy little limbs, and bright eyes, would have made that abundantly plain. No, Jacky was in a *peculiar* frame of mind—that was all. He chose to sit beside Peter, and, as he never condescended to give a reason for his choice, we cannot state one. He appeared to be meditatively inclined that day. Perhaps he was engaged in the concoction of some excruciating piece of wickedness—who knows?

Suddenly Jacky turned with a look of earnest gravity towards his companion, who was a woebegone spectacle of exhaustion. "I say, we'd better go on, don't you think?"

Peter looked up languidly, sighed heavily, and laid his hand on the fishing-basket full of sandwiches, which constituted his burden. It was small and light, but to the poor boy it felt like a ton. Jacky's eyes became still more owlishly wide, and his face graver than ever. He had never seen him in this condition before—indeed, Jacky's experience of life beyond the nursery being limited, he had never seen any one in such a case before.

"I say, Peter, are you desprit blow'd?"

"Desprit," sighed Peter.

Jacky paused and gazed at his companion for nearly a minute.

"I say, d'ye think you could walk if you tried?"

"Oh, yes!" (with a groan and a smile;) "come, I'll try to push ahead now."

"Here, give me the basket," cried Jacky, starting up with sudden and tremendous energy, and wrenching the basket out of Peter's hand. He did it with ease, although the small clerk was twice the size of the imp.

Peter remonstrated, but in vain. Mrs Brown, a woman of powerful frame and strong mind, could not turn Jacky from his purpose—it was not likely, therefore, that an amiable milk-and-water boy, in a state of exhaustion, could do it. Jacky swung the basket over his shoulder with an amount of exertion that made him stagger, and, commanding Peter to follow, marched up the hill with compressed lips and knitted brows.

It was an epoch in the mental development of Jacky—it was a new sensation to the child. Hitherto he had known nothing but the feeling of dependence. Up to this point he had been compelled by the force of circumstances to look up to everyone—and, alas! he had done so with a very bad grace. He had never known what it was to help any one. His mother had thoroughly spoiled him. Strange infatuation in the mother! She had often blamed the boy for spoiling his toys; but she had never blamed herself for spoiling the boy. "Darling Jacky! don't ask the child to do anything for you—he's too young yet." So Jacky was never asked to help any one in any way, except by Mrs Brown, who did not "ask," but commanded, and, although she never rewarded obedience with the laurel, either literally or figuratively, she invariably punished disobedience with the *palm*. Little Tilly always did everything she wanted done herself; and could never do enough for Jacky, so that she afforded no opportunity for her brother to exercise amiable qualities. Thus was Jacky trained to be a selfish little imp, and to this training he superadded the natural wickedness of his own little heart. But now, for the first time, the tables were turned. Jacky felt that Peter was dependent on him—that he could not get on without him.

"Poor Peter, I'll help him—he's a weak skinny chap, and I'm strong as a lion—as a elephant—as a crokindile—anything! Come on, Peter, are you getting better now?" Thus they went up the hill together.

"Ha! there they are at last, close under this mound. Why, I do believe that Jacky's carrying the basket!"

Mr Sudberry was bereft of breath at this discovery; so was everyone else. When the boy stumped up the hill and flung down the basket with an emphatic, "there!" his father turned to the small clerk—

"How now, sir, did you bid Jacky carry that?"

"Please, sir—no, sir;" (whimpering), "but Master Jacky forced it out of my hand, sir, and insisted on carrying it. He saw that I was very tired, sir—and so I am, but I would not have asked him to carry it, if I had been ever so tired—indeed I would not, sir."

"I'm not displeased, my boy," said Mr Sudberry, kindly, patting him on the head; "I only wanted to know if *he offered*."

"Of course I did," cried the imp, stoutly, with his arms akimbo—"and why not? Don't you see that the poor boy is dead beat; and was I goin' to stand by and see him faint by his-self; all alone on the mountain?"

"Certainly not!" and Mr Sudberry seized Jacky and whirled him round till he was quite giddy, and fell on the heather with a cheer, and declared that he would not budge from that spot until they had lunched. Need we say that Mr Sudberry himself was the subject of a new sensation that day,—a sensation of a peculiarly hopeful nature,—as he gazed at his youngest son; while that refined little creature crammed himself with sandwiches and ginger-bread, and besmeared his hands and visage with a pot of jam, that had been packed away by his mother for her own darling's special use?

"My poor lad, you must not come any farther with us. I had no idea you were so much fatigued. Remain here by the provisions, and rest in the sunshine till we return."

So Mr Sudberry gave Peter a plaid that had been carried up to serve as a table-cloth, and told him to wrap well up in it, lest he should catch cold. They left him there on the knoll, refreshed and happy, and with a new feeling in his breast in regard to Jacky, whom, up to that day, he had regarded as an imp of the most hopelessly incorrigible description.

"Over the mountain and over the moor" the Sudberrys wandered. The ridge was gained, and a new world of mountains, glens, gorges, and peaks was discovered on the other side of it, with the Lake of the Clouds lying, like a bright diamond, far below them. They descended into this new world with a cheer. A laugh or a cheer was their chief method of conversation now—their spirits as well as their bodies being so high. "Not a house to be seen! not a sign of man! the untrodden wilderness!" cried Mr Sudberry.

"Robinson Crusoe! Mungo Park! Pooh!" shouted George. "Hooray!" yelled Jacky. The whole party laughed again, and down the slope they went, at such a pace that it was a miracle they did not terminate their career in the lake with the poetic name.

At this point everyone was suddenly "seized." Mr Sudberry and George were seized with an irresistible desire to fish; Fred was seized with a burning desire to sketch; Lucy was seized with a passionate desire to gather wild flowers; and Jacky was seized with a furious desire to wet himself and *wade with his shoes on.* He did it too, and, in the course of an hour, tumbled into so many peat-bogs, and besmeared himself with so much coffee-coloured mud, that his own mother would have failed to recognise him. He was supremely happy—so was his father. At the very first cast he, (the father), hooked a trout of half a pound weight, and lost it, too! but that was nothing. The next cast he caught one of nearly a pound.

George was equally successful. Fortune smiled. Before evening began to close, both baskets were half full of splendid trout; Lucy's basket was quite full of botanical specimens; Fred's sketch was a success, and Jacky was as brown as a Hottentot from head to foot. They prepared to return home, rejoicing.

Haste was needful now. A short cut round the shoulder of the ridge was recommended by George, and taken. It conducted them into a totally different gap from the one which led to their own valley. If followed out, this route would have led them to a spot ten miles distant from their Highland home; but they were in blissful ignorance of the fact. All gaps and gorges looked much the same to them. Suddenly Mr Sudberry paused:—

"Is this the way we came?"

Grave looks, but no reply.

"Let us ascend this ridge, and make sure that we are right."

They did so, and made perfectly certain that they were wrong. Attempting to correct their mistake, they wandered more hopelessly out of their way, but it was not until the shades of night began to fall that Mr Sudberry, with a cold perspiration on his brow, expressed his serious belief that they were "lost!"

Story 1—Chapter 10

Lost on the Mountains

Did ever the worthy London merchant, in the course of his life, approach to the verge of the region of despair, it was on that eventful night when he found himself and his family lost among the mountains of Scotland.

"It's dreadful," said he, sitting down on a cold grey rock, and beginning slowly to realise the utter hopelessness of their condition.

"My poor Lucy, don't be cast down," (drawing her to his breast), "after all, it will only be a night of wandering. But we *must* keep moving. We must not venture to lie down in our wet clothes. We must not even rest long at a time, lest a chill should come upon you."

"But I'm quite warm, papa, and only a very little tired. I could walk for miles yet." She said this cheerily, but she could not help looking anxious. The night was so dark, however, that no one could see her looks.

"Do let me go off alone, father," urged George; "I am as fresh as possible, and could run over the hills until I should fall in with—"

"Don't mention it, George; I feel that our only hope is to keep together. Poor Peter! what will become of that boy?"

Mr Sudberry became almost, desperate as he thought of the small clerk. He started up. "Come, we must keep moving. You are not cold, dear? are you *sure* you are not cold?"

"Quite sure, papa; why are you so anxious?"

"Because I have a flask of brandy, which I mean to delay using until we break down and cannot get on without it. Whenever you begin to get chilled I must give you brandy. Not till then, however;

spirits are hurtful when there is hard toil before you, but when you break down there is no resource left. Rest, food, sleep, would be better; but these we have no chance of getting to-night. Poor Jacky! does he keep warm, George?"

"No fear of him," cried George, with forced gaiety. "He's all right."

Jack had broken down completely soon after nightfall. Vigorously, manfully had he struggled to keep up; but when his usual hour for going to bed arrived, nature refused to sustain him. He sank to the ground, and then George wrapped him up in his shooting-coat, in which he now lay, sound asleep, like a dirty brown bundle, on his brother's shoulders.

"I'll tell you what," said Fred, after they had walked, or rather stumbled, on for some time in silence. "Suppose you all wait here for ten minutes while I run like a greyhound to the nearest height and see if anything is to be seen. Mamma must have alarmed the whole neighbourhood by this time; and if they are looking for us, they will be sure to have lanterns or torches."

"A good idea, my boy. Go, and pause every few minutes to shout, so that we may not lose you. Keep shouting, Fred, and we will wait here and reply."

Fred was off in a moment, and before he had got fifty yards away was floundering knee-deep in a peat-bog. So much for reckless haste, thought he, as he got out of the bog and ran forward with much more caution. Soon those waiting below heard his clear voice far up the heights. A few minutes more, and it rang forth again more faintly. Mr Sudberry remarked that it sounded as if it came from the clouds: he put his hands to his mouth sailor fashion, and replied. Then they listened intently for the next shout. How still it was while they sat there! What a grand, gloomy solitude! They could hear no sound but the beating of their own hearts. Solemn thoughts of the Creator of these mighty hills crept into their minds as they gazed around and endeavoured to pierce the thick darkness. But this was impossible. It was one of those nights in which the darkness was so profound that no object could be seen even indistinctly at the distance of ten yards. Each could see the other's form like a black marble statue, but no feature could be traced. The mountain peaks and ridges could indeed be seen against the dark sky, like somewhat deeper shadows; but the crags and corries, the scattered rocks and heathery knolls, the peat-bogs and the tarns of the wild scene which these circling peaks enclosed—all were steeped in impenetrable gloom. There seemed something terrible, almost unnatural, in this union of thick darkness with profound silence. Mr Sudberry was startled by the sound of his own voice when he again spoke.

"The boy must have gone too far. I cannot hear—"

"Hush!"

"Hi!" in the far distance, like a faint echo. They all breathed more freely, and Mr Sudberry uttered a powerful response. Presently the shout came nearer—nearer still; and soon Fred rejoined them, with the disheartening information that he had gained the summit of the ridge, and could see nothing whatever!

"Well, my children," said Mr Sudberry, with an assumption of cheerfulness which he was far from feeling, "nothing now remains but to push straight forward as fast as we can. We *must* come to a road of some sort in the long-run, which will conduct to somewhere or other, no doubt. Come, cheer up; forward! Follow close behind me, Lucy. George, do you take the lead—you are the most active and sharp-sighted among us; and mind the bogs."

"What if we walk right over a precipice!" thought Fred. He had almost said it, but checked himself for fear of alarming the rest unnecessarily. Instead of cautioning George, he quietly glided to the front, and took the lead.

Slowly, wearily, and painfully they plodded on, stumbling at times over a rugged and stone-covered surface, sometimes descending a broken slope that grew more and more precipitous until it became dangerous, and then, fearing to go farther—not knowing what lay before—they had to retrace their steps and search for a more gradual descent. Now crossing a level patch that raised their hopes, inclining them to believe that they had reached the bottom of the valley; anon coming suddenly upon a steep ascent that dashed their hopes, and induced them to suppose they had turned in the wrong direction, and were re-ascending instead of descending the mountain. All the time Jacky slept like a top, and George, being a sturdy fellow, carried him without a murmur.

Several times Fred tried to make him give up his burden, but George was inexorably obstinate. So they plodded on till nearly midnight.

"Is that a house?" said Fred, stopping short, and pointing to a dark object just in front of them. "No, it's a lake."

"Nonsense, it's a mountain."

A few more steps, and Fred recoiled with a cry of horror. It was a precipice full a hundred feet deep—the dark abyss of which had assumed such varied aspects in their eyes!

A long *détour* followed, and they reached the foot in safety. Here the land became boggy.

Each step was an act fraught with danger, anxiety, and calculation. Whether they should step knee-deep into a hole full of water, or trip over a rounded mass of solid turf, was a matter of absolute uncertainty until the step was taken.

"Oh that we had only a gleam of moonshine," said Lucy with a sigh. Moonshine! How often had George in the course of his life talked with levity, almost amounting to contempt, of things being "all a matter of moonshine!" What would he not have given to have had only a tithe of the things which surrounded him at that time converted into "moonshine!"

A feeble cheer from Fred caused an abrupt halt:—

"What is it?"

"Hallo!"

"What now?"

"The lake at last!—Our own loch! I know the shape of it well! Hurrah!"

Everyone was overjoyed. They all gazed at it long and earnestly, and unitedly came to the conclusion that it was the loch—probably at the distance of a mile or so. Pushing forward with revived spirits, they came upon the object of their hopes much sooner than had been anticipated. In fact, it was not more than two hundred yards distant. A wild yell of laughter mingled with despair burst from Fred as the lake galloped away in the shape of a *white horse*! The untravelled reader may possibly doubt this. Yet it *is a fact* that a white horse was thus mistaken for a distant lake!

The revulsion of feeling was tremendous. Everyone sighed, and Mr Sudberry groaned, for at that moment the thought of poor Peter recurred to his mind. Yet there remained a strange feeling of kindliness in the breast of each towards that white horse. It was an undeniable proof of the existence of animal life in those wild regions, a fact which the deep solitude of all around had tempted them madly to doubt—unknown even to themselves. Besides, it suggested the idea of an owner to the horse; and by a natural and easy process of reasoning they concluded that the owner must be a human being, and that, when at home, he probably dwelt in a house. What more probable than that the house was even then within hail?

Acting on the idea, Mr Sudberry shouted for two minutes with all his might, the only result of which was to render himself extremely hoarse. Then George tried it, and so did Fred, and Jacky awoke and began to whimper and to ask to be let down. He also kicked a little, but, being very tired, soon fell asleep again.

"You *must* let me carry him now!" said Fred.

"I won't!"

Fred tried force, but George was too strong for him, so they went on as before, Lucy leaning somewhat heavily on her father's arm.

Presently they heard the sound of water. It filled them with mitigated joy and excitement, on the simple principle that *anything* in the shape of variety was better than *nothing*. A clap of thunder would have raised in their depressed bosoms a gleam of hope. A flash of lightning would have been a positive blessing. Mr Sudberry at once suggested that it must be a stream, and that they could follow its course—wade down its bed, if necessary—till they should arrive at "something!" Foolish man! he had been long enough in the Highlands by that time to have known that to walk down the bed of a mountain-burn was about as possible as to walk down the shaft of a coal-mine. They came to the edge of its banks, however, and, looking over, tried to pierce its gloom. There was a pale gleam of white foam—a rumbling, rustling sound beneath, and a sensation of moisture in the atmosphere.

"It rains!" said Mr Sudberry.

"I rather think it's the spray of a fall!" observed George.

Had Mr Sudberry known the depth of the tremendous gulf into which he was peering, and the steep cliff on the edge of which he stood, he would have sprung back in alarm. But he did not know—he did not entertain the faintest idea of the truth so he boldly, though cautiously, began to clamber down, assisting Lucy to descend.

Man, (including woman), knows not what he can accomplish until he tries. Millions of glittering gold would not have induced any member of that party to descend such a place in the dark, had they known what it was—yet they accomplished it in safety. Down, down they went!

"Dear me, when shall we reach the foot? We must be near it now."

No, they were not near it; still down they went, becoming more and more alarmed, yet always tempted on by the feeling that each step would bring them to the bottom.

"What a noise the stream makes! why, it must be a river!"

No, it was not a river—it was a mere burn; quite a little burn, but—what then? Little men are always fussier and noisier than big men; little boys invariably howl more furiously than big boys. Nature is full of analogies; and little streams, especially mountain streams, always make more ado in finding their level than big rivers.

They got down at last, and then they found the stream rushing, bursting, crashing among rent and riven rocks and boulders as if it had gone furiously mad, and was resolved never more to flow and murmur, but always to leap and roar. It was impassable; to walk down its banks or bed was impossible, so the wanderers had to re-ascend the bank, and roam away over black space in search of another crossing. They soon lost the sound in the intricacies of cliffs and dells, and never again found that stream. But they found a narrow path, and Fred announced the discovery with a cheer. It was an extremely rugged path, and appeared to have been macadamised with stones the size of a man's head. This led them to suspect that it must be a ditch, not a path; but it turned out to be the dry bed of a mountain-torrent—dry, at least, as regards running water, though not dry in respect of numerous stagnant pools, into which at various times each member of the party stepped unintentionally. It mattered not—nothing could make them wetter or more miserable than they were—so they thought. They had yet to learn that the thoughts of men are forever misleading them, and that there is nothing more certain than the uncertainty of all human calculations.

Story 1—Chapter 11

Still Lost!

Meanwhile, Mrs Sudberry was thrown into a species of frenzied horror, which no words can describe, and which was not in any degree allayed by the grave shaking of the head with which Mr McAllister accompanied his vain efforts to comfort and re-assure her. This excellent man quoted several passages from the works of Dugald Stewart and Locke, tending to show, in common parlance, that "necessity has no law," and that the rightly constituted human mind ought to rise superior to all circumstances—quotations which had the effect of making Mrs Sudberry more hysterical than ever, and which induced Mrs Brown to call him who offered such consolation a "brute!"

But McAllister did not confine his efforts solely to the region of mind. While he was earnestly administering doses of the wisdom of Stewart and Locke to the agitated lady in the parlour, Dan and Hugh, with several others, were, by his orders, arming themselves in the kitchen for a regular search.

"She's ready," said Dan, entering the parlour unceremoniously with a huge stable lantern.

"That's right, Dan—keep away up by the slate corrie, and come down by the red tarn. If they've taken the wrong turn to the right, you're sure to fall in wi' them thereaway. Send Hugh round by the burn; I'll go straight up the hill, and come down upon Loch Cognahoighliey. Give a shout now and then, as ye goo."

Dan was a man of action and few words: he vouchsafed no reply, but turned immediately and left the room, leaving a powerful odour of the byre behind him.

Poor Mrs Sudberry and Tilly were unspeakably comforted by the grave business-like way in which the search was gone about. They recalled to mind that a search of a somewhat similar nature, in point of manner and time, was undertaken a week before for a stray sheep, and that it had been successful; so they felt relieved, though they remained, of course, dreadfully anxious. McAllister refrained from administering any more moral philosophy. As he was not at all anxious about the lost party, and was rather fond of a sly joke, it remains to this day a matter of doubt whether he really expected that his nostrums would be of much use. In a few minutes he was breasting the hill like a true mountaineer, with a lantern in his hand, and with Hobbs by his side.

"Only think, ma'am," said Mrs Brown, who was not usually judicious in her remarks, "only think if they've been an' fell hover a precipice."

"Shocking!" exclaimed poor Mrs Sudberry, with a little shriek, as she clapped her hands on her eyes.

"Poor Jacky, ma'am, p'raps 'e's lyin' hall in a mangled 'eap at the foot of a—"

"Leave me!" cried Mrs Sudberry, with an amount of sudden energy that quite amazed Mrs Brown, who left the room feeling that she was an injured woman.

"Darling mamma, they will come back!" said Tilly, throwing her arms round her mother's neck, and bursting into tears on her bosom. "You know that the sheep—the lost sheep—was found last week, and brought home quite safe. Dan is *so* kind, though he does not speak much, and Hugh too. They will be sure to find them, darling mamma!"

The sweet voice and the hopeful heart of the child did what philosophy had failed to accomplish—Mrs Sudberry was comforted. Thus we see, not that philosophy is a vain thing, but that philosophy and feeling are distinct, and that each is utterly powerless in the domain of the other.

When Peter was left alone by his master, as recorded in a former chapter, he sat himself down in a cheerful frame of mind on the sunny side of a large rock, and gave himself up to the enjoyment of thorough repose, as well mental as physical. The poor lad was in that state of extreme lassitude which renders absolute and motionless rest delightful. Extended at full length on a springy couch of heath, with his eyes peeping dreamily through the half-closed lids at the magnificent prospect of mountains and glens that lay before him, and below him too, so that he felt like a bird in mid-air, looking down upon the world, with his right arm under his meek head, and both pillowed on the plaid, with his countenance exposed to the full blaze of the sun, and with his recent lunch commencing to operate on the system, so as to render exhaustion no longer a pain, but a pleasure, Peter lay on that knoll, high up the mountain-side, in close proximity to the clouds, dreaming and thinking about nothing; that is to say, about everything or anything in an imbecile sort of way: in other words, wandering in his mind disjointedly over the varied regions of memory and imagination; too tired to originate an idea; too indifferent to resist one when it arose; too weak to follow it out; and utterly indifferent as to whether his mind did follow it out, or cut it short off in the middle.

We speak of Peter's mind as a totally distinct and separate thing from himself. It had taken the bit in its teeth and run away. He cared no more for it than he did for the nose on his face, which was, at that time, as red as a carrot, by reason of the sun shining full on its tip. But why attempt to describe Peter's thoughts? Here they are—such as they were—for the reader to make what he can out of them.

"Heigh ho! comfortable now—jolly—what a place! How I hate mountains—climbing them—dreadful!—Like 'em to lie on, though—sun, I like your jolly red-hot face—Sunday! wonder if's got to do with sun—p'raps—twinkle, twinkle, little sun, how I wonder—oh, what fun!—won't I have sich wonderful tales—tales—tails—stories are tails—stick 'em on the end of puppy-dogs, and see how they'd look—two or three two-legged puppies in the office—what a difference now!—no ink-bottles, no smashings, no quills, plenty of geese, though, and grouse and hares—what was I thinking about? Oh, yes—the office—no scribbles—no stools, no desks, No-vember—dear me, that's funny! No-vember—what's a vember? Cut him in two can't join him again—no—no—snore!"

At this point Peter's thoughts went out altogether in sleep, leaving the happy youth in peaceful oblivion. He started suddenly after an hour's nap, under the impression that he was tumbling over a precipice.

To give a little scream and clutch wildly at the heather was natural. He looked round. The sun was still hot and high. Scratching his head, as if to recall his faculties, Peter stared vacantly at the sandwiches which lay beside him on a piece of old newspaper. Gradually his hand wandered towards them, and a gleam of intelligence, accompanied by a smile, overspread his countenance as he conveyed one to his lips. Eating seemed fatiguing, however. He soon laid the remnant down, drew the plaid over him, nestled among the heather, and dropped into a heavy sleep with a sigh of ineffable comfort.

When Peter again woke up, the sun was down, and just enough of light remained to show that it was going to be an intensely dark night. Can anyone describe, can anyone imagine, the state of Peter's feelings? Certainly not! Peter, besides being youthful, was, as we have said, an extremely timid boy. He was constitutionally afraid of the dark, even when surrounded by friends. What, then, were his sensations when he found himself on the mountain alone—*lost*! The thought was horror! Peter gasped; he leaped up with a wild shout, gazed madly round, and sank down with a deep groan. Up he sprang again, and ran forward a few paces. Precipices occurred to him—he turned and ran as many paces backward. Bogs occurred to him—he came to a full stop, fell on his knees, and howled. Up he leaped again, clapped both hands to his mouth, and shouted until his eyes threatened to come out, and his face became purple, "Master! Master! George! hi! hallo–o! Jacky! ho–o–o!" The "O!" was prolonged into a wild roar, and down he went again quite flat. Up he jumped once more; the darkness was deepening. He rushed to the right—left—all round—tore his hair, and gazed into the black depths below—yelled and glared into the dark vault above!

Poor Peter! Thus violently did his gentle spirit seek relief during the first few minutes of its overwhelming consternation.

But he calmed down in the course of time into a species of mild despair. A bursting sob broke from him occasionally, as with his face buried in his hands, his head deep in the heather, and his eyes tight shut, he strove in vain to blind himself to the true nature of his dreadful position. At last he became recklessly desperate, and, rising hastily, he fled. He sought, poor lad, to fly from himself. Of course the effort was fruitless. Instead of distancing himself— an impossibility at all times—doubly so in a rugged country—he

tumbled himself over a cliff, (fortunately not a high one), and
found himself in a peat-bog, (fortunately not a deep one). This
cooled and somewhat improved his understanding, so that he
returned to the knoll a wiser, a wetter, and a sadder boy. Who shall
describe the agonies, the hopes, the fears, the wanderings, the
faggings, and the final despair of the succeeding hours? It is
impossible to say who will describe all this, for *we* have not the
slightest intention of attempting it.

Towards midnight Dan reached a very dark and lonely part of
the mountains, and was suddenly arrested by a low wail. The sturdy
Celt raised his lantern on high. Just at that moment Peter's despair
happened to culminate, and he lifted his head out of the heather to
give free vent to the hideous groan with which he meant, if
possible, to terminate his existence. The groan became a shriek,
first of terror, then of hope, after that of anxiety, as Dan came
dancing towards him like a Jack-o'-lantern.

"Fat is she shriekin' at?" said Dan.

"Oh! I'm *so* glad—I'm so–o–ow–hoo!"

Poor Peter seized Dan round the legs, for, being on his knees,
he could not reach higher, and embraced him.

"Fat's got the maister?"

Peter could not tell.

"Can she waalk?"

Peter couldn't walk—his limbs refused their office.

"Here, speel up on her back."

Peter could do that. He did it, and hugged Dan round the neck
with the tenacity of a shipwrecked mariner clinging to his last
plank. The sturdy Celt went down the mountain as lightly as if
Peter were a fly, and as if the vice-like grip of his arms round his
throat were the embrace of a worsted comforter.

"Here they are, ma'am!" screamed Mrs Brown.

She was wrong. Mrs Brown was usually wrong. Peter alone was
deposited before the eager gaze of Mrs Sudberry, who fainted away
with disappointment. Mrs Brown said "be off" to Peter, and
applied scent-bottles to her mistress. The poor boy's grateful heart
wanted to embrace somebody; so he went slowly and sadly
upstairs, where he found the cat, and embraced *it*. Hours passed
away, and the Sudberry Family still wandered lost, and almost
hopeless, among the mountains.

Story 1—Chapter 12

Found

We left Mr Sudberry and his children in the nearly dry bed of a mountain-torrent, indulging the belief that matters were as bad as could be, and that, therefore, there was no possibility of their getting worse.

A smart shower of rain speedily induced them to change their minds in this respect. Seeking shelter under the projecting ledge of a great cliff, the party stood for some time there in silence.

"You are cold, my pet," said Mr Sudberry.

"Just a little, papa; I could not help shuddering," said Lucy, faintly.

"Now for the brandy," said her father, drawing forth the flask.

"Suppose I try to kindle a fire," said George, swinging the bundle containing Jacky off his shoulder, and placing it in a hollow of the rocks.

"Well, suppose you try."

George proceeded to do so; but on collecting a few broken twigs he found that they were soaking wet, and on searching for the match-box he discovered that it had been left in the provision-basket, so they had to content themselves with a sip of brandy all round—excepting Jacky. That amiable child was still sound asleep; but in a few minutes he was heard to utter an uneasy squall, and then George discovered that he had deposited part of his rotund person in a puddle of water.

"Come, let us move on," said Mr Sudberry, "the rain gets heavier. It is of no use putting off time, we cannot be much damper than we are."

Again the worthy man was mistaken; for, in the course of another hour, they were all so thoroughly drenched, that their previous condition might have been considered, by contrast, one of absolute dryness.

Suddenly, a stone wall, topped by a paling, barred their further progress. Fred, who was in advance, did not see this wall—he only felt it when it brought him up.

"Here's a gate, I believe," cried George, groping about. It *was* a gate, and it opened upon the road! For the first time for many hours a gleam of hope burst in upon the benighted wanderers. Presently a ray of light dazzled them.

"What! do my eyes deceive me—a cottage?" cried Mr Sudberry.

"Ay, and a witch inside," said George.

"Why, it's old—no, impossible!"

"Yes, it is, though—it's old Moggy's cottage."

"Hurrah!" cried Fred.

Old Moggy's dog came out with a burst of indignation that threatened annihilation to the whole party; but, on discovering who they were, it crept humbly back into the cottage.

"Does she never go to bed?" whispered George, as they approached and found the old woman moping over her fire, and swaying her body to and fro, with the thin dirty gown clinging close to her figure, and the spotlessly clean plaid drawn tightly round her shoulders.

"Good-evening, old woman," said Mr Sudberry, advancing with a conciliatory air.

"It's mornin'," retorted the old woman with a scowl.

"Alas! you are right; here have we been lost on the hills, and wandering all night; and glad am I to find your fire burning, for my poor daughter is very cold and much exhausted. May we sit down beside you?"

No reply, save a furtive scowl.

"What's that?" asked Moggy, sharply, as George deposited his dirty wet bundle on the floor beside the fire opposite to her.

The bundle answered for itself; by slowly unrolling, sitting up and yawning violently, at the same time raising both arms above its head and stretching itself. Having done this, it stared round the room with a vacant look, and finally fixed its goggle eyes in mute surprise on Moggy.

The sight of this wet, dirty little creature acted, as formerly, like a charm on the old woman. Her face relaxed into a smile of deep tenderness. She immediately rose, and taking the child in her arms carried him to her stool, and sat down with him in her lap. Jacky made no resistance; on the contrary, he seemed to have made up his mind to submit at once, and with a good grace, to the will of this strange old creature—to the amazement as well as amusement of his relations.

The old woman took no further notice of her other visitors. She incontinently became stone deaf; and apparently blind, for she did not deign to bestow so much as a glance on them, while they circled close round her fire, and heaped on fresh sticks without asking leave. But she made up for this want of courtesy by bestowing the most devoted attentions on Jacky. Finding that that young gentleman was in a filthy as well as a moist condition, she quietly undressed him, and going to a rough chest in a corner of the hut drew out a full suit of clothing, with which she speedily invested him. The garb was peculiar—a tartan jacket, kilt, and hose; and these seemed to have been made expressly for him, they fitted so well. Although quite clean, thin, threadbare, and darned, the appearance of the garments showed that they had been much-worn. Having thus clothed Jacky, the old woman embraced him tenderly, then held him at arm's-length and gazed at him for a few minutes. Finally, she pushed him gently away and burst into tears—rocking herself to and fro, and moaning dismally.

Meanwhile Jacky, still perfectly mute and observant, sat down on a log beside the poor old dame, and stared at her until the violence of her grief began to subside. The other members of the party stared too—at her and at each other—as if to say, "What *can* all this mean?"

At last Jacky began to manifest signs of impatience, and, pulling her sleeve, he said—

"Now, g'anny, lollipops!"

Old Moggy smiled, rose, went to the chest again, and returned with a handful of sweetmeats, with which Jacky at once proceeded to regale himself, to the infinite joy of the old woman.

Mr Sudberry now came to the conclusion that there must be a secret understanding between this remarkable couple; and he was right. Many a time during the last two weeks had Master Jacky, all unknown to his parents, made his way to old Moggy's hut—attracted thereto by the splendid "lollipops" with which the subtle old creature beguiled him, and also by the extraordinary amount of affection she lavished upon him. Besides this, the child had a strong dash of romance in his nature, and it was a matter of deep interest to him to be a courted guest in such a strange old hovel, and to be fondled and clothed, as he often was, in Highland costume, by one who scowled upon everyone else—excepting her little dog, with which animal he became an intimate friend. Jacky did not trouble himself to inquire into the reason of the old woman's partiality—sufficient for him that he enjoyed her hospitality and her favour, and that he was engaged in what he had a vague idea must needs be a piece of clandestine and very terrible wickedness. His long absences, during these visits, had indeed been noticed by his mother; but as Jacky was in the habit of following his own inclinations in every thing and at all times, without deigning to give an account of himself; it was generally understood that he had just strayed a little farther than usual while playing about.

While this was going on in Moggy's hut, George had been despatched to inform Mrs Sudberry of their safety. The distance being short, he soon ran over the ground, and burst in upon his mother with a cheer. Mrs Sudberry sprang into his arms, and burst into tears; Mrs Brown lay down on the sofa, and went into quiet hysterics; and little Tilly, who had gone to bed hours before in a condition of irresistible drowsiness, jumped up with a scream, and came skipping down-stairs in her night-gown.

"Safe, mother, safe!"

"And Jacky?"

"Safe, too, all of us."

"Oh! I'm *so* thankful."

"No, not *all* of us," said George, suddenly recollecting Peter.

Mrs Sudberry gasped and turned pale. "Oh! George! quick, tell me!"

"Poor Peter," began George.

"Please, sir, I've bin found," said a meek voice behind him, at which George turned round with a start—still supporting his mother.

Mrs Brown, perceiving the ludicrous nature of the remark, began to grow violent on the sofa, and to kick a little. Then Mrs Sudberry asked for each of the missing ones individually—sobbing between each question—and at each sob Tilly's sympathetic bosom heaved, and Mrs Brown gave a kick and a subdued scream. Then George began to tell the leading features of their misfortunes rapidly, and Mrs Brown listened intently until Mrs Sudberry again sobbed, when Mrs Brown immediately recollected that she was in hysterics, and recommenced kicking.

"But where *are* they?" cried Mrs Sudberry, suddenly.

"I was just coming to that—they're at old Moggy's hut, drying themselves and resting."

"Oh! I'll go down at once. Take me there."

Accordingly, the poor lady threw on her bonnet and shawl and set off with George for the cottage, leaving Mrs Brown, now relieved from all anxiety, kicking and screaming violently on the sofa, to the great alarm of Hobbs, who just then returned from his fruitless search.

"My son, my darling!" cried Mrs Sudberry, as she rushed into the cottage, and clasped Jacky in her arms. She could say no more, and if she had said more it could not have been heard, for her appearance created dire confusion and turmoil in the hovel. The lost and found wanderers started up to welcome her, the little dog sprang up to bark furiously and repel her, and the old woman ran at her, screaming, with intent to rescue Jacky from her grasp. There was a regular scuffle, for the old woman was strong in her rage, but George and Fred held her firmly, though tenderly, back, while Mr Sudberry hurried his alarmed spouse and their child out of the hut, and made for home as fast as possible. Lucy followed with George almost immediately after, leaving Fred to do his best to calm and comfort the old woman. For his humane efforts Fred received a severe scratching on the face, and was compelled to seek refuge in flight.

Story 1—Chapter 13

Visiting the Poor

For some time after this the Sudberry Family were particularly careful not to wander too far from their mountain home. Mr Sudberry forbade everyone, on pain of his utmost displeasure, to venture up among the hills without McAllister or one of his lads as a guide. As a further precaution, he wrote for six pocket compasses to be forwarded as soon as possible.

"My dear," said his wife, "since you are writing home, you may as well—"

"My dear, I am not writing—"

"You're writing to London for compasses, are you not?"

"No," said Mr Sudberry with a smile. "I believe they understand how to manufacture the mariner's compass in Scotland—I am writing to my Edinburgh agent for them."

"Oh! ah well, it did not occur to me. Now you mention it, I think I have heard that the Scotch have sort of scientific tendencies."

"Yes, they are 'feelosophically' inclined, as our friend McAllister would say. But what did you want, my love?"

"I want a hobby-horse to be sent to us for Jacky; but it will be of no use writing to Edinburgh for one. I suppose they do not use such things in a country where there are so few real horses, and so few roads fit for a horse to walk on."

Mr Sudberry made no reply, not wishing to incur the expense of such a useless piece of furniture, and his wife continued her needlework with a sigh. From the bottom of her large heart she pitied the Scottish nation, and wondered whether there was the remotest hope of the place ever being properly colonised by the English, and the condition of the aborigines ameliorated.

"Mamma, I'm going with Flora Macdonald to visit her poor people," said Lucy, entering at the moment with a flushed face,—for Lucy was addicted to running when in a hurry,—and with a coquettish little round straw hat.

"Very well, my love, but do take that good-natured man to guide you—Mr What's-his-name, I've *such* a memory! Ah! McCannister; do take him with you, dear."

"There is no need, mamma. Nearly all the cottages lie along the road-side, and Flora is quite at home here, you know."

"True, true, I forgot that."

Mrs Sudberry sighed and Lucy laughed gaily as she ran down the hill to meet her friend. The first cottage they visited was a little rough thatched one with a low roof; one door, and two little windows, in which latter there were four small panes of glass, with a knot in each. The interior was similar to that of old Moggy's hut, but there was more furniture in it, and the whole was pervaded by an air of neatness and cleanliness that spoke volumes for its owner.

"This is Mrs Cameron's cottage," whispered Flora as they entered. "She was knocked over by a horse while returning from church last Sunday, and I fear has been badly shaken.—Well, Mrs Cameron, how are you to-day?"

A mild little voice issued from a box-bed in a corner of the room. "Thankee, mem, I'm no that ill, mem. The Lord is verra kind to me."—There was a mild sadness in the tone, a sort of "the world's in an awfu' state,—but no doot it's a' for the best, an' I'm resigned to my lot, though I wadna objec' to its being a wee thing better, oo-ay,"—feeling in it, which told of much sorrow in years gone by, and of deep humility, for there was not a shade of complaint in the tone.

"Has the doctor been to see you, my dear granny?" inquired Flora, sitting down at the side of the box-bed, while Lucy seated herself on a stool and tried to pierce the gloom within.

"Oo, ay, he cam' an' pood aff ma mutch, an' feel'd ma heed a' over, but he said nothin'—only to lie quiet an' tak a pickle water-gruel, oo-ay."

As the voice said this its owner raised herself on one elbow, and, peering out with a pair of bright eyes, displayed to her visitor the small, withered, yet healthy countenance of one who must have been a beautiful girl in her youth. She was now upwards of seventy, and was, as Lucy afterwards said, "a sweet, charming, dear old woman." Her features were extremely small and delicate, and her eyes had an anxious look, as if she were in the habit of receiving periodical shocks of grief, and were wondering what shape the next one would take.

"I have brought you a bottle of wine," said Flora; "now don't shake your head—you *must* take it; you cannot get well on gruel. Your daughter is at our house just now: I shall meet her on my way home, and will tell her to insist on your taking it."

The old woman smiled, and looked at Lucy.

"This is a friend whom I have brought to see you," said Flora, observing the glance. The old woman held out her hand, and Lucy pressed it tenderly. "She has come all the way from London to see our mountains, granny."

"Ay?" said the old woman with a kind motherly smile: "it's a lang way to Lunnon, a lang way, ay. Ye'll be thinkin' we're a wild kind o' folk here-away; somewhat uncouth we are, no doot."

"Indeed, I think you are very nice people," said Lucy, earnestly. "I had no idea how charming your country was, until I came to it."

"Oo-ay! we can only get ideas by seein' or readin'. It's a grawnd thing, travellin', but it's wonderfu' what readin' 'll do. My guid-man, that's deed this thirteen year,—ay,—come Marti'mas, he wrought in Lunnon for a year before we was marrit, an' he sent me the newspapers reglar once a month—ay, the English is fine folk. My guid-man aye said that."

Lucy expressed much interest in this visit of the departed guid-man, and, having touched a chord which was extremely sensitive and not easily put to rest after having been made to vibrate, old Mrs Cameron entertained her with a sweet and prolix account of the last illness, death, and burial of the said guid-man, with the tears swelling up in her bright old eyes and hopping over her wrinkled cheeks, until Flora forbade her to say another word, reminding her of the doctor's orders to keep quiet.

"Oo-ay, ye'll be gawin' to read me a bit o' the book?"

"I thought you would ask that; what shall it be?"

"Oo, ye canna go wrang."

Flora opened the Bible, and, selecting a passage, read it in a slow, clear tone, while the old woman lay back and listened with her eyes upturned and her hands clasped.

"Isn't it grawnd?" said she, appealing to Lucy with a burst of feeling, when Flora had concluded.

Lucy was somewhat taken aback by this enthusiastic display of love for the Bible, and felt somewhat embarrassed for an appropriate answer; but Flora came to her rescue:

"I have brought you a book, granny; it will amuse you when you are able to get up and read. There now, no thanks—you positively *must* lie down and try to sleep. I see your cheek is flushed with all this talking. Good-day, granny!"

"The next whom we will visit is a very different character," said Flora, as they walked briskly along the road that followed the windings of the river; "he dwells half a mile off."

"Then you will have time to tell me about old Moggy," said Lucy. "You have not yet fulfilled your promise to tell me the secret connected with her, and I am burning with impatience to know it."

"Of course you are; every girl of your age is set on fire by a secret. I have a mind to keep you turning a little longer."

"And pray, grandmamma," said Lucy, with an expressive twinkle in her eyes, "at what period of your prolonged life did you come to form such a just estimate of character in girls of *my* age?"

"I'll answer that question another time," said Flora; "meanwhile, I will relent and tell you about old Moggy. But, after all, there is not much to tell, and there is no secret connected with her, although there is a little mystery."

"No secret, yet a mystery! a distinction without a difference, it seems to me."

"Perhaps it is. You shall hear:—

"When a middle-aged woman, Moggy was housekeeper to Mr Hamilton, a landed proprietor in this neighbourhood. Mr Hamilton's gardener fell in love with Moggy; they married, and, returning to this their native hamlet, settled down in the small hut which the old woman still occupies. They had one daughter, named Mary, after Mr Hamilton's sister. When Mary was ten years old her father died of fever, and soon afterwards Moggy was taken again into Mr Hamilton's household in her old capacity; for his sister was an invalid, and quite unfit to manage his house. In the course of time little Mary became a woman and married a farmer at a considerable distance from this neighbourhood. They had one child, a beautiful fair-haired little fellow. On the very day that he was born his father was killed by a kick from a horse. The shock to the poor mother was so great, that she sank under it and died. Thus the little infant was left entirely to the care of his grandmother. He was named Willie, after his father.

"Death seemed to cast his shadow over poor Moggy's path all her life through. Shortly after this event Mr Hamilton died suddenly. This was a great blow to the housekeeper, for she was much attached to her old master, who had allowed her to keep her little grandson beside her under his roof. The sister survived her brother about five years. After her death the housekeeper returned to her old hut, where she has ever since lived on the interest of a small legacy left her by her old master. Little Willie, or wee Wullie, as she used to call him, was the light of old Moggy's eyes, and the joy of her heart. She idolised and would have spoiled him, had that been possible; but the child was of a naturally sweet disposition, and would not spoil. He was extremely amiable and gentle, yet bold as a young lion, and full of fun. I do not wonder that poor old Moggy was both proud and fond of him in an extraordinary degree. The blow of his removal well-nigh withered her up, body and soul—"

"He died?" said Lucy, looking up at Flora with tearful eyes.

"No, he did not: perhaps it would have been better if the poor child *had* died; you shall hear. When Willie was six years old a gang of gypsies passed through this hamlet, and, taking up their abode on the common, remained for some time. They were a wild, dangerous set, and became such a nuisance that the inhabitants at last took the law into their own hands, and drove them away. Just before this occurred little Willie disappeared. Search was made for him everywhere, but in vain. The gypsies were suspected, and their huts examined. Suspicion fell chiefly on one man, a stout ill-favoured fellow, with an ugly squint and a broken nose; but nothing could be proved either against him or the others, except that, at the time of the child's disappearance, this man was absent from the camp. From that day to this, dear little Willie has never been heard of.

"At first, the poor old grandmother went about almost mad with despair and anxiety, but, as years passed by, she settled down into the moping old creature you have seen her. It is five years since that event. Willie will be eleven years old now, if alive; but, alas! I fear he must be dead."

"What a sad, sad tale!" said Lucy. "I suppose it must be because our Jacky is about the age that Willie was when he was stolen, that the poor woman has evinced such a fondness for him."

"Possibly; and, now I think of it, there is a good deal of resemblance between the two, especially about the hair and eyes, though Willie was much more beautiful. You have noticed, no doubt, that Moggy wears a clean plaid—"

"Oh, yes," interrupted Lucy; "I have observed that."

"That was the plaid that Willie used to wear in winter. His grandmother spends much of her time in washing it; she takes great pains to keep it clean. The only mystery about the old woman is the old chest in one corner of her hut. She keeps it jealously locked, and no one has ever found out what is in it, although the inquisitive folk of the place are very anxious to know. But it does not require a wizard to tell that. Doubtless it contains the clothing and toys of her grandson. Poor old Moggy!"

"I can enlighten you on that point," said Lucy, eagerly opening the lid of a small basket which hung on her arm, and displaying the small suit of Highland clothing in which Jacky had been conveyed home on the night when the Sudberrys were lost on the hills. "This suit came out of the large chest; and as I knew you meant to visit Moggy to-day, I brought it with me."

The two friends reached the door of a small cottage as Lucy said this, and tapped.

"Come in!" gruffly said a man's voice. This was one of Flora's difficult cases. The man was bed-ridden, and was nursed by a grand-daughter. He was quite willing to accept comfort from Flora, especially when it took the shape of food and medicine; but he would not listen to the Bible. Flora knew that he liked her visits, however; so, with prayers in her heart and the Bible in her hand, she persevered hopefully, yet with such delicacy that the gruff old man became gruffer daily, as his conscience began to reprove him for his gruffness.

Thus, from hut to hut she went, with love to mankind in her heart and the name of Jesus on her lip; sometimes received with smiles and sent away with blessings, occasionally greeted with a cold look, and allowed to depart with a frigid "good-day!"

Lucy had often wished for some such work as this at home, but had not yet found courage to begin. She was deeply sympathetic and observant. Old Moggy was the last they visited that day. Flora was the only female she would tolerate.

"I've been tryin' to say't a' night an' I *canna* do't!" she said stoutly, as the ladies entered.

"You forget the words, perhaps, dear Moggy—'The Lord gave, and the Lord hath—'"

"Na, na, I dinna forget them, but I *canna* say them." So Flora sat down on a stool, and gently sought, by means of the Bible, to teach the old woman one of the most difficult lessons that poor human nature has got to learn in this world of mingled happiness and woe.

Story 1—Chapter 14

A Surprise and a Battle

"Here! halloo! hi! Hobbs! I say," shouted Mr Sudberry, running out at the front door, after having swept Lucy's work-box off the table and trodden on the cat's tail. "Where has that fellow gone to? He's always out of the way. Halloo!" (looking up at the nursery window), "Mrs Brown!"

Mrs Brown, being deeply impressed with the importance of learning, (just because of Mrs Sudberry's contempt thereof), was busily engaged at that moment in teaching Miss Tilly and Master Jacky a piece of very profound knowledge.

"Now, Miss Tilly, what is the meaning of procrastination?" ("Ho! hi! halloo-o-o-o," from Mr Sudberry; but Mrs Brown, supposing the shout is meant for any one but herself; takes no notice of it.)

Tilly.—"Doing to-day what you might have put off till to-morrow." ("Halloo! ho! don't you hear? hi!" from below.)

Mrs Brown.—"No, you little goose! What is it, Jacky?"

Jacky.—"Doing to-morrow what you might have put off till to-day." ("Hi! halloo! are you deaf up there?")

Mrs Brown.—"Worse and worse, stupid little goose!"

Jacky, (indignantly).—"Well, then, if it's neither one thing nor t'other, just let's hear what *you* make it out to be—" ("Hi! ho! halloo! Mrs Bra–a–own!")

"Bless me, I think papa is calling on me. Yes, sir. Was you calling, sir?" (throwing up the window and looking out.)

"Calling! no; I wasn't 'calling.' I was shrieking, howling, yelling. Is Hobbs there?"

"No, sir; 'Obbs is not 'ere, sir."

"Well, then, be so good as to go and look for him, and say I want him directly to go for the letters."

"'Ere I am, sir," said Hobbs, coming suddenly round the corner of the house, with an appearance of extreme haste.

Hobbs had, in fact, been within hearing of his master, having been, during the last half-hour, seated in McAllister's kitchen, where the uproarious merriment had drowned all other sounds. Hobbs had become a great favourite with the Highland family, owing to his hearty good humour and ready power of repartee. The sharp Cockney, with the easy-going effrontery peculiar to his race, attempted to amuse the household—namely, Mrs McAllister, Dan, Hugh, and two good-looking and sturdy-limbed servant-girls—by measuring wits with the "canny Scot," as he called the farmer. He soon found, however, that he had caught a Tartar. The good-natured Highlander met his raillery with what we may call a smile of grave simplicity, and led him slyly into committing himself in such a way that even the untutored servants could see how far the man was behind their master in general knowledge; but Hobbs took refuge in smart reply, confident assertion, extreme volubility, and the use of hard words, so that it sometimes seemed to the domestics as if he really had some considerable power in argument. Worthy Mrs McAllister never joined in the debate, except by a single remark now and then. She knew her son thoroughly, and before the Sudberrys had been a week at the White House she understood Hobbs through and through.

She was wont to sit at her spinning-wheel regarding this intellectual sparring with grave interest, as a peculiar phase of the human mind. A very sharp encounter had created more laughter than usual at the time when Mr Sudberry halloed for his man-servant.

"You must be getting deaf, Hobbs, I fear," said the master, at once pacified by the man's arrival; "go down and fetch—"

"Pray do not send him away just now," cried Mrs Sudberry: "I have something particular for him to do. Can you go down yourself, dear?"

The good man sighed. "Well, I will go," and accordingly away he went.

"Stay, my dear."

"Well."

"I expect one or two small parcels by the coach this morning; mind you ask for 'em and bring 'em up."

"Ay, ay!" and Mr Sudberry, with his hands in his pockets, and his wideawake thrust back and very much on one side of his head, sauntered down the hill towards the road.

One of the disadvantageous points about the White House was its distance from any town or market. The nearest shop was four miles off, so that bread, butter, meat, and groceries, had to be ordered a couple of days beforehand, and were conveyed to their destination by the mail-coach. Even after they were deposited at the gate of Mr McAllister's farm, there was still about half a mile of rugged cart-road to be got over before they could be finally deposited in the White House. This was a matter of constant anxiety to Mr Sudberry, because it was necessary that someone should be at the gate regularly to receive letters and parcels, and this involved constant attention to the time of the mail passing. When no one was there, the coachman left the property of the family at the side of the road. Hobbs, however, was usually up to time, fair weather and foul, and this was the first time his master had been called on to go for the letters.

Walking down the road, Mr Sudberry whistled an extremely operatic air, in the contentment of his heart, and glanced from side to side, with a feeling amounting almost to affection, at the various objects which had now become quite familiar to him, and with many of which he had interesting associations.

There was the miniature hut, on the roof of which he usually laid his rod on returning from a day's fishing. There was the rude stone bridge over the burn, on the low parapet of which he and the family were wont to sit on fine evenings, and commune of fishing, and boating, and climbing, and wonder whether it would be possible ever again to return to the humdrum life of London. There was the pool in the same burn over which one day he, reckless man, had essayed to leap, and into which he had tumbled, when in eager pursuit of Jacky. A little below this was the pool into which the said Jacky had rushed in wild desperation on finding that his father was too fleet for him. Passing through a five-barred gate into the next field, he skirted the base of a high, precipitous crag, on which grew a thicket of dwarf-trees and shrubs, and at the foot of which the burn warbled. Here, on his left, stood the briar bush out of which had *whirred* the first live grouse he ever set eyes on. It was at this bird, that, in the madness of his excitement, he had flung first his stick, then his hat, and lastly his shout of disappointment and defiance. A little further on was that other bush out of which he had started so many grouse that he now never approached it without a stone in each hand, his eyes and nostrils dilated, and his breath restrained. He never by any chance on these occasions sent his artillery within six yards of the game; but once, when he approached the bush in a profound reverie, and without the usual preparation, he actually saw a bird crouching in the middle of it! To seize a large stone and hit the ground at least forty yards beyond the bush was the work of a moment. Up got the bird with a tremendous whizz! He flung his stick wildly, and, hitting it, (by chance), fair on the head, brought it down. To rush at it, fall on it, crush it almost flat, and rise up slowly holding it very tight, was the result of this successful piece of poaching. Another result was a charming addition to a dinner a few days afterwards.

At all these objects Mr Sudberry gazed benignantly as he sauntered along in the sunshine, indulging in sweet memories of the recent past, and whistling operatically.

The high-road gained, he climbed upon the gate, seated himself upon the top bar to await the passing of the mail, and began to indulge in a magnificent air, the florid character of which he rendered much more effective than the composer had intended by the introduction of innumerable flourishes of his own.

It was while thus engaged, and in the middle of a tremendous shake, that Mr Sudberry suddenly became aware of the presence of a man not more than twenty yards distant. He was lying down on the embankment beside the road, and his ragged dress of muddy-brown corduroy so resembled the broken ground on which he lay that he was not a very distinct object, even when looked at point-blank. Certainly Mr Sudberry thought him an extremely disagreeable object as he ended in an ineffective quaver and with a deep blush; for that man must be more than human, who, when caught in the act of attempting to perpetrate an amateur concert in all its parts, does not *feel* keenly.

Being of a sociable disposition, Mr Sudberry was about to address this ill-favoured beggar—for such he evidently was—when the coach came round a distant bend in the road at full gallop. It was the ordinary tall, top-heavy mail of the first part of the nineteenth century. Being a poor district, there were only two horses, a white and a black; but the driver wore a stylish red coat, and cracked his whip smartly. The road being all down hill at that part, the coach came on at a spanking pace, and pulled up with a crash.

The beggar turned his face to the ground, and pretended to be asleep.

Mr Sudberry noticed this; but, being interested in his own affairs, soon forgot the circumstance.

"Got any letters for me to-day, my man?"

Oh, yes, he has letters and newspapers too. Mr Sudberry mutters to himself as they are handed down, "Capital!—ha!—business; hum!—private; ho!—compasses; good! Any more?"

There are no more; but there is a parcel or two. The coachman gets down and opens the door of the box behind. The insides peep out, and the outsides look down with interest. A great many large and heavy things are pulled out and laid on the road.

Mr Sudberry remarks that it would have been "wiser to have stowed *his* parcels in front."

The coachman observes that *these* are *his* parcels, shuts the door, mounts the box, and drives away, with the outsides grinning and the insides stretching their heads out, leaving Mr Sudberry transfixed and staring.

"'One or two small parcels,'" murmured the good man, recalling his wife's words; "'and mind you bring 'em up.' One salmon, two legs of mutton, one ham, three dozen of beer, a cask of—of—something or other, and a bag of—of—ditto, (groceries, I suppose), 'and mind you bring 'em up!' How! *'that* is the question!'" cried Mr Sudberry, quoting Hamlet, in desperation.

Suddenly he recollected the beggar-man. "Halloo! friend; come hither."

The man rose slowly, and rising did not improve his appearance. He was rather tall, shaggy, loose-jointed, long-armed, broad-shouldered, and he squinted awfully. His nose was broken, and his dark colour bespoke him a gypsy.

"Can you help me up to yonder house with these things, my man?"

"No," said the man, gruffly, "I'm footsore with travellin', but I'll watch them here while you go up for help."

"Oh! ahem!" said Mr Sudberry, with peculiar emphasis; "you seem a stout fellow, and might find more difficult ways of earning half a crown. However, I'll give you that sum if you go up and tell them to send down a barrow."

"I'll wait here," replied the man, with a sarcastic grin, limping back to his former seat on the bank.

"Oh! very well, and I will wait *here*," said Mr Sudberry, seating himself on a large stone, and pulling out his letters.

Seeing this, the gypsy got up again, and looked cautiously along the road, first to the right and then to the left. No human being was in sight. Mr Sudberry observed the act, and felt uncomfortable.

"You'd better go for help, sir," said the man, coming forward.

"Thank you, I'd rather wait for it."

"This seems a handy sort of thing to carry," said the gypsy, taking up the sack that looked like groceries, and throwing it across his shoulder. "I'll save you the trouble of taking this one up, anyhow."

He went off at once at a sharp walk, and with no symptom either of lameness or exhaustion. Mr Sudberry was after him in a moment. The man turned round and faced him.

"Put that where you took it from!" thundered Mr Sudberry.

"Oh! you're going to resist."

The gypsy uttered an oath, and ran at Mr Sudberry, intending to overwhelm him with one blow, and rob him on the spot. The big blockhead little knew his man. He did not know that the little Englishman was a man of iron frame; he only regarded him as a fiery little gentleman. Still less did he know that Mr Sudberry had in his youth been an expert boxer, and that he had even had the honour of being knocked flat on his back more than once by *professional* gentlemen—in an amicable way, of course—at four and sixpence a lesson. He knew nothing of all this, so he rushed blindly on his fate, and met it—that is to say, he met Mr Sudberry's left fist with the bridge of his nose, and his right with the pit of his stomach; the surprising result of which was that the gypsy staggered back against the wall.

But the man was not a coward, whatever other bad qualities he might have been possessed of. Recovering in a moment, he rushed upon his little antagonist, and sent in two sledge-hammer blows with such violence that nothing but the Englishman's activity could have saved him from instant defeat. He ducked to the first, parried the second, and returned with such prompt good-will on the gypsy's right eye, that he was again sent staggering back against the wall; from which point of observation he stared straight before him, and beheld Mr Sudberry in the wildness of his excitement, performing a species of Cherokee war-dance in the middle of the road. Nothing daunted, however, the man was about to renew his assault, when George and Fred, all ignorant of what was going on, came round a turn of the road, on their way to see what was detaining their father with the letters.

"Why, that's father!" cried Fred.

"Fighting!" yelled George.

They were off at full speed in a moment. The gypsy gave but one glance, vaulted the wall, and dived into the underwood that lined the banks of the river. He followed the stream a few hundred yards, doubled at right angles on his course, and in ten minutes more was seen crossing over a shoulder of the hill, like a mountain hare.

Story 1—Chapter 15

A Dream and a Ball

That evening Mr Sudberry, having spent the day in a somewhat excited state—having swept everything around him, wherever he moved, with his coat-tails, as with the besom of destruction—having despatched a note to the nearest constabulary station, and having examined the bolts and fastenings of the windows of the White House—sat down after supper to read the newspaper, and fell fast asleep, with his head hanging over the back of his chair, his nose turned up to the ceiling, and his mouth wide open. His loving family—minus Tilly and Jacky, who were abed—encircled the table, variously employed; and George stood at his elbow, fastening up a pair of bookshelves of primitive construction, coupled together by means of green cord.

While thus domestically employed, they heard a loud, steady thumping outside. The Sudberrys were well acquainted by this time with that sound and its cause. At first it had filled Mrs Sudberry with great alarm, raising in her feeble mind horrible reminiscences of tales of burglary and midnight murder. After suffering inconceivable torments of apprehension for two nights, the good lady could stand it no longer, and insisted on her husband going out to see what it could be. As the sound appeared to come from the cottage, or off-shoot from the White House, in which the McAllisters lived, he naturally went there, and discovered that the noise was caused by the stoutest of the two servant-girls. This sturdy lass, whose costume displayed a pair of enormous ankles to advantage, and exhibited a pair of arms that might have made a prize-fighter envious, was standing in the middle of the floor, with a large iron pot before her and a thick wooden pin in her hands, with the end of which she was, according to her own statement, "champin' tatties."

Mrs McAllister, her son, Hugh and Dan, and the other servant-girl, were seated round the walls of the room, watching the process with deep interest, for their supper was in that pot. The nine dogs were also seated round the room, watching the process with melancholy interest; for their supper was *not* in that pot, and they knew it, and wished it was.

"My dear," said Mr Sudberry, on returning to the parlour, "they are 'champing tatties.'"

"What?"

"'Champing tatties,' in other words, mashing potatoes, which it would seem, with milk, constitute the supper of the family."

Thus was Mrs Sudberry's mind relieved, and from that night forward no further notice was taken of the sound.

But on the present occasion the champing of the tatties had an unwonted effect on Mr Sudberry. It caused him to dream, and his dreams naturally took a pugilistic turn. His breathing became quick and short; his face began to twitch; and Lucy suggested that it would be as well to "awake papa," when papa suddenly awaked himself; and hit George a tremendous blow on the shoulder.

"Hallo! father," cried George remonstratively, rubbing the assaulted limb; "really, you know, if you come it in this way often, you will alienate my affections, I fear."

"My dear boy!—what?—where? Why, I was dreaming!"

Of course he was, and the result of his dream was that everybody in the room started up in surprise and excitement. Thereafter they sat down in a gay and very talkative humour. Soon afterwards a curious squeaking was heard in the adjoining cottage, and another thumping sound began, which was to the full as unremitting as, and much more violent than, that caused by "champin' tatties." The McAllister household, having supped, were regaling themselves with a dance.

"What say to a dance with them?" said George.

"Oh!" cried Lucy, leaping up.

"Capital!" shouted Mr Sudberry, clapping his hands.

A message was sent in. The reply was, "heartily welcome!" and in two minutes Mr Sudberry and stout servant-girl Number 1,

George and stout girl Number 2, Hugh and Lucy, Dan and Hobbs, (the latter consenting to act as girl Number 3), were dancing the Reel o' Tullochgorum like maniacs, to the inspiring strains of McAllister's violin, while Peter sat in a corner in constant dread of being accidentally sat down upon. Fred, in another corner, looked on, laughed, and was caressed furiously by the nine dogs. Mrs Sudberry talked philosophy in the window, with grave, earnest Mrs McAllister, whose placid equanimity was never disturbed, but flowed on, broad and deep, like a mighty river, and whose interest in all things, small and great, seemed never to flag for a moment.

The room in which all this was going on was of the plainest possible description. It was the hall, the parlour, the dining-room, the drawing-room, and the library of the McAllister Family. Earth was the floor, white-washed and uneven were the walls, non-existent was the ceiling, and black with peat-smoke were the rafters. There was a dresser, clean and white, and over it a rack of plates and dishes. There was a fire-place—a huge yawning gulf; with a roaring fire, (for culinary purposes only, being summer),—and beside it a massive iron gallows, on which to hang the family pot. Said pot was a caldron; so big was it that there was a species of winch and a chain for raising and lowering it over the fire; in fact, a complicated sort of machinery, mysterious and soot-begrimed, towered into the dark depths of the ample chimney. There was a brown cupboard in one corner, and an apoplectic eight-day clock in another. A small bookshelf supported the family Bible and several ancient and much-worn volumes. Wooden benches were ranged round the walls; and clumsy chairs and tables, with various pails, buckets, luggies, troughs, and indescribable articles, completed the furniture of the picturesque and cosy apartment. The candle that lighted the whole was supported by a tall wooden candlestick, whose foot rested on the ground, and whose body, by a simple but clumsy contrivance, could be lengthened or shortened at pleasure, from about three to five feet.

But besides all this, there was a world of *matériel* disposed on the black rafters above—old farm implements, broken furniture, an old musket, an old claymore, a broken spinning-wheel, etcetera, all of which were piled up and so mingled with the darkness of the vault above, that imagination might have deemed the spot a general rendezvous for the aged and the maimed of "still life."

Fast and furious was the dancing that night. Native animal spirits did it all. No artificial stimulants were there. "Tatties and mulk" were at the bottom of the whole affair. The encounter of that forenoon seemed to have had the effect of recalling the spirit of his youth to Mr Sudberry, and his effervescing joviality gave tone to all the rest.

"Now, Fred, you must take my place," said he, throwing himself in an exhausted condition on a "settle."

"But perhaps your partner may want a rest?" suggested Fred.

Lass Number 1 scorned the idea: so Fred began.

"Are your fingers not tired?" asked Mr Sudberry, wiping his bald forehead, which glistened as if it had been anointed with oil.

"Not yet," said McAllister quietly.

Not yet! If the worthy Highlander had played straight on all night and half the next day, he would have returned the same answer to the same question.

"You spend a jolly life of it here," said Mr Sudberry to Mrs McAllister.

"Ay, a pleasant life, no doot; but we're not *always* fiddling and dancing."

"True, but the variety of herding the cattle on these splendid hills is charming."

"So it is," assented Mrs McAllister; "we've reason to be contented with our lot. Maybe ye would grow tired of it, however, if ye was always here. I'm told that the gentry whiles grow tired of their braw rooms, and take to plowterin' aboot the hills and burns for change. Sometimes they even dance wi' the servants in a Highland cottage!"

"Ha! you have me there," cried Mr Sudberry, laughing.

"Let me sit down, pa, pray do!" cried Lucy. Her father rose quickly, and Lucy dropped into his place quite exhausted.

"Come, father, relieve me!" cried Fred. "I'm done up, and my partner *won't* give in."

To say truth, it seemed as if the said partner, (stout lass Number 1), never would give in at all. From the time that the Sudberrys entered she had not ceased to dance reel after reel, without a minute of breathing-time. Her countenance was like the sun in a fog; her limbs moved as deftly and untiringly, after having tired out father and son, as they did when she began the evening; and she now went on, with a quiet smile on her face, evidently resolved to show their English guests the nature of female Highland metal.

In the midst of all this the dogs suddenly became restive, and began to growl. Soon after, a knock came to the door, and the dogs rushed at it, barking violently. Mr McAllister went out, and found that a company of wandering beggars had arrived, and prayed to be allowed to sleep in the barn. Unfortunate it was for them that they came so soon after Mr Sudberry's unpleasant rencounter with one of their fraternity. The good man of the house, although naturally humane and hospitable to such poor wanderers, was on the present occasion embittered against them; so he ordered them off.

This incident brought the evening to an abrupt termination, as it was incumbent on the farmer to see the intruders safely off his premises. So the Sudberrys returned, in a state of great delight, excitement, and physical warmth, to their own parlour.

The only other fact worth recording in regard to this event is, that the Sudberrys were two hours late for breakfast next morning!

Story 1—Chapter 16

The Effects of Compasses

The first few weeks of the Sudberrys' residence in their Highland home were of an April cast—alternate sunshine and shower. Sometimes they had a day of beaming light from morning till night; at other times they had a day of unmitigated rain, or, as Mr Sudberry called it, "a day of cats and dogs;" and occasionally they had a day which embraced within its own circuit both conditions of weather—glorious bursts of sunshine alternating with sudden plumps of rain.

Thus far the weather justified and strengthened the diverse opinions of both husband and wife.

"Did I not tell you, my love, that the climate was charming?" was Mr Sudberry's triumphant remark when a dazzling blaze of light would roll over flood and fell, and chase the clouds away.

"There, didn't I say so?" was the withering rejoinder of Mrs Sudberry, when a black cloud rolled over the sky and darkened the landscape as with a wipe of ink.

Hitherto victory leaned decidedly to neither side, the smile of triumph and the humbled aspect of defeat rested alternate on either countenance, so that both faces taken together formed a sort of contradictory human barometer, which was not a bad one—at all events it was infinitely superior to that instrument of the banjo type, which Mr Sudberry was perpetually tapping in order to ascertain whether or not its tendencies were dropsical.

When father was up at "set fair," mother was certain to be depressed, inclining to much rain; yet, strangely enough, it was on such occasions *very dry*! When mother was "fair," (barometrically speaking, of course), father was naturally down at "changeable"! Yet there was wonderful contradiction in the readings of this barometer; for, when mother's countenance indicated "much rain," father sometimes went down to "stormy," and the tails of his coat became altogether unmanageable.

But, towards the middle of the holidays, father gained a decided victory. For three weeks together they had not a drop of rain—scarcely a cloud in the sky; and mother, although fairly beaten and obliged to confess that it was indeed splendid weather, met her discomfiture with a good grace, and enjoyed herself extremely, in a quiet way.

During this bright period the Sudberry Family, one and all, went ahead, as George said, "at a tremendous pace." The compasses having arrived, Mr Sudberry no longer laid restrictions on the wandering propensities of his flock but, having given a compass to each, and taught them all the use of it, sent them abroad upon the unexplored ocean of hills without fear. Even Jacky received a compass, with strict injunctions to take good care of it. Being naturally of an inquiring disposition, he at once took it to pieces, and this so effectually that he succeeded in analysing it into a good many more pieces than its fabricator had ever dreamed of. To put it together again would have taxed the ingenuity of the same fabricator—no wonder that it was beyond the power of Jacky altogether. But this mattered nothing to the "little darling," as he did not understand his father's learned explanation of the uses of the instrument. To do Mr Sudberry justice, he had not expected that his boy could understand him; but he was aware that if he, Jacky, did not get a compass as well as the rest of them, there would be no peace in the White House during *that* season. Moreover, Jacky did not care whether he should get lost or not. In fact, he rather relished it; for he knew that it would create a pleasant excitement for a time in the household, and he entertained the firm belief that McAllister and his men could find any creature on the hills, man or beast, no matter how hopelessly it should be lost.

There being, then, no limit to the wanderings of the Sudberrys, they one and all gave themselves over deliberately to a spirit of riotous rambling. Of course they all, on various occasions, lost themselves, despite the compasses; but, having become experienced mountaineers, they always took good care to find themselves again before sunset. George and Fred candidly declared that they preferred to steer by "dead reckoning," and left their compasses at home. Lucy always carried hers, and frequently consulted it, especially when in her father's presence, for she was afflicted, poor girl, with that unfashionable weakness, an earnest desire to please her father even in trifles. Nevertheless, she privately confided to Fred one day that she was often extremely puzzled by her compass, and that she had grave doubts as to whether, on a certain occasion, when she had gone for a long ramble with Hector and Flora Macdonald, and been lost, the blame of that disaster was not due to her compass. Fred said he thought it was, and believed that it would be the means of compassing her final disappearance from the face of the earth if she trusted to it so much.

As for Mr Sudberry himself; his faith in the compass was equal to that of any mariner. The worthy man was, or believed himself to be, (which is the same thing, you know!) of profoundly scientific *tendencies*. He was aware, of course, that he had never really *studied* any science whatever; but he had dabbled in a number of them, and he felt that he had immense *capacity* for deep thought and subtle investigation. His mind was powerfully analytical—that's what it was. One consequence of this peculiarity of mind was that he "took his bearings" on short and known distances, as well as on long venturesome rambles; he tested himself and his compass, as it were.

One day he had walked out alone in the direction of the village, four miles distant from the White House, whence the family derived their supplies. He had set out with his rod, (he never walked near the river without his rod), intending to take a cast in what he styled the "lower pools." By degrees he fished so near to the village that he resolved to push forward and purchase a few books. Depositing rod and basket among the bushes, he walked smartly along the road, having previously, as a matter of course, taken his bearings from the village by compass. A flock of sheep met him, gazed at him in evident surprise, and passed on. At their heels came the collie dog, with his tongue out. It bestowed a mild, intelligent glance on the stranger, and also passed on. Close behind the dog came the shepherd, with plaid bonnet and thick stick.

"A fine day, friend," said Mr Sudberry.

"Oo, ay, it *is* a fine day."

He also passed on.

Another turn in the road, and Mr Sudberry met a drove of shaggy cattle, each cow of which looked sturdy and fierce enough for any ordinary bull; while the bull himself was something awful to look upon. There is nothing ladylike or at all feminine in the aspect of a Highland cow!

Mr Sudberry politely stepped to one side, and made way for them. Many of the animals paused for an instant, and gazed at the Englishman with profound gravity, and then went on their way with an air that showed they evidently could make nothing of him. The drover thought otherwise, for he stopped.

"Coot-tay to you, sir."

"Good-day, friend, good-day. Splendid weather for the—for the—"

Mr Sudberry did not know exactly for which department of agriculture the weather was most favourable, so he said—"for the cattle."

"Oo, ay, the w'ather's no that ill. Can she tell the time o' day?"

Out came the compass.

"West-nor'-west, and by—Oh! I beg your pardon," (pulling out his watch and replacing the compass), "a quarter-past two."

The drover passed on, and Mr Sudberry, chuckling at his mistake, took the bearings of a tall pine that grew on a distant knoll.

On gaining the outskirts of the village, Mr Sudberry felt a sensation of hunger, and instantly resolved to purchase a bun, which article he had now learned to call by its native name of "cookie." At the same instant a bright idea struck him—he would steer for the baker's shop by compass! He knew the position of the shop exactly—the milestone gave him the distance—he would lay his course for it. He would walk conscientiously with his eyes on the ground, except when it was necessary to refer to the compass, and he would not raise them until he stood within the shop. It would be a triumphant exhibition of the practical purposes, in a small way, to which the instrument might be applied.

Full of this idea, he took a careful observation of the compass, the sun, and surrounding nature; laid his course for the baker's shop, which was on the right side of the village, and walked straight into the butcher's, which lay on its left extremity. He was so much put out on lifting his eyes to those of the butcher, that he ordered a leg of mutton and six pounds of beefsteaks on the spot. The moment after, he recollected that two legs of mutton and a round of beef had been forwarded to the White House by coach the day before, and that there was a poached brace of moor-fowl in the larder at that moment; but, having given the order in a prompt, business tone of voice, he felt that he lacked moral courage to rescind it.

"Ye'll ha'e frien's comin' to veesit ye," observed the butcher, who was gifted with a peculiar and far-sighted faculty of "putting that and that together."

"No; we have no immediate prospect of such a pleasure."

"Ay? Hum! it's wonderfu' what an appeteet the hill air gives to strangers."

"A tremendous appetite! Good-day, friend."

Mr Sudberry said this heartily, and went off to the baker's—by dead reckoning—discomfited but chuckling.

The butcher pondered and philosophised over the subject the remainder of the afternoon with much curiosity, but with no success. Had the wisdom of Plato been mingled with his Scotch philosophy, the compound reduced to an essential oil of investigative profundity, and brought to bear on the subject in question, he would have signally failed to discover the reason of the Sudberrys' larder being crammed that week with an unreasonable quantity of butcher-meat.

Yes! during these three weeks of sunshine the Sudberrys made hay of their time as diligently as the McAllisters made hay of their grass, and the compasses played a prominent part in all their doings, and led them into many scrapes. Among other things, they led them to Glen Ogle. More of this in the next chapter.

Story 1—Chapter 17

The Trip to Glen Ogle

Without entering into minute comparisons, it may be truly said that Glen Ogle is one of the grandest and wildest of mountain passes in the highlands of Perthshire. Unlike the Trossachs, which Sir Walter Scott has immortalised in his "Lady of the Lake," Glen Ogle is a wild, rugged, rocky pass, almost entirely destitute of trees, except at its lower extremity; and of shrubs, except along the banks of the little burn which meanders like a silver thread down the centre of the glen. High precipitous mountains rise on either hand—those on the left being more rugged and steep than those on the right. The glen is very narrow throughout—a circumstance which adds to its wildness; and which, in gloomy weather, imparts to the spot a truly savage aspect. Masses of *débris* and fallen rocks line the base of the precipices, or speckle the sides of the mountains in places where the slopes, being less precipitous than elsewhere, have served to check the fallen matter; and the whole surface of the narrow vale is dotted with rocks of various sizes, which have bounded from the cliffs, and, overleaping every obstacle, have found a final resting-place on a level with the little stream.

The road follows the course of the stream at the foot of the glen; but, as it advances, it ascends the mountains on the right, and runs along their sides until the head of the pass is gained. Here it crosses, by means of a rude stone bridge, a deep chasm, at the bottom of which the waters of the burn leap and roar among chaotic rocks—a foretaste of the innumerable rushes, leaps, tumbles, and plunges, which await them all down the glen. Just beyond this bridge is a small level patch of mingled rocky and mossy ground. It is the summit of the mountain ridge; yet the highest peaks rise above it, and so hem it in that it resembles the arena of a rude amphitheatre. In the centre of this spot lies a clear, still lake, or tarn, not more than a hundred yards in diameter. This is the fountain-head of two streams. From the pools and springs, within a stone's cast of the tarn, arise the infant waters of the burn already mentioned, which, descending Glen Ogle, find their way to the Firth of Tay, through Strath Earn. From the opposite side of the tarn issues another brook, which, leaping down the other side of the mountains, mingles its waters with Loch Tay, and finds its way, by a much more circuitous route, to the same firth. The whole region is desolate and lonely in the extreme, and so wild that a Rocky Mountain hunter, transported thither by fairy power, might find himself quite at home, except in the matter of big-horned goats and grisly bears. But, for the matter of that, he would find mountain sheep with very respectable horns in their way; and, as to bears, the hill-sides are bare enough to satisfy any hunter of moderate expectations.

Up to this elevated tarn, among the hoary mountain peaks, the Sudberry Family struggled one hot, sunny, lovely forenoon. Bent on a long and bold flight, they had travelled by the stage-coach to the foot of the glen, near the head of Loch Earn. Here they were deposited at the door of a picturesque white-washed house, which was styled the Inn, and from this point they toiled up the glen on foot, intoxicating themselves on the way with deep draughts of mingled excitement, fresh air, and romance.

The whole family were out upon this occasion, including Mrs Brown, Hobbs, and Peter. The delicate Tilly was also there, and to her Master Jacky devoted himself with an assiduity worthy of even a *good* boy. He took occasion several times, however, to tell Peter, in a grave way, that, whenever he felt tired, he would be glad to carry his basket for him, and himself too, for the matter of that, if he should get quite knocked up. He indemnified himself for these concessions on the side of virtue by inflicting various little torments on the bodies and minds of Mrs Brown and his mother, such as hiding himself at some distance ahead, and suddenly darting out from behind a rock with a hideous yell; or coming up behind with eyes staring and hair flying, and screaming "mad bull," with all the force of his lungs.

Hector and Flora Macdonald were also of the party. George and Fred were particularly attentive to Flora, and Hector was ditto to Lucy. He carried her botanical box, and gave her a good deal of information in regard to plants and wild flowers, in which Lucy professed a deep interest, insomuch that she stopped frequently to gather specimens and listen to Hector's learned observations, until they were more than once left a considerable way behind the rest of the party. Indeed, Lucy's interest in science was so great that she unwittingly pulled two or three extremely rare specimens to pieces while listening to these eloquent discourses, and was only made conscious of her wickedness by a laughing remark from Hector that she "must surely have the bump of destructiveness largely developed."

Arrived at the tarn, each individual deposited his and her basket or bundle on a selected spot of dry ground, and the ladies began to spread out the viands, while Mr Sudberry took the exact bearings of the spot by compass. While thus philosophically engaged, he observed that fish were rising in the tarn.

"Hallo! Hector; why, I see fish in the pond."

"True," replied the young man, "plenty of trout; but they are small."

"I'll fish," said Mr Sudberry.

"So will I," cried George.

And fish they did for half an hour, at the end of which period they were forcibly torn away from the water-side and made to sit down and eat sandwiches—having caught between them two dozen of trout, the largest of which was about five inches long.

"Why, how did ever the creatures get up into such a lake?" inquired Mr Sudberry, eyeing the trout in surprise: "they could never jump up all the waterfalls that we have passed to-day."

"I suppose they were born in the lake," suggested Hector, with a smile.

"Born in it?" murmured Mr Sudberry, pondering the idea; "but the *first* ones could not have been born in it. How did the first ones get there?"

"The same way as what the first fishes came into the sea, of course," said Jacky, looking very pompous.

Unfortunately he unintentionally tried to perform that impossible feat which is called swallowing a crumb down the wrong throat, thereby nearly choking himself; and throwing his mother into a flutter of agitation.

There was something so exhilarating in the atmosphere of that elevated region that none of the party felt inclined to waste much time over luncheon. Mr Sudberry, in particular, was very restless and migratory. His fishing propensities had been aroused, and could not be quieted. He had, in the course of a quarter of an hour, gobbled what he deemed it his duty to eat and drink, and, during the remainder of the meal, had insisted on helping everybody to everything, moving about as he did so, and thereby causing destruction to various articles of crockery. At last he declared that he was off to fish down the burn, and that the rest of the party would pick him up on their way back to the coach, which was to start from the inn at Loch Earn Head at five in the afternoon.

"Now don't be late," said he; "be at the inn by half-past four precisely."

"Ay, ay; yes, yes," from everybody; and away he went alone to enjoy his favourite sport.

The rest of the party scattered. Some went to good points for sketching, some to botanise, and others to ascend the highest of the neighbouring peaks. Mrs Brown and Hobbs were left in charge of the *débris* of luncheon, to the eating up of which they at once devoted themselves with the utmost avidity as soon as the others were gone.

"Come, this is wot I calls comfortable," said Hobbs; (he spoke huskily, through an immense mouthful of sandwich.) "Ain't it, Mrs Brown?"

"Humph!" said Mrs Brown.

It is to be remarked that Mrs Brown was out of temper—not that that was an unusual thing; but she had found the expedition more trying than she had anticipated, and the torments of mind and body to which Jacky had subjected her were of an uncommonly irritating nature.

"Wot," continued Hobbs, attacking a cold tongue, "d'you think of the natives of this 'ere place?"

"Nothink at all," was Mrs Brown's prompt rejoinder.

Hobbs, who was naturally of a jolly, sociable disposition, felt a little depressed at Mrs Brown's repellent manner; so he changed his mode of address.

"Try some of this 'ere fowl, Mrs Brown, it's remarkably tender, it is; just suited to the tender lips of—dear me, Mrs Brown, how improvin' the mountain hair is to your complexion, if I may wenture to speak of improvin' that w'ich is perfect already."

"Get along, Hobbs!" said Mrs Brown, affecting to be displeased.

"My dear, I'm gettin' along like a game chicken, perhaps I might say like Dan, who's got the most uncommon happetite as I ever did see. He's a fine fellow, Dan is, ain't he, Mrs Brown?"

"Brute," said Mrs Brown; "they're all brutes."

"Ah!" said Hobbs, shaking his head, "strong language, Mrs Brown. But, admitting that, (merely for the sake of argument, of course), you cannot deny that they are raither clever brutes."

"I do deny it," retorted Mrs Brown, taking a savage bite out of the leg of a chicken, as if it represented the whole Celtic race. "Don't they talk the most arrant stuff?—specially that McAllister, who is forever speakin' about things that he don't understand, and that nobody else does!"

"Speak for yourself; ma'am," said Hobbs, drawing himself up with as much dignity as was compatible with a sitting posture.

"I *do* speak for myself. Moreover, I speak for *some* whom I might name, and who ain't *verra* far away."

"If, ma'am, you mean that insinivation to apply—"

"I make no insinivations. Hand me that pot of jam—no, the unopened one."

Hobbs did as he was required with excruciating politeness, and thereafter took refuge in dignified silence; suffering, however, an expression of lofty scorn to rest on his countenance. Mrs Brown observed this, and her irate spirit was still further chafed by it. She meditated giving utterance to some withering remarks, while, with agitated fingers, she untied the string of the little pot of cranberry-jam. Worthy Mrs Brown was particularly fond of cranberry-jam.

She had put up this pot in her own basket expressly for her own private use. She now opened it with the determination to enjoy it to the full, to smack her lips very much and frequently, and offer none of it to Hobbs. When the cover was removed she gazed into the pot with a look of intense horror, uttered a piercing shriek, and fell back in a dead faint.

This extraordinary result is easily accounted for. Almost every human being has one grand special loathing. There is everywhere some creature which to some individual is an object of dread—a creature to be shrunk from and shuddered at. Mrs Brown's horror was frogs. Jacky knew this well. He also knew of Mrs Brown's love for cranberry-jam, and her having put up a special pot. To abstract the pot, replace it by a similar pot with a live frog imprisoned therein, and then retire to chuckle in solitude and devour the jam, was simple and natural. That the imp had done this; that he had watched with delight the deceived woman pant up Glen Ogle with the potted frog on her arm and perspiration on her brow; that he had asked for a little cranberry-jam on the way, with an expression of countenance that almost betrayed him; and that he had almost shrieked with glee when he observed the anxiety with which Mrs Brown—having tripped and fallen—opened her basket and smiled to observe that the pot was *not* broken; that the imp, we say, had been guilty of all this, was known only to himself; but much of it became apparent to the mind of Hobbs, when, on Mrs Brown's fainting, he heard a yell of triumph, and, on looking up, beheld Master Jacky far up the heights, clearly defined against the bright sky, and celebrating the success of his plot with a maniacal edition of the Highland fling.

At a quarter-past four all the party assembled at the inn except Mr Sudberry.

Five arrived—no Mr Sudberry. The coach could not wait! The gentlemen, in despair, rushed up the bed of the stream, and found him fishing, in a glow of excitement, with his basket and all his pockets full of splendid trout.

The result was that the party had to return home in a large wagon, and it was night when at last they embarked in their boat and rowed down their own lake. It was a profound calm. The air was mild and balmy. There was just enough of light to render the surrounding mountains charmingly mysterious, and the fatigues of the day made the repose of the boat agreeable. Even Mrs Sudberry enjoyed that romantic night-trip on the water. It was so dark that there was a tendency to keep silence on landing to speak in low tones; but a little burst of delight broke forth when they surmounted the dark shoulder of the hill, and came at last in sight of the windows of the White House, glowing a ruddy welcome home.

Story 1—Chapter 18

The Family go to Church under Difficulties

It would seem to be a well-understood and undeniable fact that woman invariably gains the victory over man in the long-run; and even when she does not prove to be the winner, she is certain to come off the conqueror. It is well that it should be so. The reins of the world could not be in better hands!

But, strangely enough, woman triumphs, not only in matters over which she and man have, more or less, united control, but even in matters with which the human race cannot interfere. For instance, in regard to weather—despite the three weeks of unfailing sunshine, Mrs Sudberry maintained her original opinion, that, notwithstanding appearances being against her, the weather in the Highlands of Scotland was, as a rule, execrable. As if to justify this opinion, the weather suddenly changed, and the three weeks of sunshine were followed by *six* weeks of rain.

Whether there was something unusual in the season or not, we cannot positively say; but certain it is that, for the period we have named, it rained incessantly, with the exception of four days. During a great part of the time it rained from morning till night. Sometimes it was intermittent, and came down in devastating floods. At other times it came in the form of Scotch mist, which is simply small rain, so plentiful that it usually obliterates the whole landscape, and so penetrating that it percolates through everything except water-proof. It was a question which was the more wetting species of rain—the thorough down-pour or the heavy mist. But whether it poured or permeated, there was never any change in the leaden sky during these six weeks, and the mountains were never clearly seen except during the four accidental days already referred to.

At first Mrs Sudberry triumphed; but long before that season was over she had reached such a condition of humility that she would have actually rejoiced in a fine day.

As for the rest of the family, they bore up against it bravely for a time. On the first day of this wet season, they were rather pleased than otherwise to be obliged to stay in the house. Jacky, in particular, was delighted, as it afforded him a glorious opportunity of doing mischief, and making himself so disagreeable, that all, except his mother, felt as if they hated him. On the second day, indoor games of various kinds were proposed and entered into with much spirit. On the third day the games were tried again, with less spirit. On the fourth day they were played without any spirit at all, and on the fifth they were given up in disgust. The sixth day was devoted to reading and sulking, and thus they ended that week.

The seventh day, which chanced to be Sunday, was one of the four fine days before mentioned. The sky was blue, the sun intensely bright, and the inundated earth was steaming. The elastic spirits of the family recovered.

"Come, we'll walk to church!" cried Mr Sudberry, as they rose from breakfast.

"What, my dear!" exclaimed his wife, "and the roads knee-deep in mud and water!"

"I care not if they were waist-deep!" cried the reckless man: "I've been glued to my seat for a week; so I'll walk to church, if I should have to swim for it."

"So will I! so will I!" from George and Fred; "So will we all!" from Lucy; "And me, too!" timidly, from Tilly; with "Hurrah!" furiously from the imp,—this decided the business.

"Very well!" said the resigned mother of the flock; "then I will go too!"

So away they went to church, through mud and mire and water, with the nine collie dogs at their heels, and Mr McAllister bearing them company.

Fred and McAllister walked together in rear of the rest, conversing earnestly, for the latter was learned in theology, and the former dearly loved a philosophical discussion. Mr Sudberry and

Lucy walked in advance. As he approached the well-known bush, the force of habit induced him almost unconsciously to pick up a stone and walk on tip-toe. Lucy, who did not know the cause of this strange action, looked at her father in surprise.

Whirr! went a black-cock; bang! went the stone, and a yell instantly followed, accompanied by a hat—it was his best beaver!

"Why, dear papa, it is Sunday!"

"Dear me, so it is!" The good man was evidently much discomfited. "Ah! Lucy dear, that shows the effect and force of bad habit; that is to say, of habit, (for the simple act cannot be called bad), on the wrong day."

"You cannot call throwing your best hat in the mud a good habit on *any* day," said Mrs Sudberry, with the air of a woman who regarded her husband's chance of mending as being quite hopeless.

"It was only forgetfulness, my dear!" said the worthy man, putting his hat quite meekly on the back of his head, and pushing forward in order to avoid further remarks. Coming to a hollow of the road, they found that it was submerged a foot deep by the river, which had been swollen into a small lake at that spot. There was much trouble here. McAllister, with native gallantry, offered to carry the ladies over in his arms; but the ladies would not listen to the proposal, with the exception of Tilly, who at once accepted it gladly. The rest succeeded in scrambling along by the projecting stones at the base of the wall that ran alongside of the road, and gained the other side, after many slips, much alarm, and sundry screams.

"Oh, you *darling!*" cried Tilly, suddenly. She pointed to a hole in the wall, out of which peeped the most wide-awake weasel that ever lived. Its brown little head and sharp nose moved quickly about with little jerks, and its round lustrous black eyes seemed positively to glitter with surprise, (perhaps it was delight), at the Sudberry Family. Of course Jacky rushed at it with a yell—there was a good deal of the terrier in Jacky—and of course the weasel turned tail, and vanished like a flash of light.

When they came to the narrowest part of the pass which opened out of their own particular valley—Rasselas Vale, as Lucy had named it—Tilly was fortunate enough to set eyes on another "darling," which, in the shape of a roe deer, stood, startled and trembling, in the centre of the pass. They came on it so suddenly that it seemed to have been paralysed for a moment. A shout from the imp, however, quickly dissolved the spell; with one graceful bound it cleared the wall, and was far away among the brackens on the mountain-side before the party had recovered from their delight and surprise at having met a real live wild deer, face to face, and not twenty yards distant, in this unexpected manner.

Nothing further occurred to arrest their progress to church, which was upwards of four miles from their home among the hills.

The sermon that day was peculiar. The minister of the parish was a young man; one of those quiet, modest, humble young men, who are, as their friends think, born to be neglected in this world. He was a shrewd, sensible young fellow, however, who, if put to it, could have astonished his "friends" not a little. He was brimful of "Scotch" theology; but, strange to say, he refrained from bringing that fact prominently before his flock, insomuch that some of the wiser among them held the opinion, that, although he was an excellent, worthy young man, he was, if any thing, a little commonplace—in fact, "he never seemed to have any diffeeculties in his discoorses: an' if he had, he aye got ower them by sayin' plump oot that they were mysteries he did na pretend to unravel!"

Any one with half an eye might have seen that the young clergyman was immeasurably above his flock intellectually. A few of them, among whom was our friend McAllister, perceived this, and appreciated their minister. The most of them, good souls, thought him worthy, but weak.

Feeling that he had been appointed to preach the gospel, this youth resolved to "make himself all things to all men, in order that he might gain some." He therefore aimed at preaching Christ crucified, and kept much of his own light in the background, bringing it out only in occasional flashes, which were calculated to illuminate, but not dazzle, the minds of his people. He remembered the remark of that old woman, who, when asked what she thought of a new minister, said, "Hoot! I think naethin' o' him ava'; I understand every word he says," and he resolved rather to be thought nothing of at all than pander to the contemptible craving of those who fancy that they are drinking deep draughts of wisdom when they read or hear words that are incomprehensible, but which sound profoundly philosophical.

But we might have spared our readers all this, for the young minister did not preach that day. He was unwell, and a friend had agreed to preach for him. The friend was an old man, with bent form and silvery hair, who, having spent a long life in preaching the gospel, had been compelled, by increasing age, to retire from active service. Yet, like a true warrior, he could, when occasion required, buckle on his Christian armour, and fight stoutly, as of old, for his beloved Master and for the salvation of human souls.

His eye was dim and his voice was weak, and it brought tears to the eyes of the sympathetic among the people to see the old man lose his place and unconsciously repeat his sentences. But not a shadow of disrespect mingled with their feelings. There was no mistaking the glow of love and the kindly fire which flushed the pale face when salvation was the theme. When he mentioned the name of Jesus, and urged sinners to flee from the wrath to come, the people felt the truth of that word, "God's strength is perfected in man's weakness."

The Sudberrys felt very happy that day on returning home. They overtook old Moggy, stumping along through mud and water, with tears bedewing her cheeks.

"Why, Moggy, you are all wet!" said Fred, hastening towards her.

"Ay, I fell into a dub as I cam out o' the kirk. But, ech! sirs, I've heard blessed words this day."

The Sudberrys spent that evening in their usual way. They went to a particular spot, which Lucy had named the Sunny Knoll, and there learned hymns off by heart, which were repeated at night, and commented on by Mr Sudberry. After supper they all got into what is called "a talk." It were presumptuous to attempt to explain what that means. Everyone knows what it is. Many people know, also, that "a talk" can be got up when people are in the right spirit, on any subject, and that the subject of all others most difficult to get up this "talk" upon, is religion. Mr Sudberry knew this; he felt much inclined at one time that night to talk about fishing, but he laid strong constraint on himself; and gave the conversation a turn in the right direction. The result was "a talk"—a hearty, free, enthusiastic communing on the Saviour, the soul, and eternal things, which kept them up late and sent them happy to bed— happier than they had yet been all that season.

Story 1—Chapter 19

A Strange Home-Coming

Master Jacky made two discoveries next day, both of which he announced with staring eyes and in breathless haste, having previously dashed into the parlour like a miniature thunderbolt.

The first was that the bathing-pool was clean swept away by the floods, not a vestige of it being left. The whole family rushed out to see with their own eyes. They saw and were convinced. Not a trace of it remained. Even the banks of the little stream had been so torn and altered by gushing water and tumbling rocks that it was almost impossible to say where that celebrated pool had been. The rains having commenced again on Monday, (just as if Sunday had been allowed to clear up in order to let people get to church), the family returned to the house, some to read and sketch, Mr Sudberry and George to prepare for a fishing excursion, despite the rain.

The second discovery was more startling in its nature. Jacky announced it with round eyes and a blazing face, thus—

"Oh! ma, old Moggy's d–dyin'!"

The attractive power of "sweeties" and a certain fondness for the old woman in the boy's heart had induced Jacky to visit the hut so frequently, that it at last came to be understood, that, when the imp was utterly lost, he was sure to be at old Moggy's! He had sauntered down, indifferent to rain, to call on his friend just after discovering the destruction of the bathing-pool, and found her lying on the bundle of rags which constituted her bed. She was groaning woefully. Jack went forward with much anxiety. The old woman was too ill to raise herself; but she had sufficient strength to grasp the child's hand, and, drawing him towards her, to stroke his head.

"Hallo! Moggy, you're ill!"

A groan and a gasp was the reply, and the poor creature made such wry faces, and looked altogether so cadaverous, that Jacky was quite alarmed. He suggested a drink of water, and brought her one. Then, as the old woman poured out a copious stream of Gaelic with much emphasis, he felt that the presence of some more able and intelligent nurse was necessary; so, like a sensible boy, he ran home and delivered his report, as has been already described.

Lucy and Fred hastened at once to the hut of the old woman, and found her in truth in a high fever, the result, no doubt, of the severe wetting of the day before, and having slept in damp clothes. Her mind was wandering a little when Lucy knelt at her side and took her hand, but she retained sufficient self-control to look up and exclaim earnestly, "I can say'd noo—I can say'd noo! I can say, *Thy will be done!*"

She became aware, as she said so, that the visitor at her side was not the one she had expected.

"Eh! ye're no' Miss Flora."

"No, dear granny, but I am quite as anxious to help you, and Flora will come very soon. We have only just heard of your illness, and have sent a message to Flora. Come, tell me what is the matter; let me put your poor head right."

Old Moggy submitted with a groan, and Lucy, assisted by Fred, endeavoured to make her bed a little more comfortable, while the anxious and staring Jacky was sent back to the house for some tea and a dry flannel gown. Before his return, however, Flora Macdonald, who chanced to be in the neighbourhood, came in to see Moggy, and immediately took the case in hand, in a way that greatly relieved Fred and Lucy, because they felt that she was accustomed to such incidents, and thoroughly understood what to do.

Hobbs, who came in a few minutes later with the Sudberry medicine chest, was instantly despatched by Flora for the doctor, and George, who entered a few minutes after that, was sent about his business, as were also a number of gossips, whose presence would ere long have rendered the small hut unbearably warm, but for Flora's decision.

Meanwhile all this unusual bustle had the effect of diverting the mind of the patient, who ceased to groan, and took to wandering instead.

Leaving them all thus engaged, we must beg the reader to accompany us to a very different scene.

It is a dense thicket within the entrance of the pass, to which reference has been made more than once. Here a band of wandering beggars or gypsies had pitched their camp on a spot which commanded an extensive view of the high-road, yet was itself concealed from view by the dwarf-trees which in that place covered the rugged hill-side.

There was a rude hut constructed of boughs and ferns, underneath which several dark-skinned and sturdy children were at play. A dissipated-looking young woman sat beside them. In front of this hut a small fire was kindled, and over it, from a tripod, hung an iron pot, the contents of which were watched with much interest, and stirred from time to time by a middle-aged woman of forbidding aspect. Beside her stood our amiable friend with the squint and the broken nose, who has already been mentioned as having received a merited thrashing from Mr Sudberry.

"Yes, the little brute has come back," said the gypsy, grinding his teeth in a way that might have led one to suppose he would have been glad to have had the "little brute" between them.

"Serves ye right for stealin' him away!" said the woman.

"Serves me right!" echoed the man, bitterly. "Did I not vow that I would have my revenge on that old witch? Did she not stand up in court and witness again' me, so that I got two year for a job that many a fellow gits off with six months for?"

"Well, you know you deserved it!" was the woman's comforting rejoinder. "You committed the robbery."

"So I did; but if that she-wolf had not made it out so bad, I'd have got off with six months. Ha! but I knew how to touch her up. I knew her weakness! swore, afore I left the dock, that I'd steal away the little cub she was so fond of—and *I did it!*"

There was a gleam of triumph in the gypsy's face as he said this, but it was quickly followed by a scowl when the woman said—

"Well, and much you have made of it. Here is the brat come back at the end o' five years, to spoil our harvest!"

"How could I know he'd do that? I paid the captain a goodish lump o' tin to take him on a long voyage, and I thought he was so young that he'd forget the old place."

"How d'ye know that he hasn't forgot it?" inquired the woman.

"'Cause, I seed him not twenty miles from this, and heerd him say he'd stop at the Blue Boar all night, and come on here in the morning—that's to-morrow—so I come straight out to ask you wot I'm to do."

"Ha! that's like you. Too chicken-hearted to do any thing till I set you on, an' mean enough to saddle it on me when ye'r nabbed."

"Come, that's an old story!" growled the man. "You know wot *I* am, and I knows wot *you* are. But if something's not done, we'll have to cut this here part o' the country in the very thick o' the season, when these southern sightseers are ranging about the hills."

"That's true!" rejoined the woman, seriously. "Many a penny the bairns get from them, an there's no part so good as this. Ye couldn't *put him out o' the way*, could ye?"

"No," said the man, doggedly.

The woman had accompanied her question with a sidelong glance of fiendish meaning, but her eyes at once dropped, and she evinced no anger at the sharp decision of her companion's reply.

"Mother!" cried the young woman, issuing from the hut at the moment, "don't you dare to go an' tempt him again like that. Our hands are black enough already; don't you try to make them *red*, else I'll blab!"

The elder woman assumed an injured look as she said, "Who spoke of makin' them red? Evil dreaders are evil doers. Is there no way o' puttin' a chick out o' the way besides murderin' him?"

"Hush!" exclaimed the man, starting and glancing round with a guilty look, as if he fancied the bare mention of the word "murder" would bring the strong arm of the law down on his head.

"I won't hush!" cried the woman. "You're cowards, both of you. Are there no corries in the hills to hide him in—no ropes to tie him with—that you should find it so difficult to keep a brat quiet for a week or two?"

A gleam of intelligence shot across the ill-favoured face of the gypsy.

"Ha! you're a wise woman. Come, out with your plan, and see if I'm not game to do it."

"There's no plan worth speakin' of," rejoined the woman, somewhat mollified by her companion's complimentary remarks. "All you've to do is to go down the road to-morrow, catch him, and bring him to me. I'll see to it that he don't make his voice heard until we've done with this part of the country. Then we can slip the knot, and let the brat go free."

"I'll do it!" said the man, sitting down on a stone and beginning to fill his pipe.

"I thought he was dead!" said the woman.

"So did I; but he's not dead yet, an' don't look as if he'd die soon."

"Maybe," said the woman, "he won't remember ye. It's full five year now sin' he was took away."

"Won't he?" retorted the man, with an angry look, which did not tend to improve his disagreeable visage. "Hah! I heerd him say he'd know me if he saw me in a crowd o' ten thousand. I would ha' throttled the cub then and there, but the place was too public."

A short silence ensued, during which the gypsies ate their food with the zest of half-starved wolves.

"You'd better go down and see old Moggy," suggested the woman, when the man had finished his repast and resumed his pipe. "If the brat escapes you to-morrow, it may be as well to let the old jade know that you'll murder both him and her, if he dares to blab."

The man shook his head. "No use!" said he. But the woman repeated her advice in a tone that was equivalent to a command, so the man rose up sulkily and went.

He was not a little surprised, on drawing near to the hut, to find it in a state of bustle, and apparently in possession of the Sudberrys. Not daring to show himself; he slunk back to his encampment, and informed his female companion of what he had seen.

"All the more reason to make sure work of him on the road to-morrow!" said she, with a dark frown.

"So I mean to!" replied the man doggedly. With these amiable sentiments and intentions animating their breasts, this pair crept into their booth and went to rest in the bosom of their family.

Story 1—Chapter 20

Mysterious Matters—A Happy Return, etcetera

The morning which followed the events narrated in the last chapter broke with unclouded splendour. It was the second of the four bright days which relieved the monotony of those six dreary weeks of rain.

Rejoicing in the glorious aspect of earth and sky, and in the fresh scents which the rain had called forth from every shrub and flower on the mountains, Mr Sudberry dashed about the White House—in and out—awaiting the assembling of the family to breakfast with great impatience. His coat-tails that morning proved the means of annihilating the sugar-basin—the last of the set which had graced the board on his arrival in the Highlands, and which had been left, for some time past, "blooming alone," all its former companions having been shattered and gone long ago.

According to custom, Mr Sudberry went forward to the barometrical banjo, intending to tap it—not that he expected correct information *now*. No; he had found out its falsehood, and was prepared to smile at anything it should say. He opened his eyes, however, and exclaimed "Hallo!" with unwonted energy, on observing that, as if in sheer defiance of the weather, of truth, and of public opinion, its index aimed point-blank at "stormy!"

He speedily discovered that this tremendous falsehood was the result of a careful intestine examination, to which the instrument had been privately subjected by Master Jacky the evening before; in the course of which examination the curious boy, standing below the barometer, did, after much trouble, manage to cut the bulb which held the mercury. That volatile metal, being set free, at once leaped into its liberator's bosom, and gushed down between his body and his clothes to the floor!

"I'll thrash him to within an inch—"

Mr Sudberry clinched his teeth and his fists, and burst out of the room, (it was at this moment that the last of the set became "faded and gone"), and rushed towards the nursery. "No, I won't," he muttered, suddenly wheeling round on his heel and returning slowly to the parlour. "I'll say nothing whatever about it." And Mr Sudberry kept his word—Jacky never heard of it from that day to this!

Seizing the opportunity of the fine day, Mr Sudberry and George went out to fish. They fished with worm now, the streams being too much swollen for fly.

Meanwhile, Master Jacky sauntered down alone, in a most free-and-easy independent manner, to visit old Moggy, who was thought to be in a dying state—at least the doctor said so, and it was to be presumed that he was right.

Jacky had regularly constituted himself sick nurse to the old woman. Despite the entreaties of Flora and his sister, who feared that the disease might be infectious, he could not be prevailed on to remain away. His nursing did not, indeed, consist in doing much that was useful. He confined himself chiefly to playing on the river-banks near the hut, and to making occasional inquiries as to how the patient was getting on. Sometimes he also assisted Flora in holding sundry cups, and glasses, and medicine bottles, and when Flora was away he amused himself by playing practical jokes on the young woman who had volunteered to act as regular nurse to the old invalid.

Towards the afternoon, Jacky put his hands behind his back—he would have put them under his coat-tails if he had had any, for he was very old-mannish in his tendencies—and sauntered down the road towards the pass. At this same time it chanced that another little boy, more than twice Jacky's age, was walking smartly along the same road towards the same pass from the other side of it. There were as yet several miles between the two boys, but the pace at which the elder walked bid fair to bring them face to face within an hour. The boy whom we now introduce was evidently a sailor. He wore blue trousers, a blue vest with little brass buttons, a blue jacket with bigger brass buttons, and a blue cap with a brass button on either side—each brass button, on coat, cap, and vest, having an anchor of, (apparently), burnished gold in the centre of it. He had clear blue eyes, brown curly hair, and an easy, offhand swagger, which last was the result of a sea-faring life and example; but he had a kindly and happy, rather than a boastful or self-satisfied, expression of face, as he bowled along with his hands in his pockets, kicking all the stones out of his way, and whistling furiously. Sometimes he burst into a song, and once or twice he laughed, smote his thigh, and cheered, but never for a moment did he slacken his pace, although he had walked many a mile that day.

Curiously enough, at this same time, a man was crouching behind some bushes in the centre of the pass towards which these two boys were approaching. This man had a pair of grey eyes which might have been beautiful had they not been small and ferocious-looking, and a nose which might have been aquiline had the bridge not been broken, and a head of shaggy hair which might have been elegant had it been combed, oiled, curled, and dyed, and a general appearance which might have been prepossessing had it not been that of a thorough blackguard. This lovely specimen of humanity sat down on a rock, and waited, and fidgeted; and the expression of his sweet face betrayed, from time to time, that he was impatient, and anything but easy in his mind.

As Jack walked very leisurely and stopped frequently to play, his progress towards the pass was slow, and as our waiting friend, whom the reader no doubt recognises as the gypsy, could not see far along the road in that direction, he was not aware of his approach. On the other hand, the sailor-boy came on fast, and the road was so open and straight in that direction that the gypsy saw him when he was far enough away to seem like a mere blue spot in the distance.

Presently he gained the entrance to the pass and began the ascent, which was gradual, with a riotous windlass song, in which the sentiments, yo! heave! and ho! were most frequently expressed. As he drew near, the gypsy might have been observed to grin a smile that would have been quite captivating but for some obstinate peculiarity about the muscles of the mouth which rendered it very repulsive.

Next moment the sailor-boy was abreast of him. The moment after that the bushes parted, and the gypsy confronted his victim, cutting a tremendous "heave!" short in the middle, and converting the "ho!" that should have followed, into a prolonged whistle of astonishment.

"Hah! my lad, you remember me, it seems?"

"Remember you? Yes, I just do!" answered the boy, in whose countenance every trace of boyishness was instantly swallowed up in an intense gaze of manly determination.

This mute but meaning glance had such a strange effect upon the gypsy that he actually cowered for a moment, and looked as if he were afraid he was going to "catch it." However, he forced a laugh and said—

"Come, Billy, you needn't look so cross. You know I was hard put to it w'en I sent you aboord the 'Fair Nancy,' and you shouldn't ought to owe me a grudge for puttin' ye in the way o' makin' yer fortin'."

The man kept edging towards the boy as he spoke, but the boy observed this and kept edging away, regarding the man with compressed lips and dilated eyes, but not vouchsafing a word in reply.

"I say, Billy, it's unkind, you know, to forget old times like this. I want to shake hands; and there's my old woman up on the hill as wants to see you again."

Suddenly the fierce look left the boy's face, and was replaced by a wild, waggish expression.

"Oh! your old woman wants to see me, does she? And you want to shake hands, do you? Now look here, Growler; I see through you! You thought to catch a flat, and you'll find you've caught a tartar; or, rather, that the tartar has caught *you*. But I've grown merciful since I went to sea," (the lad tucked-up his wristbands at this point, as if he really meditated a hand-to-hand encounter with his huge antagonist). "I *do* remember old times, and I know how richly you deserve to be hanged; but I don't want to mix up my home-coming, if I can help it, with dirty work. Now, I'll tell you what—I'll give you your choice o' two courses. Either take yourself off and be out o' hail of this part of the country within twelve hours, or walk with me to the nearest police station and give yourself up. There—I'll give you exactly two minutes to think over it."

The youthful salt here pulled out an enormous double-case silver watch with an air of perfect nonchalance, and awaited the result. For a few seconds the gypsy was overwhelmed by the lad's coolness; then he burst into a gruff laugh and rushed at him. He might as well have run at a squirrel. The boy sprang to one side, crossed the road at a bound, and, still holding the watch, said—

"Half a minute gone!"

Again the man rushed at his small opponent with similar result, and a cool remark, that another half minute was gone. This so exasperated the gypsy, that he ran wildly after the boy for half a minute, but the latter was as active as a kitten, and could not be caught.

"Time's up; two minutes and a quarter; so don't say that I'm not merciful. Now, follow me to the constable."

So saying, Billy, as the man had called him, turned his back towards the pass, and ran off at full speed towards the village. The gypsy followed him at once, feeling that his only chance lay in capturing the boy; but so artfully did Billy hang back and allow his pursuer to come close up, that he had almost succeeded in enticing him into the village, when the man became suddenly aware of his folly, and stopped. Billy stopped too.

"What! you're not game to come on?"

The man shook his fist, and, turning his face towards the pass, ran back towards his booth in the hills, intending to take the boy's first piece of advice, and quit that part of the country. But Billy had no idea of letting him off thus. He now became the pursuer. However fast the gypsy ran, the sailor-lad kept up with him. If the man halted, as he frequently did in a breathless condition, and tried to gain over his adversary, Billy also stopped, said he was in no hurry, thrust his hands into his jacket pockets, and began to whistle. Thus he kept him in view until they once more stood in the pass. Here the man sat down on a large stone, thoroughly exhausted. The boy sat down on another stone opposite to him, looking quite fresh and jolly. Five years of hearty devotion to a noble calling had prepared the muscles of the little sailor for that day's exercise. The same number of years spent in debauchery and crime had *not* prepared the vagabond giant for that day's work.

"What has brought you back?" said Growler, savagely.

"To see the old granny whom you stole me from," replied the boy. "Also, to have the satisfaction of puttin' you in limbo; although I did not expect to have this pleasure."

"Ha! ha!" laughed Growler, sarcastically, "you'll fail in both. It's not so easy to put me in limbo as you think—and your grandmother is dyin'."

"That's false!" cried Billy, springing half way across the road and shaking his little fist at his enemy—"you know it is. The landlord of the 'Blue Boar' told me he saw her at church strong and well last Sunday."

"She's dyin', however, may be *dead*," said the man, with a sneer so full of triumph, that it struck a chill to the heart of the poor boy.

Just at that moment, Jacky Sudberry turned slowly round a sharp angle of the road, and stood there transfixed, with his eyes like two saucers, and his mouth as round as an o.

The sight of this intruder distracted Billy's attention for a moment. Growler at once bounded over the low wall and dived into the underwood. Billy hesitated to follow him, for the last piece of information weighed heavily on his mind. That moment's hesitation was sufficient for the gypsy to make good his retreat. Although Billy leaped the wall the next moment, and darted hither and thither through the copse, he failed to catch sight of him again, and finally returned to the road, where he found Jacky seated on a stone, pondering in a state of bewilderment on what he had seen.

"Well, my boy, how goes it?" cried the sailor heartily, as he came forward, wiping his heated brow with a blue spotted cotton handkerchief.

"All right!" was Jacky's prompt reply. "I say, was you fightin' with that man?"

"Ay, that was I, and I've not done with him yet."

Jacky breathed hard and looked upon the young sailor-lad with a deep reverential awe, feeling that he was in the presence of a real Jack the Giant-killer.

"He runn'd away!" said Jacky in amazement. "Did you hit him hard?"

"Not with my fists; they ain't big enough for that yet. We've only had a sparring-match with words and legs."

Jacky glanced at Billy's legs as if he regarded them in the light of dire engines of destruction. Indeed, his active mind jumped at once to the conclusion that the sailor's must be a kicking mode of warfare; but he was too much amazed to make any rejoinder.

"Now, my boy, I'm going this way, so I'll bid you good-day," said Billy. Jacky informed him that he was going the same way,—having only been taking a stroll,—and would willingly go back: whereupon Billy put his arm round his shoulder, as boys are wont to do, and Jacky grasped Billy round the waist, and thus they wandered home together.

"I say, you're a funny chap," observed the young sailor, in a comic vein, as they went along.

"So are you," replied Jacky, with intense gravity, being deeply serious.

Billy laughed; but as the two friends at that moment emerged from the pass and came in sight of the White House, the laugh was suddenly checked, and was followed by a sound that was not unlike choking. Jacky looked up in alarm, and was surprised to see tears hopping over his companion's brown cheeks. To find a lad who could put a giant to flight was wonderful enough, but to find one who could cry without any reason at all was beyond belief. Jacky looked perplexed and said, "I say, what's the matter?"

"Oh! nothing; only this is my old home, and my scrimmage with that villain has made me come plump on it without thinkin'. I was born here. I know every stone and bush. I—I—there's the old—"

He choked again at this point, and Jacky, whose mind was only opening, stood looking on in silent wonder.

"My old granny lives here; old Moggy—"

The expression of Jacky's face caused Billy to stop.

"Why, what's wrong, boy?"

"Is—is—o–old Moggy *your* granny?" cried Jacky, eagerly, stumbling over his words as if he had come upon stepping-stones in the dark.

"Ay; what then?"

"Eh! *I* know her."

"Do you, my boy?"

"Ye–yes; sh–she's dyin'!"

The result of this remark was that the sailor-boy turned deadly pale, and stared at his little friend without being able to utter a word. Mere human nature taught Jacky that he had made a mistake in being so precipitate: but home education had not taught him to consider the feelings of others. He felt inclined to comfort his new friend, but knew not how to do it. At last a happy thought occurred to him, and he exclaimed eagerly—

"B–but *sh–she's not dead yet!*"

"Does she live in the same cottage?" asked the boy, in a low, husky voice, not considering that his companion could not know what cottage she had occupied in former days. Jacky, also ignoring this fact, nodded his head violently, being past speech with excitement, and pointed in the direction of the hut.

Without another word, Billy, (more correctly speaking, Willie), at once took to his heels, and was followed by Jacky as fast as his short legs could carry him.

Flora Macdonald was administering a glass of hot wine and water to her patient, when the door was quickly, yet gently, opened, and a sailor-lad sprang into the room, fell on his knees beside the lowly couch, seized the old woman's hand, gazed for a few seconds into her withered face, and then murmuring, "Granny, it's me," laid his head on her shoulder and burst into tears.

Flora gently drew the boy away.

"Willie, is it possible; can it be you?"

"Is she dyin'?" said Willie, looking up in Flora's face with an expression of agony.

"I trust not, dear boy; but the doctor says she is very ill, and must be kept quiet."

"Hoot, awa' wi' the doctor! He's wrang," cried old Moggy, suddenly raising herself with great energy on one elbow; "don't I see my ain Willie there, as I've seen him in my dreams mony and mony a night?" (Flora grasped Willie's arm to prevent his running towards her, and pointed to Jacky, who had at that moment entered the room, and was at once recognised by Moggy.) "Ay, little did I think when I said yestreen, 'Thy wull be done,' that He wad send my ain laddie back again!"

She folded Jacky, who had gone to the bedside, in her arms, and was with difficulty prevailed on to let him go. It was quite evident that her mind was wandering.

The effect of this little episode on Willie was powerful and twofold. A pang of jealousy at first shot through his heart like a flash of lightning; but when he perceived that the loving embrace was meant for his old self he broke down, and the tears once more tumbled over his brown cheeks.

"She cannot recognise you just now, dear Willie," said Flora, deeply touched by the sorrow of the lad; "and, even if she could, I fear it would do her harm by exciting her too much. Come, my poor fellow," (leading him softly to the door), "I am just going up to visit a kind English family, where they will be only too glad to put you up until it is safe to let her know that you have returned."

"But she may die, and never know that I have returned," said Willie, almost passionately, as he hung back.

"She is in God's loving hands, Willie."

"Can I not stay and help you to nurse her?" asked the boy, in pitiful tones.

Flora shook her head, and Willie meekly suffered himself to be led out of the hut.

This, then, was the home-coming that he had longed for so intensely; that he had dreamed of so often when far away upon the sea! No sooner was he in the open air than he burst away from Flora without a word, and ran off at full speed in the direction of the pass. At first he simply sought to obtain relief to his feelings by means of violent muscular exercise. The burning brain and throbbing heart were unbearable. He would have given the world for the tears that flowed so easily a short time before; but they would not now come. Running, leaping, bounding madly over the rough hill-side—*that* gave him some relief; so he held on, through bush and brake, over heathery knoll and peat swamp, until the hut was far behind him.

Suddenly his encounter with the gypsy occurred to him. The thought that he was the original cause of all this misery roused a torrent of indignation within him, and he resolved that the man should not escape. His wild race was no longer without purpose now. He no longer sprang into the air and bounded from rock to rock like a wild goat, but, coursing down the bed of a mountain-torrent, came out upon the road, and did not halt until he was in front of the constabulary station.

"Hallo! laddie, what's wrong?" inquired a blue-coated official, whose language betokened him a Lowland Scot.

"I've seen him; come with me—quick! I'll take you to his whereabouts," gasped Willie.

"Seen whae?" inquired the man, with slow deliberation.

"The gypsy, Growler, who stole me, and would have murdered me this morning if he could have caught me; but quick, please! He'll get off if you don't look alive!"

The earnestness and fervour of the lad had the effect of exciting even the constable's phlegmatic nature; so, after a short conversation, he summoned a comrade, and set off for the pass at a round trot, led by Willie.

"D'ye think it's likely he'll ken ye've come here to tell on him?" inquired the constable, as they ran.

"I said I would have him nabbed," replied the boy.

"Hoot! mon; that was na wise-like. But after a' ye're ony a bairn. Here, Tam, ye'd better gang up by the Stank burn an' keep a look-oot ower the hills, an' I'll start him."

Thus advised, the second constable diverged to the right, and, plunging into the copsewood, was instantly out of sight.

Soon afterwards, Willie came to the place where he had met the gypsy. Here a consultation was held as to where the booth might probably be.

"He jumped over the wall here," said Willie, "and I'm sure he took the hill in this direction at *first*."

"Ay, laddie; but chiels o' his stamp never gang straight to their mark. We'll follow him up *this* way. Hoe long is't sin' ye perted wi' him, said ee?" examining the place where the gypsy had entered the copse.

Willie returned no answer. The unusual amount of fatigue and the terrible mental excitement which he had undergone that day were too much for him. A feeling of deadly sickness came suddenly on him, and when the constable looked round he was lying on the road in a swoon.

This unexpected incident compelled the man to abandon further pursuit for the time. Giving utterance to a "puir laddie," he raised the boy in his arms and carried him to the nearest hut, which happened to be that of old Moggy! No one was there but the young woman who acted as nurse to the invalid. It chanced that Moggy had had a sleep, and she awoke with her mental faculties much cleared, when the constable entered and laid Willie on a mat not far from her bed.

The old woman gazed long and earnestly in the boy's face, and seemed much troubled and perplexed while the nurse applied water to his temples. At last Willie opened his eyes. Moggy at once recognised him. She strove eagerly to reach her long-lost child, and Willie, jumping up, sprang to her side; but ere they met she raised both arms in the air, and, uttering a long piercing cry, fell back insensible upon the bed.

Story 1—Chapter 21

The End

Rain, rain, rain; continual, pertinacious, unmitigated rain! The White House was no longer white, it was grey. Things were no longer damp, they were totally flooded. Mr McAllister's principal hay-field was a pond—every ditch was a rivulet; "the burn" was a destructive cataract; the white torrents that raged down the mountains everywhere, far and near, looked like veins of quartz, and the river had become a lake with a strong current in the middle of it. There was no sunshine now in the Highlands,—not a gleam!

Nevertheless there was sunshine in the hearts of some who sojourned there. Mr Sudberry had found out that he could fish just as well in wet weather as in dry, and that the fish were more eager to be caught. That was sunshine enough for him! Lucy found a new and engrossing amusement, of a semi-scientific kind, in laying down and pressing her botanical specimens, and writing Latin names under the same, being advised thereto and superintended by Hector Macdonald. That was sunshine enough for her, and for him too apparently, for he came every day to help her, (and she declared she could not get on without help), and it was quite wonderful to observe how very slowly the laying-down progressed, although both of the semi-philosophers were intensely interested in their work. Flora was so sunny by nature that she lightened up the place around her wherever she went; she was thus in some measure independent of the sun. George was heard to say more than once that her face was as good as a sunbeam any day! Mrs Sudberry, poor woman, was so rampantly triumphant in the total discomfiture of her husband touching the weather, that she resigned herself to Highland miseries in a species of happy contentment, and thus lived in what may be likened to a species of mild moonshine of her own. Tilly, poor, delicate, unobtrusive Tilly, was at all times satisfied to bask in the moonlight of her mother's countenance. As for Jacky—that arch-imp discovered that wet weather usually brought his victims within doors, and therefore kept them constantly within reach of his dreadful influence. He was supremely happy—"darling child." Fred finished up his sketches—need we say that that was sunshine to him? The servants too shared in the general felicity. Indeed, they may, in a sense, be said to have been happier than those they served, for, having been transported to that region to *work*, they found the little bits of fun and amusement that fell to their lot all the more pleasant and enjoyable, that they were unexpected, and formed a piquant contrast to the monotonous routine of daily duty.

But the brightest blaze of internal sunshine—the most effulgent and dazzling beams of light were shed forth in the lowly hut of Jacky's particular friend. Old Moggy did *not* die after all! To the total discomfiture of the parish doctor, and to the reflected discredit of the medical profession generally, that obstinate old creature got well in spite of the emphatic assurances of her medical adviser that recovery was impossible. The doctor happened to be a misanthrope. He was not aware that in the *Materia Medica* of Nature's laboratory there is a substance called "joy," which sometimes effects a cure when all else fails—or, if he did know of this medicine, he probably regarded it as a quack nostrum.

At all events this substance cured old Moggy, as Willie said, "in less than no time." She took such deep draughts of it, that she quite surprised her old friends. So did Willie himself. In fact, these two absolutely took to tippling together on this medicine. More than that, Jacky joined them, and seemed to imbibe a good deal—chiefly through his eyes, which were always very wide open and watchful when he was in the old hut. He drank to them only with his eyes and ears, and could not be induced to enter into conversation much farther than to the extent of yes and no. Not that he was shy—by *no* means! The truth was that Jacky was being opened up—mentally. The new medicine was exercising an unconscious but powerful influence on his sagacious spirit. In addition to that he was fascinated by Willie—for the matter of that, so was old Moggy—for did not that small sailor-boy sing, and laugh, and talk to them for hours about sights and scenes of foreign travel of which neither of them had dreamed before? Of course he did, and caused both of them to stare with eyes and mouths quite motionless for half-hours at a time, and then roused them up with a joke that made Jacky laugh till he cried, and made Moggy, who was always crying more or less, laugh till she couldn't cry! Yes, there was very brilliant sunshine in the hut during that dismal season of rain—there was the sunshine of human love and sympathy, and Flora was the means of introducing and mingling with it sunshine of a still brighter and a holier nature, which, while it intensified the other, rendered it also permanent.

At last the end of the Sudberrys' rustication arrived; the last day of their sojourn dawned. It happened to be bright and beautiful—so bright and lovely that it made one feel as if there never had been a bad day since the world began, and never would be another bad one to the end of time. It was the fourth fine day of the six dreary weeks—the third, which occurred some days before, was only half-and-half; and therefore unworthy of special notice. Nevertheless, the Sudberrys felt sad. They were *going away*! The mental sunshine of the rainy season was beclouded, and the physical sunshine was of no avail to dispel such clouds.

"My dear," said Mr Sudberry at breakfast that morning, in a very sad tone, "have you any further use for me?"

"My dear, no," replied his partner, sorrowfully.

From the nature of these remarks and the tone in which they were uttered, an ignorant spectator might have imagined that Mr Sudberry, having suspected his wife of growing indifference, and having had his worst fears confirmed from her own lips, meant to go quietly away to the river and drown him in a deep pool with a strong eddy, so that he might run no chance of being prematurely washed upon a shallow. But the good man merely referred to "the packing," in connection with which he had been his wife's right hand during the last three or four days.

"Well, then, my love, as the heavy baggage has gone on before, and we are ready to start with the coach, which does not pass until the afternoon, I will go and take a last cast in the river."

Mrs Sudberry made no objection; so Mr Sudberry, accompanied by George and Fred, went down to the "dear old river," as they styled it, for the last time.

Now it must be known, that, some weeks previous to this time, Hobbs had been allowed by his master to go out for a day's trout-fishing, and Hobbs, failing to raise a single fin, put on a salmon fly in reckless desperation.

He happened, by the merest chance, to cast over a deep pool in which salmon were, (and still are), wont to lie. To his amazement, a *"whale,"* as he styled it, instantly rose, sent its silvery body half out of the water, and fell over with a tremendous splash, but missed the fly. Hobbs was instantly affected with temporary insanity. He cast in violent haste over the same spot, as if he hoped to hook the fish by the tail before it should get to the bottom. Again! again! and over again, but without result. Then, dancing on the bank with excitement, he changed the fly; tried every fly in the book; the insanity increasing, tried two flies at once, back to back; put on a bunch of trout-flies in addition; wound several worms round all; failed in every attempt to cast with care; and finished off by breaking the top of the rod, entangling the line round his legs, and fixing the hooks in his coat-tails; after which he rushed wildly up to the White House, to tell what he had seen and show what he had done!

From that day forward Mr Sudberry always commenced his day's sport at the "Salmon Pool."

As usual, on this his last day, he went down to the salmon pool, but he had so often fished there in vain, that hope was well-nigh extinguished. In addition to this, his spirits were depressed, so he gave the rod to Fred.

Fred was not naturally a fisher, and he only agreed to take the rod because he saw that his father was indifferent about it.

"Fred, my boy, cast a little farther over, just below yon curl in the water near the willow bush—ah! that's about the place. Hobbs declares that he raised a salmon there; but I can't say I've ever seen one myself; though I have fished here every other morning for many weeks."

Mr Sudberry had not quite finished speaking when Fred's rod was bent into the form of a large hoop.

"Hallo! here, father, take it—I don't know what to do."

What a blaze of excitement beamed on the father's countenance!

"Hurrah! hold on, Fred,—no, no, *no*! ease off—he'll break all away."

The caution was just in time. Fred was holding on like a true Briton. He suddenly let the rod down and allowed the line to run out, which it did like lightning.

"What now, father? Oh! *do* take it—I shall certainly lose the fish."

"No, no, boy; it is *your* fish; try to play it out." No one but the good man himself knew what a tremendous effort of self-denial Mr Sudberry made on this occasion. But Fred felt certain that the fish would get off. He also knew that his father would give fifty pounds down on the spot to land a salmon: so he said firmly, "Father, if you don't take the rod, I'll throw it down!"

This settled the question. Father took the rod under protest, and, having had considerable experience in trout-fishing, began to play the salmon with really creditable skill, considering the difficulty of the operation, and the fact that it was his first "big fish."

What varied expression flitted across the countenance of the enthusiastic sportsman on this great occasion! He totally forgot himself and his sons; he forgot even that this was his last day in the Highlands. It is an open question whether he did not forget altogether that he was *in* the Highlands, so absorbed, so intensely concentrated, was his mind on that salmon. George and Fred also became so excited that they lost all command of themselves, and kept leaping about, cheering, giving useless advice in eager tones, tripping over stones and uneven places on the banks, and following their father closely, as the fish led him up and down the river for full two hours. They, too, forgot themselves; they did not know what extraordinary faces they went on making during the greater part of the time!

Mr Sudberry began the battle by winding up the line, the salmon having begun to push slowly up stream after its first wild burst. In a moment it made a dart towards the opposite bank, so sudden and swift that the rod was pulled straight, and the line ran out with a whiz of the most violent description. Almost simultaneously with the whiz the salmon leaped its entire length out of the water, gave a tremendous fling in the air, and came down with a heavy splash!

Fred gasped; George cheered, and Mr Sudberry uttered a roar of astonishment, mingled with alarm, for the line was slack, and he thought the fish had broken off. It was still on, however, as a wild dash down stream, followed by a spurt up and across, with another fling into the air, proved beyond a doubt. The fish was very wild— fortunately it was well hooked, and the tackle was strong. What with excitement and the violent action that ensued at each rush, Mr Sudberry was so dreadfully blown in the first minutes, that he trembled from head to foot, and could scarce wind up the line. For one moment the thought occurred that he was too old to become a salmon-fisher, and that he would not be able to fight the battle out. He was quite mistaken. Every minute after this he seemed to gain fresh strength. The salmon happily took it into his head to cease its antics for half a minute, just when the fisher was at his worst. That half-minute of breathing-space was all that was wanted.

"Geo'ge—hah!—cut—wata!"

George could not make out what his agitated parent wanted.

"Water! water! —chokin'!" reiterated his father.

"Oh, all right!" George scooped up a quantity of water in a leathern cup, and ran with it to his choking sire, who, holding the rod tight with both hands, turned his head aside and stretched over his left arm, still, however, keeping his eyes fixed on the line.

"Here, up with't lips."

The lips were projected, and George raised the cup to them, but the salmon moved at the moment, and the draught was postponed. The fish came to another pause soon after.

"Now, Geo'ge, try 'gain."

Once more the lips were projected, once again the cup was raised, but that salmon seemed to know what was going on, for, just as the cup and the lips met, it went off in an unusually fierce run down the river. The cup and its contents were knocked into George's face, and George himself was knocked over by his father as he sprang down the bank, and ran along a dry patch of gravel, which extended to the tail of the pool.

Hitherto the battle had been fought within the limits of one large pool, which the fish seemed to have an objection to quit. It now changed its tactics, and began to descend the river tail foremost, slowly, but steadily. The round face of the fisher, which had all this time been blazing red with eager hope, was now beclouded with a shade of anxiety.

"Don't let him go down the rapids, father," said George; "you'll never get past the thick bushes that overhang the bank."

Mr Sudberry stopped, and held on till the rod bent like a giant hoop and the line became rigid; but the fish was not to be checked. Its retrograde movement was slow, but steady and irresistible.

"You'll smash everything!" cried Fred. Mr Sudberry was constrained to follow, step by step. The head of the rapid was gained, and he had to increase the pace to a quick walk; still farther down, and the walk became a smart run. The ground here was more rugged, and the fisher's actions became quite acrobatic. George and Fred kept higher up the bank, and ran along, gazing in unspeakable amazement at the bounds and leaps which their fat little sire made with the agility of a roe deer.

"Hold on! the bushes! let it break off!"

Mr Sudberry scorned the advice. The part of the bank before him was impassable; not so the river, which rushed past him like a mill-race. He tried once more to stop the fish; failed, of course, and deliberately walked into the water. It was waist-deep, so he was carried down like a cork with his toes touching the ground so lightly, that, for the first time in his life, he rejoiced in those sensations, which he had hitherto believed belonged exclusively to harlequins and columbines; namely, swift motion without effort! Fifty yards at the rate of ten miles an hour brought him to an eddy, into which the salmon had dashed just before him. Mr Sudberry gave vent to another roar as he beheld the fish almost under his nose. The startled creature at once flashed out of his sight, and swept up, down, and across the stream several times, besides throwing one or two somersaults in the air, before it recovered its equanimity. After this it bolted into a deep, dark pool, and remained there quite motionless.

Mr Sudberry was much puzzled at this point. To let out line when the fish ran up or across stream, to wind in when the fish stopped, and to follow when the fish went down stream—these principles he had been taught by experience in trout-fishing; but how to act when a fish would not move, and could not be made to move, was a lesson which he had yet to learn.

"What's to be done?" said he, with a look of exasperation, (and no wonder; he had experienced an hour and a quarter of very rough treatment, and was getting fagged).

"Pull him out of that hole," suggested George.

"I can't."

"Try."

Mr Sudberry tried and failed. Having failed he sat down on a stone, still holding the rod very tight, and wiped his heated brow. Then, starting up, he tried for the next ten minutes to pull the fish out of the hole by main force, of course never venturing to pull so hard as to break the line. He went up the stream and pulled, down the stream and pulled, he even waded across the stream at a shallow part and pulled, but all in vain. The fish was in that condition which fishers term "the sulks."

At last Fred recollected to have heard Hector Macdonald say that in such cases a stone thrown into the pool sometimes had the effect of starting the sulky one. Accordingly a stone was thrown in, and the result was that the fish came out at full speed in a horrible fright, and went down stream, not *tail* but *head* foremost. Now, when a salmon does this, he knows by instinct that if he does not go down *faster* than the stream the water will force itself into his gills and drown him; therefore when he goes down head first, (which he seldom does, except when on his way to the sea), he goes at full speed, and the fisher's only chance of saving his fish is to run after him as fast as he can, in the hope that he may pause of his own accord in some opportune eddy.

A fine open space of bank enabled Mr Sudberry to run like a deer after his fish for nigh a quarter of a mile, but, at the end of this burst, he drew near to "the falls"—a succession of small cataracts and rapids which it seemed impossible for any fisher to go down without breaking his neck and losing his fish. George and Fred roared, "Hold on!" Mr Sudberry glanced at the falls, frowned, and compressed his lips. He felt that he was "in for it;" he resolved not to be beat, so on he went! The fish went right down the first fall; the fisher leaped over a ledge of rock three feet high, scrambled across some rough ground, and pulled up at an eddy where the fish seemed disposed to rest. He was gratified here by seeing the fish turn up the white of his side—thus showing symptoms of exhaustion. But he recovered, and went over another fall.

Here he stopped again, and George and Fred, feeling convinced that their father had gone mad, threw off their coats and ran to the foot of the fall, ready to plunge into the stream and rescue him from the fate which they thought they saw impending. No such fate awaited the daring man. He succeeded in drawing the fish close to a gravelly shallow, where it gave an exhausted wallop or two, and lay over on its side. George came up, and leaping into the water tried to kick it out. He missed his kick and fell. Fred dashed in, and also missed. Mr Sudberry rushed forward and gave the salmon such a kick that he sent it high and dry on the bank! But in doing so he fell over George and tripped up Fred, so that all three were instantly soaked to the skin, and returned to the bank without their hats. Mr Sudberry flung himself on the conquered fish and held it fast, while George and Fred cheered and danced round him in triumphant joy.

Thus Mr Sudberry landed his first and last salmon—a ten-pounder—and thus, brilliantly, terminated his three-months' rustication in the Highlands.

But this was not the end of the whole affair—by no means. Mr Sudberry and family returned to London, and they took that salmon with them. A dinner-party of choice friends was hastily got up to do honour to the superb fish, and on that occasion Fred and his father well-nigh quarrelled on the point of, "who caught the salmon!" Mr Sudberry insisting that the man who hooked the fish was the real catcher of it, and Fred scouting the ridiculous notion, and asserting that he who played and landed it was entitled to all the honour. The point was settled, however, in some incomprehensible way, without the self-denying disputants coming to blows; and everyone agreed that it was, out of sight, the best salmon that had ever been eaten in London. Certainly, it was one of the merriest parties that ever ate a salmon, for Mr Sudberry's choice friends were of an uncommonly genial stamp. Jones, the head clerk, (the man with the red nose and humble aspect), was there, and so brilliant was Mr Sudberry that Jones was observed to smile!—the first instance on record of his having given way to levity of demeanour. Lady Knownothing was there too, and before the evening was over she knew a few things that surprised but did not in the least convince her. Oh, no! she knew everything so thoroughly that there was no possibility on earth of increasing *her* stock of knowledge! Truly it was a happy party, and Mr Sudberry enjoyed himself so much that he volunteered the Highland fling in the drawing-room—George whistling the music—on which occasion he, (Mr Sudberry), swept nearly half the tea-service off the table with his coat-tails, and Mrs Sudberry was so happy that she didn't care a button—and said so!

But this was not the end of it yet, by any means. That winter Hector and Flora Macdonald visited London and were received by the Sudberrys with open arms. The result was that Lucy became intensely botanical in her tastes, and routed out the old plants. Of course Hector could not do less than assist her, and the finale was, that these two scientific individuals were married, and dwelt for many years thereafter in the Highlands. Strange to say, George and Flora fell in love with each—But why say more? We do not mean to write the history of these two families. It is enough to say, that every summer, for many years after that, the Sudberrys spent two or three months in the Highlands with the Macdonalds, and every winter the Macdonalds spent a similar period with the Sudberrys. On the former of these occasions Fred renewed his intercourse with Mr McAllister, and these two became so profoundly, inconceivably, deep and metaphysical, besides theological, in their converse, that they were utterly incomprehensible to everyone except themselves.

Best of all, Jacky became a good boy! Yes; that day on the hills with Peter was the beginning of it—old Moggy, Willie, and Flora, were the continuation of it—and Jacky became good, to the unspeakable joy of his mother.

Old Moggy lived to a fabulous age, and became at last as wrinkled as a red herring. For all we know to the contrary, she may be alive yet. Willie lived with her, and became a cultivator of the soil. But why go on? Enough has been said to show that no ill befell any individual mentioned in our tale. Even Mrs Brown lived to a good old age, and was a female dragon to the last. Enough has also been said to prove, that, as the old song has it, "we little know what great things from little things may rise."

Story 2—Chapter 1

Why I did not become a Sailor

There is mystery connected with the incidents which I am about to relate. Looked at from one point of view, the whole affair is mysterious—eminently so; yet, regarded from another point of view, it is not so mysterious as it seems. Whatever my reader may think about it as he goes along, I entreat him to suspend his judgment until he has reached the conclusion of my narrative. My only reason for bringing this mysterious matter before the public is, that, in addition to filling me with unutterable surprise, it had the effect of quenching one of my strongest desires, and effectually prevented my becoming a sailor.

This, I freely admit, is not in itself a sufficient reason to justify my rushing into print. But when I regard the matter from what may be termed a negative point of view, I do feel that it is not absolutely presumptuous in me to claim public attention. Suppose that Sir John Franklin had never gone to sea; what a life of adventure and discovery would have been lost to the world! what deeds of heroism undone, and, therefore, untold! I venture to think, that if that great navigator had not gone to sea, it would have been a matter of interest, (knowing what we now know), to have been told that such was the case. In this view of the matter I repeat it, as being of possible future interest, that the incident I am about to relate prevented my becoming a sailor.

I am said to be a soft boy—that is to say, I *was* said to be soft. I'm a man now, but, of course, I was a boy once. I merely mention this to prove that I make no pretension whatever to unusual wisdom; quite the reverse. I hate sailing under false colours—not that I ever did sail under any colours, never having become a sailor—and yet I shouldn't say that, either, for that's the very point round which all the mystery hangs. I *did* go to sea! I'm rather apt to wander, I find, from my point, and to confuse my own mind, (I trust not the reader's). Perhaps the shortest way to let you understand how it was is to tell you all about it.

My name is Robert Smith—not an unusual name, I am given to understand. It was of little use to me during the period of my boyhood, for I never got any other name than Bob—sometimes *soft* was added. I had a father. He loved me. As a natural consequence, I loved him. He was old, partially bald, silver-haired, kind, affectionate, good, five feet six, and wore spectacles. I, at the time I write of; was young, stout, well-grown, active, and had a long nose—much too long a nose: it was the only point in regard to which I was sensitive. It was owing to the length of this member, I believe, that I once went by the name of Mozambique. You see, I conceal nothing. The remarkable—the mysterious—the every way astonishing incidents I am about to relate, require that I should be more than usually careful and particular in stating things precisely as I saw them and understood them at the time.

In this view of the matter I should remark that the softness with which I was charged did not refer to my muscles—they were hard and well developed—but to my intellect. I take this opportunity of stating that I think the charge unjust. But, to conclude my description of myself; I am romantic. One of my dearest companions used to say that my nose was the same, minus the tic! What he meant by that I never could make out. I doubt if he himself knew.

My chief delight in my leisure hours was to retire to my bedroom and immerse myself in books of travel and adventure. This was my mania. No one can conceive the delight I experienced in following heroes of every name over the pathless deep and through the trackless forests of every clime. My heart swelled within me, and the blood rushed through my veins like liquid fire, as I read of chasing lions, tigers, elephants, in Africa; white bears and walrus in the Polar regions; and deer and bisons on the American prairies. I struggled long to suppress the flame that consumed me, but I could not. It grew hotter and hotter. At last, it burst forth—and this brings me to the point.

I thought—one dark, dismal night in the middle of November—I thought, (mind, I don't say I determined; no, but I thought), of running away from home and going to sea!

I confess it with shame. The image of my dear father rose before me with a kind and sorrowful look. I repented; started to my feet, and seized the book I was reading with the intention of tossing it into the fire. In doing so, I accidentally turned over a leaf. There was an illustration on the page. I looked at it. An African savage firing the whole contents of a six-barrelled revolver down the throat of a Bengal tiger, without, apparently, doing it any harm! I thought not of the incongruous combination. My soul was fired anew. Once again I thought of running away from home and going to sea—not by any means with the intention of remaining at sea, but for the purpose of reaching foreign—if possible—unknown lands.

Having conceived the thought, I rose calmly, shut the book carefully, but with decision, thrust my hands firmly into my pockets, knitted my brows, and went out in search of my bosom friend John Brown—also a commonplace name, I believe—at least, so it is said.

Jack, as I used to call him, had a mother, but no father—his father died when Jack was an infant. I've often fancied that there was a delicate bond of union between us here. He had a mother, but no father. I had a father, but no mother. Strange coincidence! I think the fact helped to draw us together. I may be wrong, but I think so. Jack was on a visit to us at the time, so I had only to cross the passage to reach his room.

"Come in," he cried, as I knocked.

"Jack, come to my room. It's more comfortable than yours. I want your advice."

He rose, in some surprise, and followed me.

If John Brown's name was commonplace his person was certainly not so. He looked like a young lord. He was a noble fellow, by nature if not by birth. A clear, sunny face, masculine chin and nose, sweet, firm mouth, the eye of an eagle, and the soft, curly, golden hair of a child. Tall, broad-shouldered, elegant, bold as a lion, gentle and kind as a lamb—such was my best, my dearest friend, Jack.

"Jack," said I, "I'm going to run away!"

My friend fell into a chair, put both legs straight out, and looked at me in speechless amazement for a second; then he burst into an uncontrollable fit of laughter.

"Jack," I repeated, "I'm going to run away."

"You'll do nothing of the sort," said he.

"And," I continued, regardless of his remark, "I mean that you shall run away with me."

"I'll do nothing of the sort," he replied. "But come, Bob, my boy, you're joking. Surely this is not the object for which you called me out of my room."

"Indeed it is. Listen to me, Jack." (I looked at him impressively. He returned the look, for Jack was earnest as well as gay.) "You know that my dear father positively refused to let me go abroad, although I have entreated him to do so again and again. Now I think that's hard, you know. I love my dear father very much, but—"

"You love yourself better. Is that it?"

"Well, put it so if you choose. I don't care. I'm going to run away, and if you won't go with me you can stay at home—that's all."

"Come, come, Bob, don't be cross," said Jack, kindly; "you know you don't mean it."

"But I do; and I'm sure I don't see what it is that prevents you from going too," said I, testily.

"H'm! well, there is a small matter, a sort of moral idea, so to speak, that prevents."

"And what is that?"

"Respect for my mother! Bob, my boy, I've been too deeply imbued with that in my babyhood to shake it off now, even if I wished to do so; but I don't, Bob, I don't. I'm proud of my mother, and, moreover, I remember her teachings. There's one little verse I used to repeat to her every Sunday night, along with the rest of the ten commandments, 'Honour thy father and thy mother,' etcetera. It seems to me that running away is rather flying in the face of that. Doesn't it strike you in that light, Bob?"

I was silent. I felt that I had no argument against such reasoning. Jack rose.

"It's late, Bob; we are to start on our fishing expedition to-morrow morning at six, so it behoves us to get into bed. Good-night! and think over it!"

I seized his hand and pressed it warmly.

"Good-night, Jack, I will!"

Story 2—Chapter 2

My bedroom was a small one, with little furniture in it. A small iron stove in the fire-place acted instead of a grate, and as I was accustomed to read late my father allowed me to light it in cold weather. It was blazing cheerfully when Jack left me, and the bright gleams of ruddy light that darted through the chinks of the door and fell on the opposite wall, threw the light of my solitary candle quite into the shade.

I have already remarked that the night was dark and dismal. In addition to that, it was stormy. The wind moaned drearily among the venerable elms that surrounded our quiet country residence, and ever and anon came in sharp, fitful gusts that caused the window-frames to rattle, and even shook the house, at times, to its foundation. Heavy drops of rain fell occasionally on the window-panes, and in a few minutes the storm broke forth in full violence.

As the old house had stood many such in years gone by, I did not give myself much concern about the gale; but pulled down the blind, placed my little table and books near the stove, and, drawing in my chair, sat down to think. How long I remained in this condition I cannot tell; but my reveries were broken by the large clock on the stairs striking twelve.

I started up, and clinching my hands exclaimed aloud, "No! I've made up my mind, I *won't* run away!" Under the impulse of the feeling I threw open the door of the stove and heaped on fresh coals, muttering to myself; as I did so, "No, I won't run away, I won't run away; no, no, no, I won't run a—"

I was checked suddenly by my eye falling a second time on that terrific African savage sending from his revolver a charge down the throat of that magnificent Bengal tiger, that would have blown the inside entirely out of any living creature smaller than an elephant. I sat down. I gazed at the picture. I read the account. I followed up the adventurous savage. My head reeled with excitement. A strange terrible heat seemed to dart like lightning through my veins, and the book began to flicker before my eyes. I became alarmed.

"Surely some terrible fever is seizing on me!" I exclaimed, and in the terror of the thought I started up and paced my room rapidly. But the fire increased, and my head swam. I meditated ringing the bell and alarming the household; but the thought of this quieted me, and gradually I became calmer.

It was at this moment that my former resolution returned upon me with tenfold violence. "I'll submit to this no longer," I growled between my teeth; "I *will* run away!"

The instant I said that, I felt as if I were imbued with a determination that nothing could shake. Jack's reasoning never once came into my mind. I took down the knapsack that hung on a nail ready packed for the intended fishing expedition of the morrow. I buckled it on; put on my thickest shoes, and, seizing a stout cudgel, issued softly from my apartment, and tapped gently at Jack's door.

"Come in!"

I entered, and was overwhelmed with surprise at finding my friend standing in the middle of the room accoutred for the road just like myself. He put his finger to his lips.

"Hush! Bob. I was on the point of going to your room to say that I've made up my mind to run away with you."

I was staggered. I did not relish this unaccountable change. If I had persuaded him to go, it would have been all right; but to find him thus ready and eager was unnatural. I felt as if I were accountable for this change in his opinions and actions, and immediately, strange to say, experienced a tendency to dissuade him.

"But, Jack, you forget what you said to me some hours ago."

"No, I don't," he answered, gloomily.

"Perhaps we'd better think over it again."

"No, we won't. Come, Bob, don't show the white feather now. Don't waste time. It's about dawn. It's too late to reason. You have tempted me, and I have given in."

Saying this, he seized me by the collar and pushed me before him.

And now the mysterious events which I am about to relate began. The conduct of my friend Jack on this occasion was in itself a mystery. He was by nature the gentlest and most inoffensive of human beings, except when circumstances required him to act vigorously: then he was a lion—irresistible. Since the commencement of our acquaintance, which was of many years' standing, he had never by word or look given me the slightest cause for anger; and yet here he was grasping me violently by the collar and pushing me forcibly before him.

I did not get angry. My conscience smote me. I said to myself; "Ah! this is the result of evil conduct. I have tempted Jack to act against his judgment; he is no longer what he was."

Instead of melting under this feeling, I became hardened. I stepped out, and so dragged my friend after me down the back stairs which led to the lower part of the house, where the servants slept. Jack whispered, "All right," and let go his hold.

"Now we must be cautious," I said, in a low tone, as we proceeded to traverse the passage, on each side of which were the rooms occupied by the servants. We took off our shoes and advanced on tip-toe. At the far end of the passage we heard a sound like a trombone. That was the butler; we knew of his snoring propensities, and so were not alarmed. His door was open; so was his mouth—I could see that plainly, as I passed, by the dim light of a candle which he always burned at night. The butler was excessively fat. I merely mention this because it accounts for the fact of his not awaking when we unlocked the street door. Fat people are not easily wakened.

The lock of the door was an old-fashioned large one. It grated slightly as Jack turned the key; then at a certain point the key lost control over it, and it shot back with a report like a pistol-shot! My heart flew to my mouth, and almost choked me. The butler gave a double snort and turned in his bed as Jack and I darted round an angle of the wall and hid in a dark corner. The butler soon gave unquestionable evidence that he had not been thoroughly aroused, and we were about to issue from our place of concealment, when the door of our man-servant's room opened, and he peeped out.

Edwards—that was his name—was a stout young fellow, and we felt certain that he would not rest satisfied until he had found out the cause of the noise.

We were right. He stepped cautiously into the passage with a poker in his hand. My heart sank within me. Just at that moment a cat darted across the passage with its back and tail up, and its eyes glaring. Edwards flung the poker at it, missed the cat, and knocked over an old tin umbrella-stand, with which the poker made a hideous clatter on the stone floor of the passage.

"Ha! you brute! Wot? it's you as is makin' all that row, is it?"

"Oh, dear, Edwards, what's happened?" cried a shrill voice from the other end of the passage—it was cook.

"Oh, nothin', only the cat," replied the man as he sauntered into the butler's room. The butler seemed at that moment to have been smitten with a fit of apoplexy—we could see him from our dark corner;—he grew purple in the face, gasped once or twice, choked awfully, and then sat up in bed staring like a maniac.

"Oh! Jack," I whispered in horror.

"Don't be alarmed; it's only his usual way of waking up. I've seen him do it often."

"What noise is that? What's going on down there?" cried a deep bass voice in the distance. It was my father. No one replied. Presently my father's bedroom bell rang with extreme violence. Edwards rushed out of the butler's room. The butler fell back, opened his mouth, and pretended to be asleep—snoring moderately. This of itself would have undeceived any one, for when the old hypocrite was really asleep he never snored *moderately*. The cook and housemaid uttered two little shrieks and slammed their respective doors, while the bell rang violently a second time.

"Now for it," whispered Jack. He opened the back door softly, and we darted out. A streak of pale light on the horizon indicated the approach of day. We tried to close the door behind us, but we heard the butler choke, gasp, and shout at the top of his voice, "Hi! hallo!" At the same instant the old dinner-gong sent a peal of horrible sound through the house, and we took to flight filled with unutterable terror.

Oh, how we did run! We had scarcely cleared the offices and got fairly into the avenue when we heard Edwards shout as he started in pursuit.

We were both good runners, but Jack soon took the lead, and kept it by about five yards. Our feet scarcely touched the ground. I felt as if I had wings, so great was my terror. We reached the end of the avenue. The gate was full five feet high. To my inexpressible amazement, Jack went clear over it with one bound!

I have never been able to analyse my feelings and impulses on that occasion. I am, and always was, rather a poor jumper; yet, without hesitation, without even a doubt as to my ability to clear it, I went at that gate like an Irish hunter at a stone wall, and leaped fairly over it! The leap did not even check my pace for an instant. I remember, in the whirl and confusion of the moment, that I attributed my almost superhuman powers to terror; but the feeling that we were pursued again absorbed all my faculties.

We dashed on at a killing pace, and, strange to say, without feeling the slightest fatigue. Having cleared the avenue, we mounted the high ground in the neighbourhood, passed the church, entered the village, and went through it like a railway train; came out upon the road beyond, and reached a wooded part of the country where several roads and by-paths diverged from the highway. All this time Edwards kept close on our heels. He did not gain on us, but we felt that we did not distance him. "Down here!" cried Jack, doubling suddenly into a lane.

We passed a small bridge that crossed a mill-lake. Beyond, there was a farm-yard. The path-way was high, and we could look down on the tops of the stacks. One of these, a haystack, stood about ten feet from the low wall that skirted the road. It had been half pulled down, and the hay was loose. Without a word or warning Jack sprang completely across this space, turned right over, and plunged head first into the hay. I followed instantly, and disappeared. We lay for a few seconds perfectly still, and heard Edwards pass at full speed. Then we struggled out and watched him out of sight.

Sliding down, we regained the lane, returned to the high-road, and continued our flight.

We saw no more of Edwards.

About eight miles from my father's house there was a small seaport town. We made for this, and reached it just as the sun rose in all his golden glory on the distant edge of the sleeping sea.

Story 2—Chapter 3

On entering the village we found it in a state of unusual bustle. I had often been there before, and had thought it rather a quiet place for a seaport. But now there was a sort of bustling activity and an air of mystery about it that I could not understand. I mentioned my feelings to Jack, but he did not answer me, which was a piece of rudeness so unusual that I could only suppose that his mind was so deeply affected with the circumstances in which we had placed ourselves, as to render him somewhat absent.

On arriving at the chief, indeed the only, inn of the place, we discovered the reason of all the bustle. A strange ship had arrived the night before—a large ship, fitted out for an expedition to some distant part of the world. She had come to complete her supply of provisions and to engage a few extra hands.

Here then was a fortunate opportunity! We asked at once where we could find the captain. He was in the bar-room of the inn. We entered it and found him there, standing with his back to the fire and a coat-tail under each arm. He was a big fat man, with a savage expression of countenance, and ragged head and beard, and a red nose.

"He was a big fat man, with a savage expression of countenance, and ragged head and beard, and a red nose."

"Sir," said Jack, "we wish to ship with you."

The captain stared, took a pencil-case out of his pocket, picked his teeth therewith, and surveyed us from head to foot.

"Oh, you do, do you? You wish to ship with me?"

"Yes."

"Suppose I don't want you."

"Then we shall have to try elsewhere."

The captain smiled grimly, shut up the pencil-case, and said—

"What can ye do?"

"We can read, and write, and count," said I, taking the words out of Jack's mouth; for I felt that his brusque manner of replying was not calculated to commend us to the captain.

"Oh, you can read, and write, and count, can ye?" repeated the captain, with deep sarcasm. "If ye had said ye could feed, and fight, and shout, it would have bin more to the purpose."

"Perhaps we can do a little of that sort of thing, too," suggested Jack, with a broad grin.

"Hah?" ejaculated the captain. "Wot else can ye do?"

"Oh, anything," said Jack.

"I gin'rally find," observed the captain, "that w'en a boy says he can do anything, he very soon proves that he can do nothing."

"Well, I don't mean that exactly," rejoined Jack; "I mean we can *try* anything."

"Ha! that's more to the pint. Where did ye come from?"

We looked at each other. "That," said I, "is a matter of no importance to any one but ourselves. We have run away from home, and we want to go to sea as fast as possible. If you are willing to take us, we are willing to go. What say you?"

"Run away! ho! ho!—run away!" said the captain, chuckling; "you are just the lads I want. Nothing like runaway boys for me. I wouldn't give a pinch of snuff for your good boys that do wot they're bid. Commend me to the high-spirited fellers that runs away, and that folk are so wicked as to call bad boys. That's the sort o' stuff that suits *our* service."

I did not by any means relish the manner and tone in which all this was said: so I asked him what particular service he belonged to.

"You'll know that time enough," he replied, laughing; "but after all, why shouldn't I tell ye? there's nothing to conceal. We're a discovery-ship; we're goin' to look for Sir John Franklin's expedition, and after we've found it we're going to try the North Pole, and then go right through the Nor'-west passage, down by Behring's Straits, across the Pacific, touchin' at the Cannibal Islands in passin', and so on to China. Havin' revictualled there, we'll bear away for Japan, Haustralia, Cape o' Good Hope, and the West Indies, and come tearin' across the Atlantic with the Gulf-stream to England! Will that suit ye?"

It may seem strange, and the reader will hardly believe me when I say, that, transparently absurd though this statement was, nevertheless I believed every word of it—and so did Jack. I saw that by his glowing eye and heightened colour.

"And when do you sail?" I inquired joyfully.

"In half an hour; so get aboard, boys, and don't give so much tongue. I've other matters to mind just now. Come, be off!"

We retreated precipitately to the door.

"What's her name?" inquired Jack, looking back.

"'The Ring-tailed Smasher,'" cried the captain, fiercely.

"The what?"

"'The Ring-tailed Smasher,'" roared the captain, seizing the poker.

We vanished. In five minutes we were on board the ship. To this hour I have no remembrance of how we got on board. My brain swam with intense excitement. I felt as if I were flying, not walking, as I ran about the deck and clambered up the rigging.

Shortly after the captain came aboard. The rope that attached the vessel to the quay was cast off, the sails flew out as if by magic, and the shore began to fall rapidly astern.

It was now, for the first time, that a full sense of what I had done came over me. I leaned over the stern of the ship, and gazed at my native shore as it grew fainter in the distance, until the familiar hills became a mere line of blue on the horizon, and were finally blotted from my view by the blinding tears that sprang suddenly to my eyes. Oh! the agony of that moment I shall never forget. The words that Jack had quoted to me the night before— "Honour thy father and thy mother"—seemed to be stamped in letters of fire within my brain. I felt keenly that, in a moment of passionate self-will, I had done that which would cause me the deepest sorrow all my life.

In that dark hour I forgot all my romantic notions of travel in foreign lands; I cared not a straw for hunting, or fighting, or wild adventures. I would have cheerfully given worlds, had I possessed them, to be permitted to undo the past—to hasten to my dear father's feet, and implore forgiveness of the evil that I had done. But regret was now unavailing. The land soon sank below the horizon, and, ere many hours had passed, our ship was scudding before a stiff breeze and leaping wildly over the waves of the Atlantic Ocean.

Story 2—Chapter 4

"Ho! tumble up there, tumble up! All hands, ahoy! tumble up! Look alive, lads; there's work to do, my hearties!"

Such were the words, uttered in the most terrifically violent bass tones, that awoke me on the first morning after I went to sea. Instantly all the men around me leaped out of their hammocks. They were all half-dressed, and I noticed that the greater part of them completed their toilet in the short interval between quitting their hammocks and gaining the deck. Jack and I had lain down in our clothes, so we were on deck almost as soon as the others.

Here the most unexpected sights assailed us. It seemed to me as if a miraculous change had taken place on everybody and everything during the night. The ship when she had set sail was as untidy and lumbered about the decks as a merchantman usually is on quitting port. Now everything was clean, in its place, snugly fastened, and in order. The sails appeared to have undergone some modification. I fancied, too, that the masts raked aft a good deal more than they had done, and round the foot of them were ranged muskets, pistols, cutlasses, and boarding-pikes, where masses of cordage and handspikes had been before. The hencoops had vanished, and in their place were rows of brass carronades, while in the centre of the deck an enormous swivel gun occupied the place on which the long-boat had formerly rested. Even the captain seemed to have changed. His costume was somewhat Eastern in its character, and his whole aspect was much more ferocious than when I first saw him.

Vague and terrible suspicions crossed my mind as I viewed these wonderful transformations; but I had no time to indulge them, for the men had hastened with the promptitude of men-of-war's men to their stations, leaving Jack and me alone in the middle of the deck.

"Hallo, boys!" shouted the captain, "no idlers allowed aboard this ship. Here, stand by this gun, and lend a hand with the ropes when you're told to. Obey orders,—that's the only duty I've got to lay on you."

We hastened to the gun pointed out, and while I was standing there waiting for orders, I looked over the side, and, for the first time, became aware of the cause of these proceedings.

About two miles to leeward of us, just off our larboard bow, I saw a large ship running under a press of canvas. She was a huge clumsy-looking merchantman, and I heard our first mate say she was an East-Indiaman.

"Then why chase her?" thought I, "and why these warlike preparations?"

It struck me at the time, I remember, that the captain must have guessed my thoughts, for he glanced at me quickly, and then turning to the mate, with a sarcastic smile, said—

"I thought you had better sight than you seem to have. In my judgment that's a Russian merchantman, and as we happen to be at war with Russia just now I'll take the liberty of overhauling her."

Instead of replying to this the mate burst into a loud laugh in which, strangely enough, he was joined by the captain and all the men who were within hearing. I felt uneasy at this, and expressed my feelings in a whisper to Jack, who shook his head and looked at me mysteriously, but said nothing.

I felt that, even though we were at war with Russia, we, as a discovery-ship, had no right whatever to interfere in the capacity of a war-ship, and I was about to remonstrate with the captain at all hazards, when my thoughts were suddenly changed by the order being given to fire a shot across the stranger's bows. The gun at which I was stationed was run out.

"Stand by!" cried the captain.

"Fire!"

In the excitement of the moment, and without knowing what I had to do, though deeply impressed with the feeling that something ought to be done when an order was given, I pulled violently at the rope which I had in my hand; the effect of which was to move the gun very slightly when it exploded. The result was that the ball, instead of passing well ahead of the strange vessel, passed close to its bow and carried away half of the bowsprit.

The captain turned on me a face absolutely blazing with wrath. He seized a handspike, and I thought he was about to dash out my brains on the spot. He hissed at me between his clinched teeth; then, suddenly bursting into a shout of fiendish laughter, he cried—

"Well, well, after all there's no harm done. It'll make them understand that we don't mean to trifle with 'em. Clear the boarding-pikes there. Are the grappling-irons ready?"

"Ay, ay, sir."

By this time the stranger had hove-to, and we were bearing down on her so rapidly that a few minutes more would bring us alongside. Our men stood ready for action. They were the worst-looking set of scoundrels I ever beheld.

"Ship ahoy!" shouted our captain as we drew near, "what ship's that?"

A smart young officer leaped on the bulwarks, and cried, "Come alongside and I'll tell you. Show your colours."

At the word our colours went up, as colours are usually hoisted, rolled up like a ball. I watched with intense interest, for I felt that now at last I should know our true character. The ball of what seemed to be dark-blue bunting reached the masthead and hung for one instant—then its folds fell heavily, and were swept out by the breeze. The flag was black, and in the centre were a white skull and crossbones!

I almost fainted at the sight. I looked at Jack, who stood beside me. He was as white as a sheet; but his lips were firmly compressed, and his brows knitted.

"Do we deserve what we have got?" he muttered in a deep, sad voice.

I did not reply; but my conscience answered, "We do—at least I do."

We were now hove-to about a pistol-shot to leeward of the ship, and our captain, leaping on the bulwark, cried, with a dreadful oath, "Send your gig alongside instantly with your captain and papers. If you don't look sharp I'll blow you out of the water."

He had scarcely finished speaking, when a loud shout rent the air, and the bulwarks of the strange vessel swarmed with soldiers. At the same moment, twenty concealed ports flew open and twenty heavy guns were run out.

Our captain gave the word, "Fire!" as he leaped on the deck and rushed to the wheel. The word must have been given at the same moment on board the chase, for both broadsides burst simultaneously from the vessels' sides with a deafening crash that sounded ten times louder and more terrible than the loudest thunder I ever heard. We were so near that the combined volumes of smoke completely blinded and almost suffocated me. I fancied, for a moment, that our powder-magazine had blown up.

The thunder of the broadsides was followed by the most appalling shrieks I ever heard, and by the ceaseless rattle of musketry as the soldiers opened on us with deadly precision. Through the smoke I saw men falling around me, and the decks were immediately covered with blood, while bullets and splinters of wood whistled round my head like hail.

I was stunned. I felt like one in a horrid dream. Gradually the smoke cleared away, and then I saw that our captain had put down the helm and our vessel was sheering off to leeward under full sail. The rapidity with which everything was done quite took away my breath. Before we were out of gun-shot the decks had been cleared, the dead thrown into the sea, the wounded carried below, and the decks washed with buckets of water.

Just then I thought of Jack, and looked round in haste. He was not there! I rushed below! he was not in his hammock. In an agony of anxiety I went down into the horrible den of blood where our surgeon was attending to the wounded. Here, amid groaning and dying men, I found my friend stretched in a cot with a blanket over him, his handsome face was very pale, and his eyes were closed when I approached. Going down on my knees beside him, while my heart fluttered with an inexpressible feeling of dread, I whispered his name.

He opened his large eyes slowly, and a sweet sad smile lit up his face for one moment, as he took me by the hand.

"O Jack! Jack, my friend—my brother—are you wounded?" I asked.

"Yes," he replied, in a faint voice; "I'm badly hurt, I fear."

"Has the doctor dressed your wound?"

"He finished the—the—operation just before you came down."

"Operation!" I whispered, while a feeling of deadly sickness came over me. "Where—what—" I could not go further.

Poor Jack knew what I wished to ask. He gently lifted part of the blanket, and I felt as if I had been stunned by an electric shock on observing that his right leg had been amputated above the knee. For some moments I could not speak. I could not move. It was with difficulty that I could draw my labouring breath. Suddenly I clasped my hands—

"O Jack! my beloved! my—" I gasped. My throat was parched. For one moment I thought I was dying. Suddenly I started up, uttered a great agonising cry, and fell down on the deck. Then a flood of tears sprang into my burning eyes, and I sobbed as if my heart would burst asunder. I did not try to check this. It was too precious a relief to my insupportable agony. I crept close to my friend's cot, took his hand gently, and, laying my cheek upon it, wept there as I never wept before. Jack's former advice now came back to me vividly, and his words of caution, "Honour thy father and thy mother," burned deep into my throbbing brain, while my accusing conscience whispered unceasingly, "You brought him to this—you brought him to this!" My sorrow was broken in upon rudely by the first mate.

"What are you doin' here, you young blackguard?" he cried, seizing me by the collar, and dragging me to the foot of the ladder that led out of this bloody den. "Skulking, eh! *I'll* teach you to skulk; *I'll* cure you o' that, my lad! *I'll* tan your skin for you," and at each emphatic word he gave a blow with a rope's end that raised a bar of livid flesh across my back. "There," he cried, giving me a final cut, and hurling me up the first few steps of the ladder, "on deck with you!"

I did not hesitate to comply. I gained the deck with unusual rapidity, smarting with pain and burning with indignation. But what I saw going on there made me almost forget my pain. The great swivel gun amidships was being cleared for action, and our captain was giving orders beside it as coolly and quietly as if nothing unusual had occurred that day.

I was deeply impressed for a few minutes with this cool, calm indifference, which characterised the men as well as the captain; but when I had considered a little, I came to understand that they were used to battle and bloodshed, and that therefore it was quite natural. After that I ceased to wonder at anything. Indeed, the power to be astonished seemed to leave my breast altogether, and from that moment I regarded everything that happened on the pirate vessel as being quite what might be expected—mere matter of course.

I now observed that we had not yet done with the supposed Russian. We had merely run astern out of range of her guns, but not beyond the range of our large swivel. In a few minutes it was ready. The captain sighted the gun, and gave the word "Fire!"

The ship quivered with the shock, and so large was the ball that I could distinctly trace its flight. It fell short a few yards. "So, so," muttered the captain. "The next will do its work."

He was right. The next ball struck the rails that ran round the poop, carried away the binnacle, and raked the upper deck from stern to stem. I could see it quite plainly with the glass.

"Hurrah!" shouted some of the crew.

"Silence, you babies," growled the captain; "time enough to crow when our work's done."

The men who had cheered fell back abashed. I noticed that they were chiefly the younger men of the crew, whose countenances were not yet utterly unhumanised by crime.

"Load."

"Ready."

"Fire!"

Again the huge iron mass sprang from the cannon's mouth, and rushed along its deadly track. It struck the top of a wave, and bounding up passed through the sails and cordage of the Russian, cutting one or two of the lighter spars, and also the main topsail halyards, which caused the yard to come rattling down, and rendered the sail useless. Seeing this, the pirate captain ordered sail to be reduced in order to keep at a sufficient distance astern to render the guns of the chase useless. Every shot from our gun now told with terrible effect. We could see the splinters fly as every ball entered the ship's stern, or swept her deck, or crashed through her rigging. Presently she turned her broadside to us.

"She don't mean to waste her ammunition, surely," remarked the captain, with a sneer.

She did not mean to do so. She evidently meant to turn the tables by bearing suddenly down on us, and, if possible, give us a broadside before we could get out of range. The captain saw the intention instantly, and thwarted it.

"Up your helm! Square the yards! Look alive there!"

We fell off, and were soon running before the wind, with the swivel gun thundering over our stern, as it had formerly thundered over our bows. The Russian fired a broadside, and lay-to. Every ball fell short of us. We also lay-to, and now the fire was kept up steadily. The ship's fate was sealed. Those on board evidently thought so, for the colours which had hitherto been flying from the mast were presently lowered. Upon this we ceased firing, and ranged up alongside.

"Oh! you've had enough, have you?" cried our captain. "Perhaps you'll condescend to let your captain and papers come aboard *now*."

The Russian did not reply, but a boat was lowered. It was evident they meant to obey.

"Here, you boy," cried our captain, as he paced the deck, awaiting their arrival. "Here's a letter for you."

"A letter, sir!" I exclaimed, stepping forward, and touching my cap.

"Ay, your father gave it to me just afore we set sail. He told me not to give it to you until you'd seen a little rough work. You've seen some now, I think," (he accompanied this remark with a horrible leer), "so there's the letter. Go below and read it. I'll want you in half an hour for some still rougher work."

There seemed to me something very unaccountable and mysterious in this. I knew that the captain did not know my father. I had not even told him that I had a father. It seemed to me impossible that in the course of the short half-hour that intervened between the time of my engaging to serve in the *Ring-tailed Smasher*, and the time of my setting sail, my father could have found out where I had run to, have met and conversed with the captain, and have written a letter to me. Yet it seemed that such was the case. I recognised the handwriting.

"Whom did you get the letter from? Did you see my father?"

"Come, youngster, don't you go for to question me. Go below d'rectly, an' stop there till ye'r wanted."

The captain seized the end of a rope as he spoke, so I retreated at once to the bedside of my poor friend Jack, only too glad to escape from the presence of the men whom I now abhorred with all my heart.

"Jack," said I, eagerly, "here's a letter from my father!"

He evinced no surprise, but, looking up solemnly, said, in a faint voice, "Read it."

Breaking the seal, I read as follows:—

"My Beloved Son,—I forgive you. You have sinned deeply in thus leaving me; but I know that you have repented. I know that your own conscience has rebuked you more sternly than any earthly parent could do. You cannot now recall the past—you cannot undo what you have done; you must now continue your voyage, and, in order to relieve your oppressed heart, I give you my blessing. I commend you, my dear boy, to Him who is the Saviour of sinners.

"Beware of the captain. Obey him in all that is right, but do not serve him. Again, I say, beware of him. There are secrets concerning him that I cannot unfold. I have just been to see Jack's mother. She sends her forgiveness and blessing to her son. God bless you, boy.—Your loving father,

"John Smith."

My father understood human nature. No reproaches that he could have heaped upon me would have cut half so deeply into my heart as did this kind, forgiving letter. My heart was full. Yet I felt a deep undercurrent of joy at knowing that my father loved me still. I looked at Jack. He seemed to be asleep, but he was not. A single tear coursed over his pale cheek as he looked up and whispered—

"We don't deserve this, Bob."

Before I could reply, the ship was shaken by a tremendous explosion, and immediately after I heard the most appalling shrieks and yells on deck, accompanied by the clashing of swords and the scuffling of men in deadly conflict. I looked at Jack; he lay motionless, with his eyes closed. For a moment I feared that he was dead.

"Bob Smith! Hallo! tumble up there, you skulker!" shouted a voice down the hatchway. At the same moment two wounded men were carried into the place, and the surgeon appeared with his horrible instruments glittering, cold and sharp, on a wooden tray.

Seizing my cutlass, and thrusting a brace of pistols in my belt, I rushed on deck.

Story 2—Chapter 5

On reaching the deck I saw at once how matters stood. The Russian had allowed us to come alongside, and then, throwing out grappling-irons, had fired a broadside into us, and attempted to board. They were soon overcome, however, by the pirates, and driven back into their ship, whither they were immediately followed.

I resolved, come what might, that I would take no part in the fray; but I was carried, in spite of myself, on board the strange vessel in the rush that our men made when they drove their opponents back. There was a short, sharp skirmish on the deck of the Russian, and then the crew were driven below, and the hatches put on. I remembered having seen a number of soldiers on board when we first came up with this vessel. There were none now. Their mysterious disappearance struck me at first, but I soon forgot it in the thrilling scenes that followed.

In the middle of the vessel's main-deck there was a cage of wild beasts. How they had got there of course I knew not, but I at once concluded the ship must have been in southern climes, and these animals were being brought home to be presented to some menagerie or zoological garden. There were several fine specimens of lions and tigers, and the sight of blood which flowed plentifully on the decks had so excited these creatures that they were now filling the air with deafening roars, bounding against the sides of their cage, (which I expected every moment to see broken to pieces by their united strength), and glaring at us with the most awful expressions of ferocity I ever beheld.

Our captain, who looked almost as fierce as the wild brutes, could not make his voice heard for their roaring. In savage fury he rushed at the cage and made a desperate cut with his sword at the lion nearest the bars. The blood flowed from the wound freely, and the savage animal, being unable to wreak its vengeance on its cowardly assailant, attacked one of its comrades. This, and the

- 168 -

blood now flowing in the cage, quite maddened them all. An indiscriminate fight ensued. The wooden partition that separated the tigers from the lions was smashed in, and the strong cage shook as if it were made of card-board.

"Turn a gun in-board," yelled the captain, who seemed to have actually gone mad with passion.

The order was instantly obeyed.

"Load to the muzzle—grape—canister—chain shot. In with it."

He assisted in the operation; rammed home the extraordinary charge, pointed the gun at the cage, and applied the match. Instantly the gun leaped backwards as if it had been a living thing, broke down the bulwarks of the ship, and plunged overboard.

The effect of the shot was terrific. The cage was blown to atoms, and the mangled remains of the wild beasts were strewn about the deck. One animal, however, a magnificent Bengal tiger, had apparently escaped unhurt. It sprang at the captain with a hideous roar. He pointed a pistol at its open throat!

At that moment the woodcut in my book of travels flashed vividly before me. But I had not time to think. The pistol exploded, sending its contents down the creature's throat. The tiger fell short in its leap; blood poured from its mouth and nose. With another bound it cleared the bulwarks, and fell into the sea.

The calm that succeeded this thrilling incident was like a sudden lull in the midst of a furious storm. Even the pirates seemed to be solemnised by what had passed.

"Now to work," cried the captain, wiping his sword, and laying it, with a brace of loaded pistols, on the capstan. "What are you staring at, you fools?—have you lost your senses? Open the after-hatch, and bring them up, one at a time. Get the plank ready."

The first who was led bound before the captain was the steward of the ship. He was deadly pale, and trembled very much.

"Now, my man," said the captain, "answer my questions. The *truth* mind, else—" he touched the butt of a pistol significantly.

"Where did you last sail from?"

To my amazement, the man gave the name of the port from which we ourselves had sailed. I felt certain that this was a falsehood, and that the poor man's life would be forfeited. Judge, then, my surprise when the captain said—

"I know that as well as you. I saw you sneak out just the day before we did. But you didn't escape me, ha! ha! You are too good to live, my man. Stand aside here till I call someone who's not quite so frightened. Here, hold him, one of you! Bring another!"

I started. My heart almost ceased to beat when the next man was led forward. He was my father's man-servant, Edwards. In the confusion and horror of that hour I could not reason; but a vague sense of some mysterious impossibility having actually taken place oppressed me in a way that I cannot explain. The ship had sailed the day before ours did! I left Edwards behind me in the race from home! How, then, did I see him before me? Then the cage of wild beasts. How was it possible that a vessel leaving an English port could have such creatures on board? Then, my father's letter; it seemed more than ever mysterious how that letter could reach me, and through such a channel, and without a word of reference to Edwards.

He did not observe me as he passed. I tried to utter his name; but my tongue was tied. I could not speak. I could not move.

"Where did you last sail from?" began the captain.

"You'll get nothing out of me," replied Edwards, stoutly. "Do your most. Torture me if you like. I defy you to your teeth."

"Do you, my fine fellow?" said the captain, with a bitter sneer. "Then I'll just send you overboard at once. I've no time to torture you; and as I shall find plenty of your comrades willing enough to tell me all they know, I'll not trouble you any further. Ho! run out the plank there!"

I knew what that meant, and a cold shiver passed through my frame as the men obeyed, and blind-folded Edwards, preparatory to making him walk the plank. I could restrain myself no longer. Darting up to the captain, I shouted in a voice of indignation—

"Do you mean to murder an innocent man, you dastardly villain?"

He looked at me for a moment in surprise; then, snatching a pistol, felled me with it to the deck. I was not rendered quite insensible. I heard the shriek of agony uttered by poor Edwards, as he fell off the end of the plank into the sea; then I fainted.

How long I lay, I know not; probably not long, for I was restored to a state of consciousness by being plunged into the sea. I had no doubt that the captain had ordered me to be thrown overboard, just after I fell under his brutal blow.

Being a good swimmer, I struck out at once and made for the side of the pirate vessel, where I caught the end of a rope, and soon clambered on board. I was much exhausted, and sat down on the breech of a carronade to rest and recover my stunned and scattered faculties.

The crew of the pirate were so busily engaged with the captured ship that I found myself quite alone on the deck. Not a man remained in the ship. An idea suddenly occurred to me just then. I glanced up at the sails. They were all flapping in the wind except the fore-topsail. That sail had slewed round, and was drawing so that the vessel strained the ropes and grappling-irons that held her to the captured ship.

I sprang up burning with eager excitement. I heard the shrieks of the ill-fated victims, as one by one they walked the plank, which, fortunately for the success of my design, was thrust out on the other side of the ship. A crowbar enabled me to wrench off the grappling-irons. Two cuts of a large axe severed the cable that had been fastened to the bow, and the vessel's head fell slowly off. As it did so, all the sails filled with a sudden clap. This was observed: I heard a shout, and saw the pirates spring on the bulwarks of the prize. I flew rather than ran to the stern, where the cable that held the vessel was rigid as a bar of iron. One blow cut it, and the rope recoiled violently in the faces of the men who laid hold of it. Next moment the pirate ship was heading away before a stiff breeze which was quickly freshening to a gale. As I sprang to the helm, a shower of musket and pistol bullets tore up the deck round me, and I heard the captain's voice give the order to load the guns.

It was a few minutes before the *vis inertiae* of the ship was overcome, so that I was within close range when a whole broadside was fired at me. But not a shot struck. They tore up the water all round, and ricochetted over me. Before they could reload I was almost beyond range, for the gale was freshening every moment, and the canvas spread was enough almost to tear the masts out of the ship. The water hissed as she flew over the heaving waves, and in a few minutes I felt that I was *free*.

Oh the feeling of wild delight that filled me when I realised this! I lashed the helm amidships, and ran down below to tell Jack what I had done. He was asleep. By a powerful effort I restrained myself, and did not disturb him. Then I rushed on deck. My brain seemed on fire. I shouted, laughed, and sang, and wept, until I began to feel a terrible sensation of dread lest I should go mad. But this, instead of calming me, caused me to dance and sing and shout the more. A burning thirst came upon me. I ran to the water-cask and drank till I could drink no more. I was refreshed; but soon the fever returned fiercer than ever. I was mad! I knew it; I felt it; but I did not care. I saw that the storm increased; this caused me to shout again with joy at the thought that I was so quickly borne away from the scene of butchery, and from the fiends in human form with whom I had so lately associated.

The gale burst in all its fury upon us. The sails were new and strong; the ship plunged into the waves, a green billow swept inboard and burst in fury on the deck, carrying away boats and loose spars. I yelled with delight, and plunged into the brine that lashed the deck from stem to stern. I heard a noise overhead; but was so confused that I could not understand what it was. As I gazed, there came a terrific blast. The mainsail split from top to bottom. The topsails burst and were blown to ribbons. At the same moment, I received a violent blow on the head.

After that, all was darkness and oblivion.

Story 2—Chapter 6

When consciousness returned to me I found myself lying on my back on the deck of a vessel, surrounded and propped up by pillows; and Jack Brown sitting beside me reading a book.

I felt a curious sensation of weakness and emptiness in my head—as if it were hollow, and a strange disinclination, almost inability, to speak or think. Suddenly this passed away, and the events which I have related in the previous chapters rushed back upon my memory with vivid power.

"It must have been a dream," I thought, "or I must have been ill and delirious, and these things have passed through my fevered brain."

At that moment the thought of Jack's amputated leg came into my head. "That will prove it," thought I, and turned quickly to look at my friend. One glance was sufficient—a wooden stump occupied the place of his right leg. I groaned aloud and burst into tears.

"Come, Bob," said Jack in a soft, kind tone, laying down his book and bending over me. "Come, my poor fellow, keep quiet. It's about time you had your dinner. Lie still and I'll fetch it to you."

I laid my hand on his arm and detained him. "Then it's all true," said I in a tone of the deepest despondency.

"Is what all true?"

"This—this horrible—your leg; your leg—"

Jack suddenly stooped and gazed earnestly into my face. "Do you know me, Bob?" He trembled as he spoke.

"Know you, Jack! why should I not know you? When did I ever forget you?"

"Thank God!" he exclaimed fervently, taking my hand and pressing it to his breast. "You're all right again. Oh, how I have longed and prayed for this."

"All right, Jack. Have I been wrong, then?"

"That you have just," said Jack, smiling sadly. "You've just been as mad as a March hare, that's all!"

I fell flat down and gazed at him. In a minute more I raised myself on one elbow, and, looking at him earnestly, said, "How long, Jack?"

"Just three weeks to-day."

I fell flat down again, in which position Jack left me to go and fetch me some dinner. He returned quickly with a plate of soup. Before commencing to eat it I pressed my hand on my forehead, and said—

"Jack, I am surrounded by mysteries. How got you so soon well? Where got you that wooden leg? How are we here alone? Where are we going? Clear up my faculties, Jack, while I eat this soup—do, like a good fellow."

"I can easily do that, Bob. First, I got well because you took care of me."

"What! I?"

"Yes, you! At the commencement of your madness you tended me and cared for me as if you had been my mother. When you got to lose all 'method in your madness' I was well enough to take care of myself and you too. Secondly, I found this wooden leg in the carpenter's berth, and gladly availed myself of its services, though it *is* three inches too short, and causes me to hobble in a most undignified manner. Thirdly, we are here alone because there is no one else with us. You took good care of that by cutting the ropes before any of our crew could get aboard—so you told me just before you went mad."

"Oh! I remember now! I recollect it all. Go on."

"Fourthly, as to where we are going, I don't know. Our compass was smashed to pieces in the fight, and I've been running for the last three weeks right before the wind. So now you know all, and as you've finished your soup I'll go and get you a lump of boiled junk."

"Don't," said I, rising and shaking myself. "I've dined. I feel quite strong. I don't feel a bit as if I had been ill. Hallo! what land is that?"

Jack started and gazed at it with surprise. He had evidently not known that we were in the neighbourhood of land. A dense fog-bank had concealed it from us. Now that it cleared away it revealed to our gaze a stretch of yellow sand, backed by the lofty blue hills of the interior, and from the palm-trees that I could make out distinctly I judged that we must have been making for the tropical regions during the last three weeks.

Yet here again mystery surrounded me. How was it possible that we should have reached the tropics in so short a time? While I was puzzling over this question, the greatest mystery of all occurred to us. If I were not conscientiously relating events exactly as they occurred, I should expect my readers to doubt my veracity here.

As we were sailing smoothly along, our ship, without any apparent cause, began to sink. She went down gradually, but quickly—inch by inch—until the water was on a level with the decks. We struck no rock! we did not cease to advance towards the shore! I fancied that we must certainly have sprung a leak; but there had been no sound of a plank starting, and there was no noise of water rushing into the hold. I could not imagine what had occurred, but I had not much time for thought. We could do nothing to avert the catastrophe. It occurred so suddenly that we were both rendered mute and helpless. We stood gazing at the water as it crept over the deck without making the slightest effort to save ourselves.

At length the water reached the hatchway and poured in a roaring cataract into the hold. The vessel filled, gave a heavy lurch to port, a species of tremor passed through her frame as if she was a living thing and knew that her hour had come, then she went down in a whirlpool, leaving Jack and me struggling in the sea.

We were both good swimmers, so that we did not experience much alarm, especially when we felt that the sea was comparatively warm; we struck out for the shore, and, being the better swimmer of the two, I took the lead.

"At length the water reached the hatchway."

But now to our horror we found that we were followed by sharks!

No sooner did we observe this than we struck out with all the energy of terror. We never swam as we did on that occasion. It seemed to me quite miraculous. The water burst from our breasts in foam, and we left long white tracks behind us as we clove our way through the water like two boats. It was awful. I shall never forget my feelings on that occasion: they were indescribable— inconceivable!

We were about a quarter of a mile from a point of rocks when our ship sank. In an incredibly short space of time we were close on the rocks. Being several yards ahead of Jack, I was the first to clamber up, my heart fluttering with fear, yet filled with deep gratitude for my deliverance. I turned to help Jack. He was yet six yards from shore, when a dreadful shark made a rush at him.

"Oh! quick! quick!" I screamed.

He was panting and straining like a lion. Another moment and his hand would have been in mine, but at that moment I beheld the double rows of horrid teeth close upon him. He uttered a piercing shriek, and there was an indescribably horrible *scrunch* as he went down. In a moment after, he re-appeared, and making a last frightful effort to gain the rocks, caught my hand. I dragged him out of danger instantly, and then I found, to my unutterable joy, that the shark had only bitten off the half of his wooden leg!

Embracing each other fervently, we sat down in the rocks to rest and collect our thoughts.

Story 2—Chapter 7

I have often found, from experience, that the more one tries to collect one's thoughts, the more one's thoughts pertinaciously scatter themselves abroad, almost beyond the possibility of discovery. Such was the case with me, after escaping from the sea and the sharks, as related circumstantially in the last chapter. Perhaps the truth of this may best be illustrated by laying before my readers the dialogue that ensued between me and Jack on the momentous occasion referred to, as follows:—

Jack. "I say, Bob, where in all the world have we got to?"

Bob. "Upon my word, I don't know."

Jack. "It's very mysterious."

Bob. "What's very mysterious?"

Jack. "Where we've got to. Can't you guess?"

Bob. "Certainly. Suppose I say Lapland?"

Jack. (Shaking his head), "Won't do."

Bob. "Why?"

Jack. "'Cause there are no palm-trees in Lapland."

Bob. "Dear me, that's true. How confused my head is! I'll tell you what it is, Jack, I can't think. *That's it*—that's the cause of the mystery that seems to beset me, I can't tell how; and then I've been ill—that's it too."

Jack. "How can there be two causes for one effect, Bob? You're talking stuff, man. If I couldn't talk better sense than that, I'd not talk at all."

Bob. "Then why don't you hold your tongue? I tell you what it is, Jack, we're bewitched. You said I was mad some time ago. You were right—so I am; so are you. There are too many mysteries here for any two sane men." (Here Jack murmured we weren't men, but boys.) "There's the running away and not being caught—the ship ready to sail the moment we arrive; there's your joining me after all your good advice; there's that horrible fight, and the lions, and Edwards, and the sinking of our ship, and the—the—in short, I feel that I'm mad still. I'm not recovered yet. Here, Jack, take care of me!"

Instead of replying to this, Jack busied himself in fitting a piece of wood he had picked up to his wooden leg, and lashing it firmly to the old stump. When he had accomplished his task, he turned gravely to me and said—

"Bob, your faculties are wandering pretty wildly to-day, but you've not yet hit upon the cause of all our misfortunes. The true cause is that *you have disobeyed your father, and I my mother.*"

I hung my head. I had now no longer difficulty in collecting my thoughts—they circled round that point until I thought that remorse would have killed me. Then suddenly I turned with a look of gladness to my friend.

"But you forget *the letter!* We are forgiven!"

"True," cried Jack, with a cheerful expression; "we can face our fate with that assurance. Come, let us strike into the country and discover where we are. I'll manage to hop along pretty well with my wooden leg. We'll get home as soon as we can, by land if not by water, and then we'll remain at home—won't we, Bob?"

"Remain at home!" I cried; "ay, that will we. I've had more than enough of foreign experiences already. Oh! Jack, Jack, it's little I care for the sufferings I have endured—but your leg, Jack! Willingly, most willingly, my dear friend, would I part with my own, if by so doing I could replace yours."

Jack took my hand and squeezed it.

"It's gone now, Bob," he said sadly. "I must just make the most of the one that's left. 'Tis a pity that the one that's left is only the left one."

So saying he turned his back to the sea, and, still retaining my hand in his, led me into the forest.

But here unthought-of trouble awaited us at the very outset of our wanderings. The ground which we first encountered was soft and swampy, so that I sank above the ankles at every step. In these circumstances, as might have been expected, poor Jack's wooden leg was totally useless. The first step he took after entering the jungle, his leg penetrated the soft ground to the depth of nine or ten inches, and at the second step it disappeared altogether— insomuch that he could by no means pull it out.

"I say, Bob," said he, with a rueful expression of countenance, "I'm in a real fix now, and no mistake. Come to anchor prematurely. I resolved to stick at nothing, and here I have stuck at the first step. What *is* to be done?"

Jack's right leg being deep down in the ground, it followed, as a physical consequence, that his left leg was bent as if he were in a sitting posture. Observing this fact, just as he made the above remark, he placed both his hands on his left knee, rested his chin on his hands, and gazed meditatively at the ground. The action tickled me so much that I gave a short laugh. Jack looked up and laughed too, whereupon we both burst incontinently into an uproarious fit of laughter, which might have continued ever so long had not Jack, in the fulness of his mirth, given his fixed leg a twist that caused it to crack.

"Hallo! Bob," he cried, becoming suddenly very grave, "I say, this won't do, you know; if I break it short off you'll have to carry me, my boy: so it behoves me to be careful. What is to be done?"

"Come, I'll help you to pull it out."

"Oh! that's not what troubles me. But after we get it out what's to be done?"

"Jack," said I, seriously, "one thing at a time. When we get you out, then it will be time enough to inquire what to do next."

"That's sound philosophy, Bob; where did you pick it up? I suspect you must have been studying Shakespeare of late, on the sly. But come, get behind me, and put your hands under my arms, and heave; I'll shove with my sound limb. Now let us act together. Stay! Bob, we've been long enough aboard ship to know the value of a song in producing unity of action. Take the tune from me."

Suiting the action to the word, Jack gave forth, at the top of his voice, one or two of those peculiarly nautical howls wherewith seamen are wont to constrain windlasses and capstans to creak, and anchors to let go their hold.

"Now then, heave away, my hearties; yo-heave-o-hoi!"

At the last word we both strained with all our might. I heard Jack's braces burst with the effort. We both became purple in the face, but the leg remained immovable! With a loud simultaneous sigh we relaxed, and looking at each other groaned slightly.

"Come, come, Bob, never say die; one trial more; it was the braces that spoiled it that time. Now then, cheerily ho! my hearties, heave-yo-hee-o-**Hoy**!"

The united force applied this time was so great that we tore asunder all the fastenings of the leg at one wrench, and Jack and I suddenly shot straight up as if we had been discharged from a hole in the ground. Losing our balance we fell over each other on our backs—the wooden leg remaining hard and fast in the ground.

"Ah! Jack," said I sorrowfully, as I rubbed the mud off my garments, "if we had remained at home this would not have happened."

"If we had remained at home," returned Jack, rather gruffly, as he hopped towards his leg, "*nothing* would have happened. Come, Bob, lay hold of it. Out it shall come, if the inside of the world should come along with it. There now—*heave*!"

This time we gave vent to no shout, but we hove with such a will, that Jack split his jacket from the waist to the neck, and the leg came out with a crack that resembled the drawing of the largest possible cork out of the biggest conceivable bottle.

Having accomplished this feat we congratulated each other, and then sat down to repair damages. This was not an easy matter. It cost us no little thought to invent some contrivance that would prevent the leg from sinking, but at last we thought of a plan. We cut a square piece of bark off a tree, the outer rind of which was peculiarly tough and thick. In the centre of this we scooped a hole and inserted therein the end of the leg, fastening it thereto with pieces of twine that we chanced to have in our pockets. Thus we made, as it were, an artificial foot, which when Jack tried it served its purpose admirably—indeed, it acted too well, for being a broad base it did not permit the wooden leg to sink at all, while the natural leg did sink more or less, and, as the wooden limb had no knee, it was stiff from hip to heel, and could not bend, so that I had to walk behind my poor comrade, and when I observed him get somewhat into the position of the Leaning Tower of Pisa I sprang forward and supported him.

Thus we proceeded slowly through the forest, stumbling frequently, tumbling occasionally, and staggering oft; but strange to say, without either of us having any very definite idea of where we were going, or what we expected to find, or why we went in one direction more than another. In fact, we proceeded on that eminently simple principle which is couched in the well-known and time-honoured phrase, "follow your nose."

True, once I ventured to ask my companion where he thought we were going, to which he replied, much to my surprise, that he didn't know and didn't care; that it was quite certain if we did not go forward we could not expect to get on, and that in the ordinary course of things if we proceeded we should undoubtedly come to something. To this I replied, in a meditative tone, that there was much truth in the observation, and that, at any rate, if we did not come to something, something would certainly come to us.

But we did not pursue the subject. In fact, we were too much taken up with the interesting and amusing sights that met our gaze in that singular forest; insomuch that on several occasions I neglected my peculiar duty of watching Jack, and was only made aware of my carelessness by hearing him shout, "Hallo! Bob, look alive!—I'm over!" when I would suddenly drop my eyes from the contemplation of the plumage of a parrot or the antics of a monkey, to behold my friend leaning over at an angle of "forty-five." To leap forward and catch him in my arms was the work of an instant. On each of these occasions, after setting him upright, I used to give him a tender hug, to indicate my regret at having been so inattentive, and my sympathy with him in his calamitous circumstances.

Poor Jack was very gentle and uncomplaining. He even made light of his misfortune, and laughed a good deal at himself; but I could see, nevertheless, that his spirits were at times deeply affected, in spite of his brave efforts to bear up and appear gay and cheerful.

Story 2—Chapter 8

It was evening when we were cast ashore in this new country, so that we had not advanced far into the forest before night closed in and compelled us to halt; for, had we continued our journey in the dark, we should certainly have been drowned in one of the many deep morasses which abounded there, and which we had found it difficult to steer clear of, even in daylight.

As the moon arose and the stars began to glimmer in the sky, I observed, to my dismay, that all kinds of noxious creatures and creeping things began to move about, and strange hissing sounds and low dismal hootings and wails were heard at times indistinctly, as if the place were the abode of evil spirits, who were about to wake up to indulge in their midnight orgies.

"Oh! Jack," said I, shuddering violently, as I stopped and seized my companion by the arm. "I can't tell what it is that fills me with an unaccountable sensation of dread. I—I feel as if we should never more get out of this horrible swamp, or see again the blessed light of day. See! see! what horrid creature is that?"

"Pooh! man," interrupted Jack, with a degree of levity in his tone which surprised me much. "It's only a serpent. All these kind o' things are regular cowards. Only let them alone and they're sure to let you alone. I should like above all things to tickle up one o' these brutes, and let him have a bite at my wooden toe! It would be rare fun, wouldn't it, Bob, eh? Come, let us push on, and see that you keep me straight, old fellow!"

I made no reply for some time. I was horrified at my comrade's levity in such circumstances. Then, as I heard him continue to chuckle and remark in an undertone on the surprise the serpent would get on discovering the exceeding toughness of his toe, it for the first time flashed across my mind that his sufferings had deranged my dear companion's intellect.

The bare probability of such a dreadful calamity was sufficient to put to flight all my previous terrors. I now cared nothing whatever for the loathsome reptiles that wallowed in the swamps around me, and the quiet glidings and swelterings of whose hideous forms were distinctly audible in the stillness of approaching night. My whole anxiety was centred on Jack. I thought that if I could prevail on him to rest he might recover, and proposed that we should encamp; but he would not hear of this. He kept plunging on, staggering through brake and swamp, reedy pond and quaking morass, until I felt myself utterly unable to follow him a step farther.

Just at this point Jack stopped abruptly and said—

"Bob, my boy, we'll camp here."

It was a fearful spot. Dark, dismal, and not a square foot of dry ground.

"Here, Jack?"

"Ay, here."

"But it's—it's all wet. Excuse me, my dear comrade, I've not yet acquired the habit of sleeping in water."

"No more have I, Bob; we shall sleep on a fallen tree, my boy. Did you never hear of men sleeping in a swamp on the top of a log? It's often done, I assure you, and I mean to do it to-night. See, here is a good large one, three feet broad by twenty feet long, with lots of stumps of broken branches to keep us from rolling off. Come, let's begin."

We immediately began to make our arrangements for the night. With the aid of our clasp-knives we cut a quantity of leafy branches, and spread them on the trunk of a huge prostrated tree, the half of which was sunk in the swamp, but the other half was sufficiently elevated to raise us well out of the water. The bed was more comfortable than one would suppose; and, being very tired, we lay down on it as soon as it was made, and tried to sleep: having nothing to eat, we thought it well to endeavour to obtain all the refreshment we could out of sleep.

We had not lain long, when I started up in a fright, and cried—

"Hallo! Jack, what's that? See, through the reeds; it creeps slowly. Oh; horror! it comes towards us!"

Jack looked at it sleepily. "It's an alligator," said he. "If it approaches too close, just wake me; but, pray, don't keep howling at every thing that comes to peep at us."

Just at that moment, the hideous reptile drew near, and, opening its jaws, let them come together with a snap! Even Jack was not proof against this. He started up, and looked about for a defensive weapon. We had nothing but our clasp-knives. The alligator wallowed towards us.

"Oh for an axe!" gasped Jack.

The brute was within a few yards of us now. I was transfixed with horror. Suddenly an idea occurred to me.

"Your leg, Jack, your leg!"

He understood me. One sweep of his clasp-knife cut all the fastenings—the next moment he grasped the toe in both hands, and, swaying the heavy butt of the limb in the air, brought it down with all his force on the skull of the alligator. It rang like the sound of a blow on an empty cask. Again the limb was swayed aloft, and descended with extraordinary violence on the extreme point of the alligator's snout. There was a loud crash, as if of small bones being driven in. The animal paused, put its head on one side, and turning slowly round waddled away into the noisome recesses of its native swamp.

Scarcely had we recovered from the effects of this, when we heard in the distance shouts and yells and the barking of dogs. Crouching in our nest we listened intently. The sounds approached, but while those who made them were yet at some distance we were startled by the sudden approach of a dark object, running at full speed. It seemed like a man, or rather a huge ape, for it was black, and as it came tearing towards us, running on its hind-legs, we could see its eyes glaring in the moonlight, and could hear its labouring breath. It was evidently hard pressed by its pursuers, for it did not see what lay before it, and had well-nigh run over our couch ere it observed Jack standing on one leg, with the other limb raised in a threatening attitude above his head. It was too late to turn to avoid the blow.

Uttering a terrible cry the creature fell on its knees, and, trembling violently, cried—

"Oh, massa! oh, massa, spare me! Me no runaway agin. Mercy, massa! mercy!"

"Silence, you noisy villain," cried Jack, seizing the negro by the hair of the head.

"Yis, massa," gasped the man, while his teeth chattered and the whites of his eyes rolled fearfully.

"What are you? Where d'ye come from? Who's after ye?"

To these abrupt questions, the poor negro replied as briefly, that he was a runaway slave, and that his master and bloodhounds were after him.

We had guessed as much, and the deep baying of the hounds convinced us of the truth of his statement.

"Quick," cried Jack, dragging the black to the edge of our log, "get under there; lie flat; keep still;" so saying he thrust the negro under the branches that formed our couch. We covered him well up and then sat down on him. Before we had well finished our task the foremost of the bloodhounds came bounding towards us, with its eyeballs glaring and its white fangs glittering in the dim light like glow-worms in a blood-red cavern. It made straight for the spot where the negro was concealed, and would have seized him in another instant, had not Jack, with one blow of his leg, beat in its skull.

"Shove him out of sight, Bob."

I seized the dead hound and obeyed, while my comrade prepared to receive the second dog. But that animal seemed more timid. It swerved as the blow was delivered, received on its haunches, and fled away howling in another direction.

Jack at once laid down his leg and sat down on the negro, motioning me to do the same. Then pulling an old tobacco-pipe out of his pocket, he affected to be calmly employed in filling it when the pursuers came up. There were two of them, in straw hats and nankeen pantaloons, armed with cudgels, and a more ruffianly pair of villains I never saw before or since.

"Hallo! strangers," cried one, as they halted for a few moments on observing us. "Queer place to camp. Fond o' water and dirt, I guess?"

"You seem fond o' dirt and not o' water, to judge from your faces," replied Jack, calmly, attempting to light his pipe, which was rather a difficult operation, seeing that it was empty and he had no fire. "Ah! my light's out. Could you lend us a match, friend?"

"No, we can't. No time. Hain't got none. Did you see a nigger pass this way?"

"Ha! you're after him, are you?" cried Jack, indignantly. "Do you suppose I'd tell you if I did? Go and find him for yourselves."

The two men frowned fiercely at this, and appeared about to attack us. But they changed their minds, and said, "Mayhap you'll tell us if ye saw two hounds, then?"

"Yes, I did."

"Which way did they pass?"

"They haven't passed yet," replied Jack, with deep sarcasm, at the same time quietly lifting his leg, and swaying it gently to and fro; "whether they'll pass without a licking remains to be seen."

"Look 'ee, lads, we'll pay you for this," shouted the men as they turned away. "We've not time to waste now, *but we'll come back.*"

I remonstrated with my friend. "You're too rash, Jack."

"Why? We don't need to fear *two* men!"

"Ay, but there may be more in the woods."

My surmise was correct. Half an hour after, the hound was heard returning. It came straight at us, followed by at least a dozen men. Jack killed the dog with one blow, and felled the first man that came up, but we were overwhelmed by numbers, and, in a much shorter time than it takes to tell it, both of us were knocked into the mud and rendered insensible.

Story 2—Chapter 9

On recovering from the stunning effects of the blow that had felled me, I found myself lying on a hard earthen floor, surrounded by deep impenetrable darkness.

"Are you there, Jack?" I sighed faintly.

"Ay, Bob, I'm here—at least, all o' me that's left. I confess to you that I do feel a queer sensation, as if the one half of my head were absent and the other half a-wanting, while the brain lies exposed to the atmosphere. But I suppose that's impossible."

"Where are we, Jack?"

"We're in an outhouse, in the hands of planters; so I made out by what I heard them say when I got my senses back; but I've no notion of what part o' the world we're in. Moreover, I don't care. A man with only one leg, no head, and an exposed brain, isn't worth caring about. *I* don't care for him—not a button."

"Oh, Jack, dear, don't speak like that—I can't stand it."

"You're lying down, ain't you?" inquired Jack.

"Yes."

"Then how d'you know whether you can stand it or not?"

I was so overcome, and, to say the truth, surprised, at my companion's recklessness, that I could not reply. I lay motionless on the hard ground, meditating on our forlorn situation, when my thoughts were interrupted by the grating sound of a key turning in a lock. The door of the hut opened, and four men entered, each bearing a torch, which cast a brilliant glare over the hovel in which we were confined. There was almost nothing to be seen in the place. It was quite empty. The only peculiar thing that I observed about it was a thick post, with iron hooks fixed in it, which rose from the centre of the floor to the rafters, against which it was nailed. There were also a few strange-looking implements hanging round the walls, but I could not at first make out what these were intended for. I now perceived that Jack and I were chained to the wall.

Going to the four corners of the apartment, the four men placed their four torches in four stands that seemed made for the purpose, and then, approaching us, ranged themselves in a row before us. Two of them I recognised as being the men we had first seen in the swamp; the other two were strangers.

"So, my bucks," began one of the former,—a hideous-looking man, whose personal appearance was by no means improved by a closed eye, a flattened nose, and a swelled cheek, the result of Jack's first flourish of his wooden leg,—"so, we've got you, have we? The hounds have got you, eh?"

"So it appears," replied Jack, in a tone of quiet contempt, as he sat on the ground with his back leaning against the wall, his hands clasped above his solitary knee, and his thumbs revolving round each other slowly. "I say," continued Jack, an expression of concern crossed his handsome countenance, "I'm afraid you're damaged, rather, about your head-piece. Your eye seems a little out of order, and, pardon me, but your nose is a little too flat—just a little. My poor fellow, I'm quite sorry for you; I really am, though you *are* a dog."

The man opened his solitary eye and stared with amazement at Jack, who smiled, and, putting his head a little to the other side, returned the stare with interest.

"You're a bold fellow," said the man, on recovering a little from his surprise.

"I'm sorry," retorted Jack, "that I cannot return you the compliment."

I was horrified. I saw that my poor friend, probably under the influence of madness, had made up his mind to insult and defy our captors to their teeth, regardless of consequences. I tried to speak, but my lips refused their office. The man grinned horribly and gnashed his teeth, while the others made as though they would rush upon us and tear us limb from limb. But their chief, for such the spokesman seemed to be, restrained them.

"Hah!" he gasped, looking fiercely at Jack, and at the same time pointing to the implements on the wall, "d'ye see these things?"

"Not being quite so blind as you are, I do."

"D'ye know what they're for?"

"Not being a demon, which you seem to be, I don't."

"Hah! these—are," (he spoke very slowly, and hissed the words out between his teeth),—"torterers!"

"What?" inquired Jack, putting his head a little more to one side and revolving his thumbs in a contrary direction, by way of variety.

"Torterers—man-torterers! What d'ye twirl your thumbs like that for, eh?"

"Because it reminds me how easily, if I were unchained and had on my wooden leg, I could twirl you round your own neck, and cram your heels into your own mouth, and ram you down your own throat, until there was nothing of you left but the extreme ends of your shirt-collar sticking out of your eyes."

The mention of this peculiarly complicated operation seemed to be too much for the men: setting up a loud yell, they rushed upon Jack and seized him.

"Quick—the screws!" cried the man with the flattened nose.

A small iron instrument was brought, Jack's thumbs inserted therein, and the handle turned. I heard a harsh, grating sound, and observed my poor companion's face grow deadly pale and his lips turn blue. But he uttered no cry, and, to my surprise, he did not even struggle.

"Stop!" I shouted in a voice of thunder.

The men looked round in surprise. At that moment a great idea seemed to fill my soul. I cannot explain what it was. To this day I do not know what it was. It was a mystery—an indescribable mystery. I felt as one might be supposed to feel whose spirit were capable of eating material food, and had eaten too much. It was awful! Under the impulse of this sensation, I again shouted—

"*Stop!*"

"Why?"

"I cannot tell you why, until you unscrew that machine. Quick! it is of the deepest, the most vital importance to yourselves."

The extreme earnestness of my voice and manner induced the men to comply almost, I might say, in spite of themselves.

"Now, lad, what is it? Mind, *your* turn is coming; so don't trifle with us."

"*Trifle* with you!" I said, in a voice so deep, and slow, and solemn,—with a look so preternaturally awful,—that the four men were visibly impressed.

"Listen! I have a secret to tell you,—a secret that intimately concerns yourselves. It is a fearful one. You would give all you possess—your wealth, your very lives—rather than not know it. I can tell it to you; *but not now.* All the tortures of the Inquisition could not drag it out of me. Nay, you need not smile. If you did torture me *before* I told you this secret, that would have the effect of rendering my information useless to you. Nothing could then save you. I must be left alone with my friend for an hour. Go! You may leave us chained; you may lock and bar your door; you may watch and guard the house; but go, leave us. Much—too much—valuable time has been already lost. Come back in one hour," (here I pulled out my watch),—"in one hour and three minutes and five seconds, exactly; not sooner. Go! quick! as you value your lives, your families, your property. And hark, in your ear," (here I glared at them like a maniac, and sank my voice to a deep hoarse whisper), "as you value the very existence of your slaves, go, leave us instantly, and return at the hour named!"

The men were evidently overawed by the vehemence of my manner and the mysterious nature of my remarks. Without uttering a word they withdrew, and locked the door behind them. Happily they left the torches.

As soon as they were gone I threw my arms round my comrade's neck, and, resting my head on his shoulder, bemoaned our sad lot.

"Dear, dear Jack, have they hurt you?"

"Oh! nothing to speak of. But I say, Bob, my boy, what on earth can this monstrous secret be? It must be something very tremendous?"

"My poor Jack," said I, regardless of his question, "your thumbs are bruised and bleeding. Oh that I should have lived to bring you to this!"

"Come, come, Bob, enough of that. They *are* a little soreish, but nothing to what they would have been had you not stopped them. But, I say, what *is* this secret? I'm dying to know. My dear boy, you've no idea how you looked when you were spouting like that. You made my flesh creep, I assure you. Come, out with it; what's the secret?"

I felt, and no doubt looked, somewhat confused.

"Do you know, Jack," said I, solemnly, "I have no secret whatever!"

Jack gasped and stared—

"No secret, Bob!"

"Not the most distant shadow of one."

Jack pulled out his watch, and said in a low voice—

"Bob, my boy, we have just got about three-quarters of an hour to live. When these villains come back, and find that you've been humbugging them, they'll brain us on the spot, as sure as my name is John Brown and yours is Robert Smith—romantic names, both of 'em; especially when associated with the little romance in which we are now involved. Ha! ha! ha!"

I shrank back from my friend with the terrible dread, which had more than once crossed my mind, that he was going mad.

"Oh, Jack, don't laugh, pray. Could we not invent some secret to tell them?"

"Not a bad idea," returned my friend, gravely.

"Well, let us think; what could we say?"

"Ay, that's the rub! Suppose we tell them seriously that my wooden leg is a ghost, and that it haunts those who ill-treat its master, giving them perpetual bangs on the nose, and otherwise rendering their lives miserable?"

I shook my head.

"Well, then, suppose we say we've been sent by the Queen of England to treat with them about the liberation of the niggers at a thousand pounds a head; one hundred paid down in gold, the rest in American shin-plasters?"

"That would be a lie, you know, Jack."

"Come, that's good! You're wonderfully particular about truth, for a man that has just told such tremendous falsehoods about a secret that doesn't exist."

"True, Jack," I replied, seriously, "I confess that I have lied; but I did not mean to. I assure you I had no notion of what I was saying. I think I was bewitched. All your nonsense rolled out, as it were, without my will. Indeed, I did not mean to tell lies. Yet I confess, to my shame, that I did. There is some mystery here, which I can by no means fathom."

"Fathom or not fathom," rejoined my friend, looking at his watch again, "you got me into this scrape, so I request you to get me out of it. We have exactly twenty-five minutes and a half before us now."

Jack and I now set to work in real earnest to devise some plan of escape, or to invent some plausible secret. But we utterly failed. Minute after minute passed; and, as the end of our time drew near, we felt less and less able to think of any scheme, until our brains became confused with the terror of approaching and inevitable death, aggravated by previous torture. I trembled violently, and Jack became again uproarious and sarcastic. Suddenly he grew quiet, and I observed that he began to collect a quantity of straw that was scattered about the place. Making a large pile of it, he placed it before us, and then loosened one of the torches in its stand.

"There," said he, with a sigh of satisfaction, when all was arranged, "we shall give our amiable friends a warm reception when they come."

"But they will escape by the door," said I, in much anxiety, "and we only shall perish."

"Never mind that, Bob; we can only die once. Besides, they sha'n't escape; trust me for that."

As he spoke we heard approaching footsteps. Presently the key turned in the lock, and the door opened.

Story 2—Chapter 10

Punctually, to a minute, our jailors returned, and once again drew up in a row before us.

"Now, lads, wot have ye got to say?"

"My friends," began Jack, standing up and balancing himself on his one leg as well as he could, at the same time speaking with the utmost gravity and candour of expression, "my companion here in *temporary* distress—for I feel that it will be but temporary—has devolved upon me the interesting duty of making known to you the secret which has burthened his own mind for some time, and which has had so impressive and appropriate an effect upon yours. But first I must request you to lock the door, and hang the key on this nail at my elbow. You hesitate. Why? I am in chains; so is my comrade. We are two; you are four. It is merely a precaution to prevent the possibility of any one entering by stealth, and overhearing what I say."

The man with the battered face locked the door, and hung up the key as directed, merely remarking, with a laugh, that we were safe enough anyhow, and that if we were humbugging him it would be worse for us in the long-run.

"Come, now, out with yer secret," he added, impatiently.

"Certainly," answered Jack, with increased urbanity, at the same time taking down the key, (which caused the four men to start), and gazing at it in a pensive manner. "The secret! Ah! yes. Well, it's a wonderful one. D'you know, my lads, there would not be the most distant chance of your guessing it, if you were to try ever so much?"

"Well, but what is it?" cried one of the men, whose curiosity was now excited beyond endurance.

"It is this," rejoined Jack, with slow deliberation, "that you four men are—"

"Well," they whispered, leaning forward eagerly.

"The most outrageous and unmitigated asses we ever saw! Ha! I thought it would surprise you. Bob and I are quite agreed upon it. Pray don't open your eyes too wide, in case you should find it difficult to shut them again. Now, in proof of this great, and to you important truth, let me show you a thing. Do you see this torch," (taking it down), "and that straw?" (lifting up a handful), "Well, you have no idea what an astonishing result will follow the application of the former to the latter—see!"

" In two seconds the whole place was in a blaze."

To my horror, and evidently to the dismay of the men, who did not seem to believe that he was in earnest, Jack Brown thrust the blazing torch into the centre of the heap of straw.

The men uttered a yell, and rushing forward, threw themselves on the smoking heap in the hope of smothering it at once. But Jack applied the torch quickly to various parts. The flames leaped up! The men rolled off in agony. Jack, who somehow had managed to break his chain, hopped after them, showering the blazing straw on their heads, and yelling as never mortal yelled before. In two seconds the whole place was in a blaze, and I beheld Jack actually throwing somersets with his one leg over the fire and through the smoke; punching the heads of the four men most unmercifully; catching up blazing handfuls of straw, and thrusting them into their eyes and mouths in a way that quite overpowered me. I could restrain myself no longer. I began to roar in abject terror! In the midst of this dreadful scene the roof fell in with a hideous crash, and Jack, bounding through the smoking *débris*, cleared the walls and vanished!

At the same moment I received a dreadful blow on the side, and *awoke*—to find myself lying on the floor of my bedroom, and our man-servant Edwards furiously beating the bed-curtains, which I had set on fire by upsetting the candle in my fall.

"Why, Master Robert," gasped Edwards, sitting down and panting vehemently, after having extinguished the flames, "wot have you been a-doin' of?" I was standing speechless in the midst of my upset chair, table, and books, glaring wildly, when the man said this.

"Edwards," I replied, with deep solemnity, "the mystery's cleared up at last. *It has been all a dream!*"

"Wot's been all a dream? You hain't bin a bed all night, for the clo'se is never touched, an' its broad daylight. Wot has bin up?"

I might have replied, that, according to his own statement, I had been "up," but I did not. I began gradually to believe that the dreadful scenes I had witnessed were not reality; and an overpowering sense of joy kept filling my heart as I continued to glare at the man until I thought my chest would rend asunder. Suddenly, and without moving hand, foot, or eye, I gave vent to a loud, sharp, "Hurrah!"

Edwards started—"Eh?"

"Hurrah! hurrah! it's a **Dream!**"

"Hallo! I say, you know, come, this won't—"

"Hurrah!"

"Bless my 'art, Master Ro—"

Again I interrupted him by seizing my cap, swinging it round my head in an ecstasy of delight, and uttering cheer upon cheer with such outrageous vehemence, that Edwards, who thought me raving mad, crept towards the door, intending to bolt.

He was prevented from carrying out his intention, and violently overturned by the entrance of my father in dishabille. I sprang forward, plucked the spectacles off his nose, threw my arms round his neck, and kissed him on both eyes.

"I won't run away now, father, no, no, no! it's all a dream—a horrid dream! ha! ha! ha!"

"Bob, my dear boy!"

At this moment Jack, also in dishabille, rushed in. "Hallo! Bob, what's all the row?"

I experienced a different, but equally powerful gush of feeling on seeing my friend. Leaving my father, I rushed towards him, and, falling on his neck, burst into tears. Yes, I confess it without shame. Reader, if you had felt as I did, you would have done the same.

Jack led me gently to my bed, and, seating me on the edge of it, sat down beside me. I at once perceived from their looks that they all thought me mad, and felt the necessity of calming me before taking more forcible measures. This tickled me so much that I laughed again heartily, insomuch that Jack could not help joining me. Suddenly a thought flashed into my mind. My heart leaped to my throat, and I glanced downwards. *It was there!* I seized Jack's right leg, tumbled him back into the bed, and laying the limb across my knee, grasped it violently.

"All right!" I shouted, "straight, firm, muscular, supple as ever." I squeezed harder.

Jack roared. "I say, Bob, gently—"

"Hold your tongue," said I, pinching the thigh. "Do you feel *that?*"

"Ho! ah! *don't!*"

"And that?"

"Stop him! I say, my dear boy, have mercy?" Jack tried to raise himself, but I tilted him back, and, grasping the limb in both arms, hugged it.

After breakfast Jack and I retired to my room, where, the weather being unfavourable for our fishing excursion, I went all over it again in detail. After that I sent Jack off to amuse himself as he chose, and, seizing a quire of foolscap, mended a pen, squared my elbows, and began to write this remarkable account of the reason why I did not become a sailor.

I now present it to the juvenile public, in the hope that it may prove a warning to all boys who venture to entertain the notion of running away from home and going to sea.

Story 3—Chapter 1

Papers from Norway

Norway, 2nd July, 1868.

Happening to be in Norway just now, and believing that young people feel an interest in the land of the old sea-kings, I send you a short account of my experiences. Up to this date I verily believe that there is nothing in the wide world comparable to this island coast of Norway. At this moment we are steaming through a region which the fairies might rejoice to inhabit. Indeed, the fact that there are no fairies here goes far to prove that there are none anywhere. What a thought! No fairies? Why all the romance of childhood would be swept away at one fell blow if I were to admit the idea that there are no fairies. Perish the matter-of-fact thought! Let me rather conclude, that, for some weighty, though unknown, reason, the fairies have resolved to leave this island world uninhabited.

Fortune favours me. I have just come on deck, after a two days' voyage across the German Ocean, to find myself in the midst of innumerable islands, a dead calm—so dead that it seems impossible that it should ever come alive again—and scenery so wild, so gorgeous, that one ceases to wonder where the Vikings of old got their fire, their romance, their enterprise, and their indomitable pluck. It is warm, too, and brilliantly sunny.

On gazing at these tall grey rocks, with the bright green patches here and there, and an occasional red-tiled hut, one almost expects to see a fleet of daring rovers dash out of a sequestered bay, with their long yellow hair, and big blue eyes, and broad shoulders—not to mention broad-swords and ring-mail and battle-axes. But one does not always see what one expects. The days of the sea-kings are gone by; and at this moment, rowing out of one of these same sequestered bays, comes the boat of a custom-house officer. Yes, there is no doubt whatever about it. There he comes, a plain-looking unromantic man in a foraging-cap, with a blue surtout and brass buttons, about as like to a sea-king as a man-of-war is to a muffin.

Of course, the scenery is indescribable—no scenery *is* describable. In order that my reader may judge of the truth of this statement, I append the following description.

There are islands round us of every shape and size—all of them more or less barren, the greater part of their surfaces being exposed grey rock. Here and there may be seen, as I have already hinted, small patches of bright green, and, sparsely scattered everywhere, are little red-roofed wooden cottages—poor enough things the most of them; others, gaudy-looking affairs with gable-ends, white faces, and windows bordered with green. All of these are, while I write, reflected in the water as in a mirror, for there is not a breath of wind. Over the islands on my left are seen more islands extending out to sea. On the right tower up the blue hills of the interior of old Norway, and, although the weather is excessively hot, many of these are covered with snow. Everything is light, and transparent, and thin, and blue, and glassy, and fairy-like, and magically beautiful, and altogether delightful! There: have you made much of all that, good reader? If you have, be thankful, for, as I set out by saying, description of scenery, (at least to any good purpose), is impossible. The description of a man, however, is quite another thing. Here is our pilot. He is a rugged man, with fair hair, and a yellow face, and a clay-coloured chin, and a red nose. He is small in stature, and thin, insignificant in appearance, deeply miserable in aspect. His garments are black glazed oiled-cloth from head to foot, and immensely too large for him, especially the waistcoat, which is double-breasted, and seems to feel that his trousers are not a sufficient covering for such a pair of brittle looking legs, for it extends at least half way down to his knees. The flap of his sou'-wester, also, comes half way down his back. He is a wonderful object to look upon; yet he has the audacity, (so it seems to me), to take us in charge, and our captain has the foolhardiness to allow him.

If one goes out of the beaten track of "routes" in Norway, one is apt to get into difficulties of a minor kind. I happen to be travelling just now with a party of four friends, of whom three are ladies, the fourth a jolly young fellow fresh from college. A few days ago we had a few unusual experiences—even for Norway. On leaving Bergen we had made up our minds, as the steamer did not sail to within about sixty miles of our destination, to get ourselves and our luggage put down at a small hamlet at the mouth of the Nord-fjord, and there engage two large boats to transport us the remaining sixty miles up the fjord.

The ladies of our party valorously resolved to sit up all night to see the magnificent island scenery through which we were passing under the influence of the charming and subdued daylight of midnight—for there is no night here just now.

As for myself, being an old traveller, I have become aware that sleep is essential to a comfortable and useful existence. I therefore bade my friends good-night, took a farewell look at the bright sky, and the islands, and the sleeping sea, and went below to bed.

Next day we spent steaming along the island coast.

At one o'clock on the following morning we reached Moldeöen, where the steamer landed us on a rock on which were a few acres of grass and half a dozen wooden houses. We had a good deal of luggage with us, also some casks, cases, and barrels of provisions, and a piano-forte, as our place of sojourn is somewhat out of the way and far removed from civilised markets. A few poverty-stricken natives stood on the rude stone pier as we landed, and slowly assisted us to unload. At the time I conceived that the idiotical expression of their countenances was the result of being roused at untimely hours; but our subsequent experience led me to change my mind in regard to this.

In half an hour the steamer puffed away into the mysterious depths of one of the dark-blue fjords, and we were left on a desolate island, like Robinson Crusoe, with our worldly goods around us. Most of the natives we found so stupid that they could not understand our excellent Norse. One fellow, in particular, might as well have been a piece of mahogany as a man. He stood looking at me with stolid imbecility while I was talking to him, and made no reply when I had done. In fact the motion of his eyes, as he looked at me, alone betrayed the fact that he was flesh and blood.

We soon found that two boats were not to be had; that almost all the men of the place were away deep-sea fishing, and would not be back for many hours, and that when they did come back they would be so tired as to require at least half a day's rest ere they could undertake so long a journey with us. However, they sent a man off in a boat to search for as many boatmen as could be found. He was away an hour. During this period the few inhabitants who had turned out to see the steamer, disappeared, and we were left alone on the beach. There was no inn here; no one cared for us; every place seemed dirty with the exception of one house, which had a very lonely and deserted aspect, so we did not venture to disturb it.

In the course of time the messenger returned. No men were to be found except three. This was not a sufficient crew for even one large boat—we required two.

A feeling that we were homeless wanderers came over us now, and each, seating himself or herself on a box or a portmanteau, began to meditate. Seeing this, the three men coolly lay down to rest in the bow of their boat, and, drawing a sail over them, were quickly sound asleep.

The act suggested the idea that we could not do better, so we placed two portmanteaus end to end, and thus made a couch about six feet long. A box, somewhat higher, placed at one end, served for a pillow, and on this one of the ladies lay down, flat on her back of course, that being the only possible position under the circumstances. A shawl was thrown over her, and she went to sleep like an effigy on a tombstone.

Another of the ladies tried a similar couch; but as boxes of equal height could not be found, her position was not enviable. The third lady preferred an uneasy posture among the ribs and cordage of the boat, and I lay down on the paving-stones of the quay, having found from experience that, in the matter of beds, flatness is the most indispensable of qualities, while hardness is not so awful as one might suppose. Where my comrade the collegian went to I know not.

Presently one of the ladies got up and said that this would never do; that the next day was Sunday, and that we were in duty bound to do our best to reach the end of our journey on Saturday night. Thus admonished, my comrade and I started up and resolved to become "men," that is, to act as boatmen. No sooner said than done. We roused the three sleepers, embarked the most important half of our luggage; left the other half in charge of the native with the idiotic countenance, with directions to take care of it and have it forwarded as soon as possible, and, at a little after two in the morning, pulled vigorously away from the inhospitable shores of Moldeöen.

We started on our sixty-miles' journey hopefully, and went on our way for an hour or so with spirit. But when two hours had elapsed, my companion and I began to feel the effects of rowing with unaccustomed muscles rather severely, and gazed with envy at the three ladies who lay coiled up in an indescribable heap of shawls and crinolines in the stern of the boat, sound asleep. They needed sleep, poor things, not having rested for two days and two nights.

But my poor friend was more to be pitied than they. Having scorned to follow my example and take rest when he could get the chance, he now found himself unexpectedly called on to do the work of a man when he could not keep his eyes open. When our third hour began, I saw that he was fast asleep at the oar—lifting it indeed and dipping it in proper time, but without pulling the weight of an ounce upon it. I therefore took it from him, and told him to take half an hour's nap, when I would wake him up, and expect him to take the oars and give me a rest.

On being relieved he dropped his head on a sugar-cask, and was sound asleep in two minutes!

I now felt drearily dismal. I began to realise the fact that we had actually pledged ourselves to work without intermission for the next eighteen or twenty hours, of which two only had run, and I felt sensations akin to what must have been those of the galley-slaves of old. In the midst of many deep thoughts and cogitations, during that silent morning hour, when all were asleep around me save the three mechanical-looking boatmen, and when the only sounds that met my ears were the dip of the oars and the deep breathing, (to give it no other name), of the slumberers—in the midst of many deep thoughts, I say, I came to the conclusion that in my present circumstances the worst thing I could do was to *think*! I remembered the fable of the pendulum that became so horrified at the thought of the number of ticks it had to perform in a lengthened period of time, that it stopped in despair; and I determined to "shut down" my intellect.

Soon after, my shoulders began to ache, and in process of time I felt a sensation about the small of my back that induced the alarming belief that the spinal marrow was boiling. Presently my wrists became cramped, and I felt a strong inclination to pitch the oars overboard, lie down in the bottom of the boat, and howl! But feeling that this would be unmanly, I restrained myself. Just then my companion in sorrow began to snore, so I awoke him, and—giving him the oars—went to sleep.

From this period everything in the history of that remarkable day became unconnected, hazy, and confusing. I became to some extent mechanical in my thoughts and actions. I rowed and rested, and rowed again; I ate and sang, and even laughed. My comrade did the same, like a true Briton, for he was game to the backbone. But the one great, grand, never-changing idea in the day was—pull—pull—pull!

We had hoped during the course of that day to procure assistance, but we were unsuccessful. We passed a number of fishermen's huts, but none of the men would consent to embark with us. At last, late that night, we reached a small farm about two-thirds of the way up the fjord, where we succeeded in procuring another large boat with a crew of five men. Here, also, we obtained a cup of coffee; and while we were awaiting the arrival of the boat I lay down on the pier and had a short nap.

None but those who have toiled for it can fully appreciate the blessing of repose. It was a clear, calm night when we resumed our boat journey. The soft daylight threw a species of magical effect over the great mountains and the glassy fjord, as we rowed away with steady and vigorous strokes, and I lay down in the bow of the boat to sleep. The end of the mast squeezed my shoulder; the edge of a cask of beef well-nigh stove in my ribs; the corner of a box bored a hole in the nape of my neck—yet I went off like one of the famed seven sleepers, and my friend, although stretched out beside me in similarly unpropitious circumstances, began to snore in less than five minutes after he laid down.

The last sounds I heard before falling into a state of oblivion were the voices of our fair companions joining in that most beautiful of our sacred melodies, the "Evening Hymn," ere they lay down to rest in the stern of the boat. Next morning at nine we arrived at the top of the fjord, and at the end, for a time at least, of our journeying.

Story 3—Chapter 2

Salmon-Fishing Extraordinary

Norway, 14th July, 1868.

Yesterday was a peculiar day in my experience of salmon-fishing in Norway.

The day was dull when I set out for the river, seven miles distant, in a small boat, with a Norseman. A seven-miles' pull was not a good beginning to a day's salmon-fishing, the weight of my rod being quite sufficient to try the arms without that; but there was no help for it. Arrived there I got a native, named Anders, to carry the bag and gaff.

Anders is a fair youth, addicted to going about with his mouth open, with a mild countenance and a turned-up nose.

"Good weather for fishing, Anders," said I, in Norse.

"Ya," said he, "megit god," (very good).

This was the extent of our conversation at that time, for we came suddenly on the first pool in the river; and I soon perceived that, although the weather was good enough, the river was so flooded as to be scarcely fishable.

And now began a series of petty misfortunes that gradually reduced me to a state of misery which was destined to continue throughout the greater part of that day. But Hope told me flattering tales—not to say *stories*—for a considerable time; and it was not until I had fished the third pool without seeing a fin that my heart began fairly to sink. The day, too, had changed from a cloudy to a rainy one, and Anders' nose began to droop, while his face elongated visibly.

Feeling much depressed, I sat down on a wet stone, in my wet garments, and lunched off a moist biscuit, a piece of tongue, and a lump of cheese. This was consoling, as far as it went, but it did not go far. The misty clouds obliterated the mountains, the rain drizzled from the skies, percolated through the brim of my hat, trickled down my nose, and dropped upon my luncheon.

"Now we shall go up the river, Anders," said I. Anders assented, as he would have done had I proposed going down the river, or across the river, or anywhere in the wide world; for, as I said it in English, he did not understand me. Evidently he did not care whether he understood me or not!

Up the river we went, to the best pool in it. The place was a torrent—unfishable—so deep that I could not wade in far enough to cast over the spot where fish are wont to lie. In making a desperate effort to get far in, I went over the boot-top; and my legs and feet, which hitherto had been dry, had immediate cause to sympathise with the rest of my person.

Anders' face became longer than ever. All the best pools in the river were tried, but without success, and at last, towards evening, we turned to retrace our steps down the valley. On the way I took another cast into the best pool—going deeper than the waist into the water in order to cast over the "right spot."

The effort was rewarded. I hooked a fish and made for the bank as fast as possible. My legs were like solid pillars, or enormous sausages, by reason of the long boots being full to bursting with water. To walk was difficult; to run, in the event of the fish requiring me to do so, impossible. I therefore lay down on the bank and tossed both legs in the air to let the water run out—holding on to the fish the while. The water did run out—it did more; it ran right along my backbone to the nape of my neck; completing the saturation which the rain had hitherto failed to accomplish. But I had hooked a fish and heeded it not.

He was a small one; only ten pounds; so we got him out quickly and without much trouble. Yet this is not always the case. Little fish are often the most obstreperous and the most troublesome. It was only last week that I hooked and landed a twenty-eight-pound salmon, and he did not give me half the trouble that I experienced from one which I caught yesterday. Well, having bagged him we proceeded on our homeward way, Anders' face shortening visibly and his nose rising, while my own spirits began to improve. At another pool I tried again, and almost at the first cast hooked an eighteen-pounder, which Anders gaffed after about twenty-minutes' play.

We felt quite jolly now, although it rained harder than ever, and we went on our way rejoicing—Anders' countenance reduced to its naturally short proportions.

Presently we came to an old weir, or erection for catching fish as they ascend the river, where lies one of our favourite pools. The water was running down it like a mill-race. Pent up by the artificial dike, the whole river in this place gushes down in a turbulent rapid. There was one comparatively smooth bit of water, which looked unpromising enough, but being in hopeful spirits now, I resolved on a final cast. About the third cast a small trout rose at the fly. The greedy little monsters have a tendency to do this. Many a small trout have I hooked with a salmon fly as large as its own head. Before I could draw the line to cast again, the usual heavy *wauble* of a salmon occurred near the fly. It was followed by the *whir* of the reel as the line flew out like lightning, sawing right through the skin of my fingers, (which by the way are now so seamed and scarred that writing is neither so easy nor so pleasant as it used to be).

The burst that now ensued was sudden and tremendous! The salmon flashed across the pool, then up the pool, then down the pool. It was evidently bent on mischief. My heart misgave me, for the place is a bad one—all full of stumps and stones, with the furious rapid before mentioned just below, and the rough unsteady stones of the old dike as an uncertain path-way to gallop over should the fish go down the river. I held on stoutly for a few seconds as he neared the head of the rapid, but there is a limit to the endurance of rods and tackle. What made the matter worse was that the dike on which I stood terminated in a small island, to get from which to the shore necessitated swimming, and if he should go down the big rapid there was little chance of his stopping until he should reach the foot of it—far below this island.

All at once he turned tail and went down head first. I let the line fly now, keeping my fingers well clear of it.

"He's off, Anders!" I shouted, as I took to my heels at full speed.

"Hurroo-hoo-oo!" yelled the Norseman, flying after me with the gaff.

How I managed to keep my footing in the rush over the broken dike I know not. It is a marvel to me. The bushes on the island overhung the water, the earth having been cut away by the force of the rapid. I tried to pull up because they were too thick to crash through; but the fish willed it otherwise. The line was getting low on the reel; the rod bent double; presently I had to straighten it out—in another moment I was in the water over the boots, which filled of course in a moment. But this did not impede me as long as I was in deep water.

I was forsaken at this point by Anders, who sought and found a safe passage to the mainland, where he stood gazing at me with his eyes blazing and his mouth wide open.

I soon reached the end of the island, to my horror, for I had not previously taken particular note of the formation of the land there. A gulf of water of five or six yards broad of unknown depth lay between me and that shore, by which in the natural course of things I should have followed my fish as far as he chose. The rapid itself looked less tremendous than this deep black hole. I hesitated, but the salmon did not. Still down he went.

"Now, then," thought I, "hole or rapid?"

The question was settled for me, for before I could decide, I was hauled into the rapid. No doubt I was a more than half-willing captive. Anyhow, willing or not willing, down I went. Ah! what a moment of ease and relief from exertion was that when I went a little deeper than the waist, and found myself borne pleasantly along on tip-toe, as light as one of those beautiful balls with which juveniles—in these highly favoured days—are wont to sport in the fields!

And oh—ho-o! how my spirit seemed to gush out through my mouth and nose, or out at the top of my head, when the cold water encircled my neck as I lost my footing altogether, and struck out with my right hand, endeavouring the while to support my rod in the left!

I heard Anders gasp at this point; but I saw him not. In another second my knees came into violent contact with a rock, (alas! every motion of my body, as I now write, reminds me painfully of that crash!) Immediately after this I was sprawling up the bank, having handed the rod to Anders to hold, while I tossed my legs again in the air, to get rid of the water which weighed me down like lead. How earnestly I wished that I could tear these boots off and fling them away! But there was no time for that. On regaining my legs I seized the rod, and found that the salmon had brought up in an eddy created by the tail of a gravel-bank in the centre of the river between two rapids.

"Good," I gasped, blandly.

Anders smiled.

Presently I found that it was the reverse of good, for, when I tried to wind in the line and move the fish, I perceived that the resistance offered was not like that of a salmon, but a stump!

"I do believe he's gone!" I exclaimed.

Anders became grave.

"No fish there," said I, gloomily.

Anders' face elongated.

"He has wound the line round a stump, and broken off," said I, in despair.

Woe, of the deepest profundity, was depicted on Anders' visage!

For full five minutes I tried every imaginable device, short of breaking the rod, to clear the line—in vain. Then I gave the rod to Anders to hold, and, taking the gaff with me, I went sulkily up the river, and again taking to the water, made my way to the head of the gravel-bank, over which I walked slowly, oppressed in spirit, and weighed down by those abominable boots which had once more filled to overflowing! Water-proof boots are worse than useless for this sort of work. But happily this is not the usual style of thing that one experiences in Norwegian fishing. It is only occasionally that one enjoys a treat of the kind.

In the middle of the gravel-bank the water was only three inches deep, so I lay down on my back and, once again elevating my ponderous legs in the air, allowed a cataract of water to flow over me. Somewhat lightened, I advanced into the hole. It was deeper than I thought. I was up to the middle in a moment, and sighed as I thought of the boots—full again. Before I reached the line the water was up to my shoulders; but it was the still water of the eddy. I soon caught the line and found that it was round a stump, as I had feared. With a heavy heart I eased it off—when lo! a tug sent an electric shock through my benumbed body, and I saw the salmon not three yards off, at the bottom of the pool! He also saw me, and darting in terror from side to side wound the line round me. I passed it over my head, however, and was about to let it go to allow Anders to play it out and finish the work, when the thought occurred that I might play it myself, by running the line through my fingers when he should pull, and hauling in when he should stop. I tried this successfully. In half a minute more I drew him to within a yard of my side, gaffed him near the tail, and carried him up the gravel-bank under my arm.

He was not a large fish after all—only thirteen pounds. Nevertheless, had he been fresh, it would have been scarcely possible for me to hold his strong slippery body. Even when exhausted he gave me some trouble. Gaining the shallowest part of the bank I fell on my knees, crammed the fingers of my left hand into his mouth and gills, and held him down while I terminated his career with a stone. Thereafter I fixed the hook more securely in his jaw, and, launching him into the rapid, left Anders to haul him out, while I made the best of my way to the shore.

This is about the roughest experience I have yet had of salmon-fishing in Norway.

The season this year bids fair to be a pretty good one. I have had about twelve days' fishing, and have caught sixteen fish, weighing together two hundred and seventy-six pounds, two of them being twenty-eight-pounders.

Lightning Source UK Ltd.
Milton Keynes UK
UKHW040018190219
337571UK00001B/145/P